Protect Me

OAKVILLE SERIES: BOOK THREE

Protect Me

OAKVILLE SERIES: BOOK THREE

KATHY-JO REINHART

Protect Me
(Oakville Series #3)

© 2015, Kathy-Jo Reinhart
Self publishing
(kathyjoreinhart.com)

Cover Design by: Wicked By Design @ http://www.wickedbydesigncovers.com Cover
Model: Stephen Thomas
Edited by Monica Black of Word Nerd Editing
Interior Designed and Formatted by

www.emtippettsbookdesigns.com

I want to dedicate this book to my Aunt Kathy, whom our family lost this year. I feel so blessed to have known such an amazing woman. She was one of my biggest supporters and always encouraged me to keep going. There are not enough words to describe how much she'll be missed. We love you always.

Prologue

Paul

"WELL, WHICH one do you guys think she'll like?" I question Becky and Kyle. We are all gazing down at a jewelry tray full of engagement rings. It took a lot of begging on my part, but I was able to convince my best friend and one of Holly's best friends to come with me today. I understand Becky's hesitation in coming along. She hasn't known Holly for very long and wasn't sure she'd be the best choice to help me choose her engagement ring. Kyle, however, has no excuse. We've been friends for too long. He tried to pull the I-just-had-a-baby card with me. That shit didn't work. Amber just had a baby, not him.

Somehow, I was finally able to convince them both. I need this ring today. Amber and Cody are coming home from the hospital later this afternoon and Holly being Holly is throwing a little welcome home party at their house. All of the people we love will be there. Most people would propose in a quiet and romantic setting, but I know my girl. After being alone for such a long time, Holly and I never imagined we'd find each other, let alone a group of friends who are more like a family. So, asking her to be my wife in front of all the special people in our lives will be her idea of perfect. I have to admit, I kinda think it's perfect, too. That's not to say I'm not nervous as hell, though. Looking

1

down at the shiny diamond rings, my throat goes dry and my heart beats rampantly in my chest. Why? I don't know. I'm positive she'll say yes, so why am I still so fucking nervous?

"Hello? Earth to Paul. You asked us a question then zoned out on us, dumbass. Did you even hear what Becky said?" Kyle teases. He knows I've wanted to do this since the second my eyes landed on Holly. I never believed in that whole "love at first sight" bullshit until I saw her. Although, maybe it was more lust at first sight and love at first sound. Holly is a knockout, there's no doubt about it, but I think it was her take-no-shit attitude that made me fall for her. She is definitely one spunky ass redhead. Give her any shit and she will light your ass up. Though, I need to snap out of it and pay attention. This is important. My doll-face deserves the perfect ring.

"Sorry, Becky. I'm a little nervous," I admit. They both gawk at me like I've lost my mind, but who wouldn't be a little nervous in this situation? Hopefully they don't see just how nervous I really am. It has taken a long time for me to feel like I deserve to be happy at all, let alone loved by such an amazing woman. For a while, before I met Kyle, I was so fucked up in the head, I didn't care whether I lived or died. I think I would've actually preferred death.

"I remember when I was doing this and a certain someone was teasing the shit out of me for being nervous. What was it you said? Oh, yeah...'being nervous is for pussies, of course she's gonna say yes,'" Kyle playfully says between chuckles. Even Becky joins in and giggles. "At least now you get it." I'm so glad they're finding this all so amusing.

"Yes, I get it assnugget. Now, can you stop busting my balls and help me?" I joke and add a brotherly slap to the back of his head. Kyle winces in pain and steps out of slapping range. Okay, maybe it was a little harder than a brotherly slap. Becky looks between the both of us, the corners of her mouth threatening a smile.

"Wow." She shakes her head. "I have no idea why the two of you would be nervous about asking two beautiful, smart, and very mature women to marry you," Becky states sarcastically. She turns so she's facing us both with her hands resting on her hips. In this moment, I can see Holly has turned this sweet and quiet girl into her little sarcastic sidekick. The world is not prepared for two of them. "Can you two stop acting like ten year olds long enough to do what we came to do? I have a party to help with." She smiles at the both of us and goes back to examining the rings in front of her.

This is a lot harder than I thought it would be. Holly isn't really a girly girl. Buying her some big, flashy diamond won't impress her in the least. I need to find something special. Everyone has a diamond engagement ring, she would have something different. Something original. "Do you have any amethyst engagement rings?" I question the eager salesgirl. Ever since she began helping us, she's hung on every word, overacting like she really gives a damn about helping me and not just the huge commission at the end of the sale. The minute my question registers with her, all that changes. Her face tenses. The free, easy smile she wore minutes ago is gone, replaced with a hard, forced one.

"We do have amethyst rings, but traditional engagement rings are diamond. Amethyst is a much cheaper stone," she states a little too prissy for my taste. Oh, I see, she's one of those types. The total opposite of Holly. She's the girl who has to have a ring that costs more than a house. "If it's cheap you're looking for, maybe you're in the wrong place." This time, her voice has a bite to it. Her eyes scan me from head to toe, trying to determine whether I even have the means to be in this expensive store. She starts to put the tray of rings back into the display case. My body begins to tense up as sweat builds on my forehead. Her tone and the fact that she's insinuating I should go somewhere else because I don't want a diamond engagement ring pisses me off.

I glance to my right and find a massive grin on Kyle's face. He's trying his damnedest not to laugh, which fuels my anger. Seeing my expression, he raises his chin in Becky's direction. Before I can fully turn to my left to see what he's laughing at, I hear it. Becky is pissed off. I think she's more pissed at this bitch than I am. I've only seen her mad once, when Leena drugged Kyle and made everyone think she and Kyle slept together. The way she's acting right now, you'd think this girl just insulted her and not me. Her voice is calm, but you can feel the anger radiating off her. When I finally get a glimpse of her face, even I'm a little scared. Her nostrils are flaring and there's a vein raised on the side of her forehead. She just plain looks badass. I need to remember not to get on this girl's bad side — ever.

"This may come as a shock to you, but not every woman wants or even likes the traditional diamond engagement rings. The girl this ring is for isn't some superficial, prissy, materialistic Barbie Doll." She pauses, taking a deep breath, most likely trying to calm herself down.

She clenches her hands so tightly at her sides, the knuckles are turning white. "Another little known fact: just because someone doesn't buy the most expensive thing in the store doesn't mean they can't afford to." The salesgirl just stands there with her mouth hanging open and eyes wide. Becky searches the store. Something catches her eye and a sinister smirk sprouts on her lips. "You get paid on commission, correct?" The stunned salesgirl nods. "That gentleman over there in the black suit, is he your boss?" Becky points to the well-dressed man sitting behind the counter at a desk. Now the salesgirl looks nervous as she nods her head slowly. Her bottom lip is trembling, like she's going to burst into tears at any second. "Well, then, this is really going to suck for you, sweetheart. Maybe next time you'll think before you open your mouth," Becky warns as she struts toward the man in the suite.

Kyle bursts out laughing. He's doubled over, almost as if he were in pain. When he straightens up, there are tears running down his cheeks. Still standing frozen, with her mouth gaping open in disbelief, the salesgirl watches Becky introduce herself to the manager of the store. Holy shit! I don't know whether to be scared or impressed by this side of Becky we've never seen before. I never imagined she could be such a bitch. Not that this girl doesn't deserve whatever is about to happen to her — she most definitely does.

We all stand quiet and still, watching Becky and the manager talk. She points to me and the manager looks over, nods, and smiles. As soon as the conversation gets to the good part, you can see it. He glances at the now trembling girl behind the counter. They both begin to walk over to us. I glance over at the salesgirl, who now resembles a frightened caged animal. The manager stands in front of the girl while Becky eagerly watches, awaiting the girl's fate.

"We'll discuss this later, Natasha. For now, the bathrooms and break room need a good cleaning," he instructs. Natasha's expression is priceless. I don't even know how I would describe it. Shock. Horror. Anger. All of them seem to cross her face. It's quite amusing. Finally, she turns on her heels and stomps off toward the back of the store. I notice the very pleased grin plastered on Becky's face while Kyle tries to control his laughter.

"My name is Charles. Please excuse my sister. She can be a real snob sometimes," he apologizes. "How may I help you?" I explain what I'm looking for and he leads us to another counter with nothing but amethyst rings. This is more like it, more like my Holly — beautiful and unique. It doesn't take long to find the perfect ring. A large pear shaped amethyst stone sits atop a thick platinum band with diamonds in the shape of angel wings resting on each side. It's the most unique and beautiful ring I've ever seen and it just screams Holly.

As we drive back to Kyle's, I can't help but think back on my life. Never did I think I'd live past twenty-five, not with the way I went through booze, drugs, and women. One of them was sure to be the death of me at some point. The fact that I actually allowed myself to fall in love amazes me the most. That's most definitely the one thing I swore I would never let happen. I was too broken. Too lost. Too guilty. Nothing good could come from me being in love, or so I thought.

Holly

WHERE THE hell is Becky? She promised she'd be here to help me get this little "Welcome Home" party together for Amber and the baby. Though…I mainly want her here so she and Clark are around one another. There are some serious sparks between those two, but neither of them seem to want to do anything about it. So, I'm taking it upon myself to give them a little push.

"Holly, where do you want me to layout all of the food?" Clark questions, walking out of the kitchen. When he sees me struggling to blow up the extra-large blue balloons, he laughs. Filling the house with a hundred or so baby blue balloons seemed like a great idea when I was at the party store yesterday. Today, not so much. I'm dizzy and out of breath and I've only managed to completely inflate five. This sucks. Plopping down on the couch, I release the half-filled balloon from my fingers and watch it fly through the living room.

"This is useless. I'll never get these blown up before everyone gets here." Clark sits beside me as he tries to contain his laughter.

"I have one of those disposable helium tanks at the house. It was left over from Skylar's last birthday party. Would you like me to run home and grab it?" *He hasn't left yet?* I give him a 'what the fuck are you waiting for?' look. Quickly, he's on his feet and heading for the door. I don't fail to notice his laughter has returned. This is what it must feel like to have annoying little brothers. These boys just love to push my buttons. But I love them anyway. They're the only family I have.

While I wait, I decide to hang the "Welcome Home" banner. As I start to climb the ladder, Paul and Becky walk in. That's strange. What are they doing together? Becky looks nervous and Paul is hiding something. I'm pretty damn good at reading people. Except for one. Somehow, he fooled me, but that's all in the past now.

"Nice of you to finally show up to help," I tease them.

"Sorry, doll-face. I needed Kyle and Becky's help with something. No, I won't tell you what. It's a surprise," he explains as he kisses my forehead. When he pulls away, there's a shit-eating grin on his face. He's up to something and I want to know what it is. I know there's no use in pushing. Paul is the master of keeping a surprise, a surprise.

When Clark gets back, I need you to help him get the food ready," I tell Becky, not giving her a chance to protest. As if on cue, Clark comes through the front door. As soon as his eyes land on Becky, his whole face lights up. "Clark, Becky can help you with the food and Paul can help me with the rest of the decorations." He nods and they both walk into the kitchen. Paul looks at me and smiles, shaking his head. He knows exactly what I'm trying to do.

It didn't take long before Angel, Chelsie, Marcus, Taryn, and their boys showed up. Once I gave them all something to do, we finished setting up in no time. Beasley, Marty, and Anna arrived just as Kyle called saying they were five minutes away.

I want this to be memorable for both Kyle and Amber. They've both been through more shit than any two people should have to. No one was sure this day would be possible after she lost the triplets. It wasn't just the two of them who were affected by it either. We all were. We are all family. Maybe not all by blood, but family all the same. When one of us hurts, we all do. This group pulled together to do everything possible to help her get this baby here, safe and sound.

As soon as we hear Kyle's truck pull up the drive, we all rush to the door. You'd think we hadn't seen baby Cody yet. The nurses had to kick us out more than once. Since he's the first baby in our group, it's almost as if he belongs to us all. I can't wait to be called Aunt Holly. This little boy will be so spoiled. Not only by his parents, but every single one of us. His nursery is already overflowing with clothes and toys.

"I should've known you'd throw me a party. There's no way you could pass up the opportunity," Amber jokes as she hugs me tight.

"Don't flatter yourself. I'm throwing this party for Cody, not you,"

I tell her as I take the car seat from Kyle and head for the house. I hear Amber mumble bitch under her breath jokingly. "Get used to it, sweetheart, you're yesterday's news now. There's literally a new kid in town," I yell over my shoulder before everyone mobs around me, wanting to see the baby.

Once we are all stuffed from filling our faces with Clark and Marty's delicious cooking, we move outside and sit around the fire pit. It's a beautiful night. Just the right temperature and a million stars shining in the sky. I love this. All of us just hanging out and talking. This is my idea of a perfect life.

Glancing over, I see Amber and Kyle smiling down at Cody. You can almost feel the love they have for him. It radiates. They look so happy. So Content. Like all is right in their world. Watching Amber with Cody makes me a little sad. It reminds me of something I lost once. Something I may never have the chance to have again. Before the building tears have a chance to spill over, I hear Amber gasp. When I look up, her hands are covering her mouth and her eyes are as big as saucers. I follow her gaze to see Paul down on one knee holding a black velvet box. At the sight, I feel a thousand butterflies flutter around inside my stomach. The tears already threatening to spill over do, and my hands are shaking so badly, I'm afraid everyone will notice. Not until this very moment had I realized how much I've wanted Paul to propose to me.

"Holly, before I met you, I was broken. I never thought I was capable of loving, let alone being loved. Then you showed up and knocked me flat on my ass. You've repaired a heart that was beyond repair. You saved me. I love you more than I will ever be able to tell you with mere words. Instead, let me show you, every day, for the rest of our lives. Will you marry me?" he asks, staring into my eyes. I can see how nervous he is as he waits for me to answer. I'm trying to get my voice to work, but I'm so emotional after those beautiful words, nothing will come out. Finally, I give up and start nodding my head yes. I must look psychotic. A huge smile spreads across Paul's face as he places the most beautiful ring I've ever seen on my finger. How could I not love this man when he knows me so well? This ring proves it. This ring screams me.

After wiping a tear from my eye with his thumb, he leans down and kisses me. It's the most passionate kiss I've ever experienced. If it weren't for all of the catcalls and whistles from our friends, I'd have forgotten we weren't alone.

"Remember where we left off. I'd like to pick it up in the exact same spot later," I tell him as we are both bombarded with congratulations. Amber comes flying across the room, screeching loudly. She throws her arms around me with such force, it sends us both tumbling to the floor. We're both laughing so hard, neither of us can get up. When I finally think I have it under control, I turn my head to look at Amber. And just like that, we start all over again. After a few more minutes, we get ourselves under control and off the floor.

"Ahh, why'd ya stop? I was enjoying watching you lovely ladies rolling around together on the floor," Angel jokes, earning himself not only one, but two slaps to the back of the head courtesy of Paul and Kyle. "Ouch. It's not like I asked to join them," he throws out as he runs away from another head slap.

I can honestly say this is the happiest I've ever been in my entire life. I'm surrounded by people who truly care about me, who I consider my family, and I'm going to marry my soulmate. It can't get any better than this. Nothing could ruin this moment. It's absolutely perfect. The doorbell rings and I wonder who it could be. Everyone we know is here.

"I'll get it," I yell on my way to the front door. As I approach the door, I'm hit with an eerie feeling that something's wrong. I don't know what it is or why I feel this way. I hate feeling uneasy. It reminds me of a time when that's the only thing I felt. Never knowing what was coming next, but assured whatever it was wasn't good. That's a part of my life I've tried so hard to forget — ran so far away from, hoping never to see it again.

When I open the door, I realize I didn't run quite far enough. The air is knocked right out of my lungs when I see my ex-husband, Ray, standing before me.

CHAPTER
One

Twelve Years Ago

Holly

THIS HAS been the best six months of my life. Being Mrs. Ray Marconi has been better than I ever thought it would be. It's like a fairytale for a girl like me. I've spent my entire life being passed along from one foster home to another. My incubator dropped me off on the steps of a church three days after I was born. There was a note saying she didn't have the means to take care of me because she was only sixteen. Her parents hadn't known she was pregnant. She was able to hide it the whole nine months. When it came time to deliver me, she went to a friend's house. Her friend's parents were out of town and I was born on a shower floor. Not the most glamorous beginning. She didn't even name me. I spent years hating her, but as I got older, I realized she was only a scared child. She probably thought some loving couple would adopt me and I would live happily ever after.

The church's pastor and his wife adopted me. They named me Holly. When I was four, they were killed in a car accident. I don't remember them, but we all look happy in the couple of pictures I have. After that, there were a few times when I came close to being adopted, but something always happened to stop it. Eventually, I gave in to the fact that I just wasn't meant to have a family.

I kept to myself and never really made friends until my freshman year of high school. That's when I met Ray. Of course, I didn't think he'd ever give someone like me the time of day. One date and we were inseparable. His friends became mine and before I knew it, I was one of the popular kids. It was an adjustment for me. I was used to being in the shadows, not in the spotlight. But I always felt loved and safe with Ray. And that was something I'd never felt before. It was something I so desperately wanted and needed.

During our senior year, Ray asked me to marry him. Of course, I said yes. Here was this perfect man wanting to love and take care of me forever. He wanted to give me things I'd only dreamed of having, including himself. One month after graduation, we were married.

Over the last six months, I've learned a lot about Ray. He's more particular than he was when we were merely dating. Some people may call it controlling, but I don't see it that way. I'm used to rules and people who were less than nice to me usually dictated them. But this is different. Ray loves me. He's given me a beautiful home and takes very good care of me. If he like things to be a certain way in return, so be it. I had planned on getting a job after we were married. I wanted to work with kids, preferably ones in foster care who needed extra attention. When I brought this up to Ray, his response floored and disappointed me.

"A wife's job is to take care of her husband and their home. Working outside the home would keep you from doing that properly."

It seemed to make sense at the time, but after a while, I got bored sitting around the house all day alone.

He leaves at seven every morning and doesn't get home until six or seven at night. I get up in the morning to fix his breakfast and make his lunch. With it only being the two of us, the house doesn't take long to clean the way he likes it. Then, between four and five, I start cooking dinner to ensure I have it hot and on the table when Ray comes in. That stills leaves me the majority of the day with nothing to do. After five months, I was beginning to go crazy. I needed to find something to fill the empty hours in my day. One day, while reading the paper, I saw an ad. A group home for kids was looking for volunteers. Volunteering would be perfect.

For the last month, I've been going to Worthington House for a few hours a day. I'm really loving it. At least now I feel like I'm doing something worthwhile with my time. Plus, I absolutely adore all of the kids. Today, a new little girl named Courtney was brought in. Courtney is only six and from a home where violence is as common as breathing. To say she's skittish and shy is an understatement. Though, for whatever reason, she seems to like and trust me. The head Intake Counselor asks if I can stay later than normal to help out and I oblige. I can't leave this little girl alone. Ray would understand if I'm late with his dinner just this once. We never have take-out, so it will be a treat.

When I walk through the door at nine o'clock, something is off. No lights are on but I know Ray's home because his truck is in the driveway. My heart starts to beat faster the further I walk into the house. A strong sense of unease washes over me as I turn on the kitchen light and see a silhouette of Ray at the dining room table. Why is he sitting in the dark and why am I shaking?

"Where have you been, Holly?" Ray inquires. He takes a long pull from his beer as he stares me down, waiting for my answer.

Nervously, I stammer, "I was at Worthington House. I left you a message. I was the only person the little girl trusted and would let anywhere near her. They needed me to help out." I set the bag of Chinese take-out on the counter, noticing his jaw tighten at my words. Ray is most definitely mad, but never has his anger been directed at me. Slowly, he stands and stalks toward me. Not once do his eyes leave mine. My heart is beating so fast and hard against my chest, it hurts. The cold, angry look in his eyes has my palms sweating and throat dry. The closer he gets, the more nervous I become.

He stops when his face is inches from mine. The smell of beer mixed with whiskey assaults my nostrils, sending waves of nausea through me. Not only do I hate that smell, but Ray doesn't drink whiskey anymore — he loses control of himself too easily.

Ray grabs the bag of food and scrunches up his face in disgust. "What is this shit? It's cold and three hours past the time I should be having my dinner," he snaps. Taking the bag off the counter, he hurls it across the room. It hits the kitchen wall and all the food spills to the floor. His anger confuses me. For the first time in six months, his dinner hasn't been waiting for him and he loses it. It just doesn't make sense to me. "This is why you were told you couldn't have a job."

"But, Ray, I'm only volunteering. I tried to call to let you know I'd be late tonight," I try explaining. I can see by the expression on his face that opening my mouth may have been a mistake. He looks even angrier, if that's possible. Tightly, he grips my arms and shakes me. Fear immediately courses through me and tears start to flow from my eyes. "Save the waterworks. You'll get no sympathy from me. They'll only piss me off even more. You know the rules, your responsibilities, and you disregarded them. I don't ask for much, Holly, but if you can't do the few little things I ask for, you'll have to face the consequences," he fumes. Before I have a chance to respond or even think about what's coming next, there's a sharp pain radiating along the side of my face. As soon as it registers that he hit me, he does it again. There's so much force behind his punches, I'm afraid my head will snap right off my shoulders. I try to move away from him, but he has me pinned against the sink. There's no escape. Slowly, I look into his eyes and I'm startled by what I see. The love and affection I usually see in his eyes is gone, replaced with anger and hate. In this moment of rage, it's like the Ray I know and love is gone. I can't decide what hurts the most right now, the beating I'm receiving or the fact that Ray is the one giving it to me. I try to think of anything but the horror I'm living at this moment. I have no idea how long it lasts. When I feel myself begin to blackout, I welcome the darkness as long as it takes me away from what's being done to me.

Slowly, I open my eyes and tilt my head to look around. I'm still in the kitchen, laying on the floor in front of the refrigerator. Everything seems to hurt, whether I move it or not. Tears start to flood my eyes as I recall the events of last night. How could he do this to me? Was it all my fault, like he said? I gently ease myself up off the floor. I have to grab a hold of the counter to keep from falling. The room is spinning. Damn! My head is pounding and every breath I take sends a stabbing pain through my rib cage. Glancing at the clock on the stove, I see that it's eight in the morning. I look outside to see Ray's truck isn't in the driveway. He got up and went to work, leaving me passed out on the kitchen floor. How could he do that? I can't think about this anymore, my head hurts too damn bad.

After cleaning up the mess on the kitchen floor, I go upstairs to take a shower, hoping the warm water will ease some of the pain. As I'm standing in front of the mirror, I'm stunned by the sight of myself. My face is covered in bumps and bruises. There's a cut on my very swollen bottom lip. Lifting my shirt causes me to run for the toilet and empty my stomach. There are bruises all over me in the shape of Ray's hands and feet. I get into the shower and pray the water can wash this nightmare away.

I spend the rest of the day cleaning the house, making sure

everything is just like Ray likes it. For dinner, I prepare lasagna with a salad and garlic bread — his favorite. I don't dare do anything to set him off again. I have no idea what kind of mood he'll be in once he gets home and I sure as hell am not going to make it worse. The closer it gets to him coming home, the more nervous I become. My ribs still ache with every move I make and no amount of makeup will allow me to cover up the bruises on my face.

I'm just putting dinner on the table when I hear his truck pull in the driveway. Trembles wrack my body, only getting worse when the front door opens. Ray comes into the dining room holding a huge bouquet of pink roses and wearing a smile on his face. What the fuck am I missing here? I want to throw up and he's all happy and smiling like it's just another normal day. He walks up to me and presses his lips against my cheek. My whole body tenses, protesting his touch. He notices, but leaves it alone. He holds the flowers out to me and I immediately take them. Even though every fiber within me is telling me to chuck them in the trash, I pull out a vase and fill it with water before joining Ray at the table.

"Dinner smells and looks great, Holly," Ray compliments. I smile as best I can, trying to keep him happy.

"Thank you. I know it's your favorite." I know I should've been gone when he came home. I know the chances this will happen again are high. But where would I go and how would I get there? I have no one to run to and no money to get me there even if I did. I'm stuck and he knows it.

Paul

I ROLL over in my bed, pulling the pillow over my head to try to drown out the shouting coming from downstairs. My stomach twists into knots. Knots so tight I think my insides might burst at any moment. There's no chance of escaping the sounds.

"Why do you make me do this?" my father roars. Of course, there's no reply from my mom. She knows anything more than reacting to the pain will only make things worse, so she takes every punch and kick in silence. This has been going on my whole life, but it used to be only once or twice a year. Lately, it's all the time and worse than ever before. I don't know how much more I can take. For sixteen years, I've been watching my dad beat my mom. As I got older, I started to intervene, which only caused him to turn on me. I've begged and pleaded with her to leave him, but she always has an excuse — her biggest being how much she loves him.

So, here I lay, trying to make a choice. Do I stay up here knowing he's down stairs using my mom like a punching bag or do I go downstairs to protect my mom and allow him to beat on me instead? My dad is shorter than I am and after a night of drinking, I could take him with one hand tied behind my back. But I still can't bring myself to hit my own father, which has to make me all kinds of fucked up. This man beats on me and my mom and I don't have the balls to hit him back. He still makes me feel like that little scared seven year old just trying to stop his mommy from being hurt. The same mommy who stays with the man who hurts her and her child. I'm always torn in two. I want to hate them both for the agony they've put me through for sixteen years. For not allowing me the happy childhood I deserved. At the same time, I love them. They're my parents. I would rather take the beating than debate this dilemma. The beating is easier.

My mom screams out in pain and I instantly react. I'll always choose to protect her first, no matter the consequences. She used to be so happy and full of life. Now, after all these years of torture, she's just a frightened shell of the woman she once was. He's destroyed her. And they've destroyed me. If this is what it's like to be in love, I'm never letting it happen to me. A man who thinks he has the right to do whatever he pleases to the woman he loves. A woman who will sit back and take the abuse, saying she loves him too much to leave. I don't understand intentionally wanting to hurt someone you claim to love. Shouldn't you want to protect them with everything you are?

When I get to the bottom of the stairs, I notice it's gotten quiet. Too quiet. My pulse starts to pick up. A small amount of blood on the hardwood floor catches my eye as I enter the living room. Bile rises in my throat, threatening to choke me. I've always worried that one day he would go too far and kill her, maybe even me. I stand there, frozen in place, too afraid to venture into the kitchen. What if my worst fear has come true? All these years of trying to save her. All of the bruises and broken bones I've taken in her place. What was it all for? So he can just kill us all one day? I can't live like this anymore. It's obviously I'm not reason enough to make her leave and at some point, no matter how much it will kill me, I have to think of myself. My sanity. If we survive tonight, I'll beg her to leave with me one more time, but no matter what her choice is, I'm gone.

Another scream comes from the kitchen and my feet are suddenly in motion again. Sweat is dripping from my forehead. The rapid thumping of my heart is deafening. I have no idea what I'm walking into. For a split second, I think of grabbing my things, running out the door, and never looking back. Saving myself. But that goddamn protector in me won't allow it. Sometimes I really hate that I can't be a selfish bastard like my father.

Rounding the corner, I'm immobilized by the sight in front of me. My mom is sitting in a chair at the table, my father standing in front of her repeatedly bashing her in the head with a wooden rolling pin. The smell of blood and the sound of the rolling pin making contact with her skull is making me nauseous. In my head, I see myself running full force into him and just hitting him over and over again until he's the one bleeding on the floor. I wish I had the courage to do it.

"Stop it! Please!" I stammer, still unable to move any closer. The rolling pin stops inches away from her head and he slowly turns his icy gaze to me.

"Boy, I never pegged you for stupid. I thought you would've learned not to interfere by now. You know how this works. I'm gonna come over there and beat you silly, then I'll be right back over here to finish up on your momma. Why don't you turn around now and save yourself some hurt," he sneers. He's right. My interference only gives her a brief reprieve. He knows I won't hit back and when I pass out, he goes right back to her. I glance over at my mother and cringe. Her eye is swollen shut. Her nose is clearly broken, pointing to the left. Even through her swollen lips and blood, I can see teeth are missing. She sees me watching her and slumps down into the chair. He notices and it fuels his rage a little more. He grabs her by the chin and lifts her head.

"Don't get comfy, bitch! I'm nowhere near finished with you. Looks like your little pussy of a son wants to get his ass kicked for a while. I gave him a chance to walk away, but it looks like he is just as stupid as you are. Neither one of you will ever learn no matter how hard I beat the lesson into you," he rants with an evil smirk on his face. In his sick, twisted mind, he truly believes what he's doing is okay. There's no remorse at all. In his eyes, we are the ones who deserve every blow he gives.

Something inside me snaps. Like a switch being flipped on, the fear I always feel when his sights are turned to me is gone and replaced with a rage so strong, my entire body trembles. Fear flashes in his eyes, fueling my rage even more. I lunge forward, grabbing the collar of his shirt with my left hand. I use my right hand to punch him square in the nose with as much strength as I can. The sickly sound of his nose breaking mixed with the coppery smell of the blood spilling out from it makes me smile. I smile because it feels good to finally find the courage to fight back. I smile because seeing the terrified look on his face and knowing he's getting a glimpse of what we've felt all these years is a little satisfying. And I smile because when I'm finished, this son of a bitch will never lay another hand on me ever again.

Before I know it, my father is curled up in a heap on the kitchen floor. It's so fitting seeing as my mother and I have looked like that more times than I can count. I have no idea how or even why I stopped pounding on him, but I wish I would have done this years ago. I turn my attention to mom. She needs medical attention and the emergency room isn't an option. It comes with too many questions she'll refuse to answer. That only leaves the free clinic downtown. They see this type of shit all the time. They don't bother to ask questions they already know the answers to. I gently get her to the car and drive to the clinic.

After four hours at the clinic, we are on our way home. A broken nose, mild concussion, and tons of cuts and bruises are what the monster left her with this time. As long as she stays, there will be a next time and it will most likely be worse. We both need to leave him and start over — try to be happy again. We pull into the driveway and I turn off the engine. Neither one of us makes a move to exit the car. You never know what to expect when walking through those front doors. I don't think there has ever been a time when I haven't been scared to enter my house. The one place that should make me feel safe and happy is the place that breeds all my worst nightmares.

"Mom, please leave with me. We can start over and never have to worry about him hurting us again," I beg. When I hear her sniffle, I turn to look at her. She's staring at the house as tears stream steadily down her face. I know her answer before she says a word.

"I love you more than anything, son. Please always remember that. I know I'm weak and I never protected you the way a mother should've. I've never been able to stand up to him even when he was hurting you.

For that, I'm so sorry," she sobs. I reach over and hold her hand. I know she loves me and would've protected me if she could. I can't blame her for being weak when it comes to him. I was, until today. "I know you can't understand my reasoning, but I have to stay. You don't. As much as I love you, Paul, I need you to go. I want you to have a life without the fear and pain. I want you to have the life I never did."

She reaches in her purse and pulls out a small paper bag. For the first time, she faces me. Her eyes look so tired and sad. She hands me the bag then reaches over and hugs me tight. Why does it feel like this is the last time I'll ever see her again? That thought causes my tears to flow and at the moment I don't care. We both hold each other as tight as we can. As if we're hanging on for dear life.

"I've packed a bag for you. It's in the trunk. Take it and don't look back. Don't ever look back. Forget about me and this hell you once called home. Please, Paul, I need to know you can do that for me," she pleads. How can I just walk away knowing she's here and what she's going through? "It's time to save yourself and for me to be the mother I should have been a long time ago. You need to get out, Paul, and don't come back." Hugging me one last time, she gets out of the car and gets my bag from the trunk. I meet her at the back of the car, tears streaming completely unchecked down my cheeks.

"I love you, Mom," I sputter in between sobs.

"I know, baby. I love you, too. You are the only thing that's ever brought me happiness. Now, go and don't come back." She kisses my cheek and walks into the house. I stand there for what feels like hours, trying to decide whether I can really leave her behind. Finally, I glance to the house one more time before turning and hauling ass as fast as I can away from the hell I used to call home.

CHAPTER
Two

Holly

THE PAST two months have been pure hell. I never know which Ray is going to walk through the front door. Will it be the sweet, gentle Ray I fell in love with, or the cold, abusive Ray? After the first time he hurt me, he begged me to forgive him. He swore he'd never do it again. I wanted to believe him, but honestly, deep down, I knew it would happen again. And he didn't disappoint.

Two weeks later, he came home later than normal without letting me know. As a result, his dinner was cold. When I tried to explain that if he had just called me to let me know he was going to be late, I could've kept it warm, he got angry. Really angry. That beating was worse than the one before. The next one came just a week later, over the type of bread I purchased from the grocery store. Now they come at least two to three times a week and no longer does he feel the need to give me a reason.

I haven't been able to go back to Worthington House since the first beating. How could I explain the numerous bruises all over my face? As soon as they go away, he adds them right back, as if he knows they will keep me contained at home. No matter what I do, it's never good enough for him. Every time it happens, I just want to run. Run far away where he can never hurt me again. But…how? My name is on nothing. I have no credit cards, no bank account. I have no job. Ray used to give me enough cash each week to buy groceries, but lately, he's started going with me on Saturdays. I'm starting to feel like a prisoner in my own home. Ray controls everything. Even if I had the nerve to leave, I have no means to do so. My car suddenly broke down and Ray hasn't found the time to take it to the mechanic.

I stand in front of the mirror, trying my damnedest to cover up all the various stages of bruising blanket my face. It's no use. There are too many. Some black and blue. Some a dark purple. Some a yellowish-green. There's just not enough make-up in the world to help the mess that is my face. Tonight, his parents are coming for dinner. Raymond Senior and Gianna have always been nice to me and they seem to like me. How am I going to explain away all of these bruises if they ask? Why would he want them to come over knowing they'll see me this way? Do they have any idea what their son is capable of? If they did, would they help me? Or maybe they already know and that's why he doesn't care.

The hairs on the back of my neck stand at attention when I hear him enter our bedroom. My heart beats at a frantic pace as I scramble to think if there's something I could've done to set him off again. He enters the bathroom all smiles. For now, it seems he's the Ray I married. Walking up behind me, he slides his arms around my waist and nuzzles my neck. I pray for him to be in these moods, but his touch causes my stomach to turn. I try not to let my disgust show. I try to avoid anything that will surely send him into a rage.

"You need to finish getting dressed. My parents will be here very soon. Besides, if you put on any more make-up, you're gonna look like a fucking hooker," he says sweetly, as if he hadn't just insulted me. Still attempting to keep the peace, I don't react.

"I'm all finished. I'll go make sure everything's set for dinner, if that's okay?" Asking him for permission makes me want to vomit, but I've learned it makes him happy. This time is no different. He pats me on the ass, sending me toward the door.

"That's a good idea. Take out the good bottle of whiskey, would ya? It's my dad's favorite," he yells to me. Chills run down my spine at the thought of what things will be like when we're alone later after he's been drinking. There's no way I'll get through the night without another beating. I just pray to God he'll be too tired to make it a long one.

For dinner, I've made Chicken Parmesan over spaghetti with salad and garlic bread. For dessert, homemade Tiramisu. I have a lot of time on my hands so I've watched a shit ton of the Food Network. I've gotten very good at cooking; it's just too bad I'm usually too nervous to really enjoy anything I eat. I double-check the table to make sure it's set perfectly and wait until I hear them pull up in the driveway before I start to lay the food out on the table. I make sure to place the whiskey between Ray and his father's spot at the table. I've chilled a nice bottle of wine for Gianna and I — at least he still allows me to have a glass or two with dinner.

As soon as I finish placing everything on the table, Ray and his parents walk into the dining room. Gianna wraps me in a tight hug. When she breaks away, I see sympathy and recollection flash in her eyes. It's as if she knows exactly what I'm going through because she's been there. I can't picture Raymond being anything like his son. That is…until he sees me. A proud papa smile spreads across his face when he looks at his son. It takes everything in me not to throw up right there in the middle of my dining room.

"Holly, this all looks amazing. You're turning into quite the cook, dear," Gianna beams, trying to take my attention away from her husband. Things make a hell of a lot more sense now. I see why he wasn't worried about inviting them over. He learned everything he knows from his father. So, of course, neither one of them will say a word — his mother too afraid, his father too proud.

"Thank you, Mom. I want to make sure I have a happy husband," I say, trying to sound sincere with a smile on my face. It must work because Ray has a smile on his face. "Shall we all sit before it gets cold?" I ask, looking to the men for approval. They both nod and lead us to our chairs. Raymond pours two very full glasses of whiskey for Ray and himself. Ray opens the bottle of wine and pours a glass for his mother and me. If I drink it slow enough, he'll allow me to have a second glass. While the men begin to talk shop, I try to think of anything to say to Gianna just to make conversation.

"Mom, maybe one day we can get together and do a little shopping and have lunch," I suggest. I hear a fork fall against a plate and look up to see Gianna's mouth wide open and her face full of fear. Confused, I glance over to Ray and his father, who are both fuming. What the hell did I say?

"Looks like you haven't taught her enough yet, son. She needs to learn her place is at home and not out running the roads spending money that isn't hers," Raymond sneers. *He can't be serious.* "Do I need to show you how it's done or do you think you can handle it?" He wouldn't dare let his father touch me. Ray finishes the rest of the whiskey in his glass before answering.

"I'm perfectly capable of handling my own wife," Ray states as he grips my arm tight and yanks me to my feet. *Oh, God! He's going to do this now! In front of his parents.* I look to Gianna, hoping she'll do something to stop this, but her eyes are trained on her lap like a good little girl. Ray pulls me to the living room, still in view of his father.

"You are gonna pay for embarrassing me in front of my father," he hisses just before he slams his fist into the side of my head. I fall back, landing on the glass coffee table and shattering it into a million pieces. A small whimper escapes my lips as pain shoots through my back, the tiny shards of glass causing warm blood to run down my skin. When I open my eyes, Ray is above me. He grabs my head, lifting it just to crash against the hardwood floor. My ears begin to ring and my sight blurs. He continues slamming my head into the floor, over and over, until my body goes limp and darkness finally takes over.

I wake up to the sound of beeping. When I try to open my eyes, pain shoots through my head. Only one eye will open. As soon as my eye adjusts to the dim light, I realize I'm in the hospital. My pulse quickens, as does the beeping. Who brought me here? In that moment, the door opens and Ray walks in, followed by a doctor.

"Holly, I'm so happy you're awake. I've been so worried," Ray says as he squeezes my hand a little too tightly.

"What happened?" I whisper. God, I hope that wasn't the wrong thing to say, but how else will I know what Ray has told them? When the doctor glances down at his chart, Ray gives me a reassuring smile, letting me know I've done the right thing.

"You were taking your walk after dinner, like you always do, but you were gone longer than usual. I started to get worried and went to look for you. I found you unconscious on the sidewalk," Ray responds.

"I remember leaving to go on my walk, but nothing after that," I say, hoping this whole story is somewhat believable. If it's not, I'll be the one Ray blames. Thankfully, the doctor doesn't seem to disbelieve what he's being told.

"The police said your phone was missing, so it was most likely a mugging, Mrs. Marconi. You've sustained severe head trauma so not remembering isn't uncommon. I'll give you both some privacy. I'll be back later to see how you're doing," the doctor says before walking out. As soon as the door closes, I feel nauseous. Being alone with Ray frightens me. Not that being with other people did me any good either. What the hell did I get myself into?

"I'm sorry I let myself get so out of control. I didn't mean to hurt you as badly as I did. I love you so much. You know that, don't you?" Ray pleads. Not 'I'm sorry I hurt you at all', which is what he should be saying. He truly thinks what he does is okay and I will never be able to convince him otherwise. I just need to face the fact that this is my life and I have to deal with it.

"I know, Ray. I love you, too," I tell him, trying to sound as sincere as possible. Ray doesn't leave my side for the three days I'm in the hospital. The people around us see a loving and doting husband who's worried about his wife. But they have it all wrong. He's guarding his prisoner. Making sure I don't tell anyone what goes on behind closed doors. Or, even worse, make my escape. I have a sinking feeling that my only escape from his torture will be the day he loses all control, the day I skip the hospital bed and head straight to the pine box. That will be the only way he lets me go.

Paul

"DAMN IT!" I shout as I throw my phone down. It's been two months since I left and I've been leaving my mom messages for weeks. I just want to hear her voice. To hear she's okay. I never should have left without her. What kind of son leaves his mother alone with a monster?

The night I left, I started running. I didn't know where I was going, or how I was getting there, I just ran. And before I knew it, I was in Reggie's driveway, fifteen blocks away from my house. Reggie and I have been best friends since third grade and I've basically lived at his house all these years. His family is great — the total opposite of mine. They never ask me questions about my home life, even though I'm sure they have some idea of what goes on. All the bruises and broken bones over the years are pretty much a dead giveaway; there are only so many excuses a kid can use to explain them away.

When I showed up on Reggie's doorstep and explained what had happened, his parents told me I was welcome to stay as long as I wanted, to consider this my home from now on. I have to admit, it really is nice to go to bed at night without worrying about what might happen as soon as you close your eyes. For the first time in as long as I can remember, I'm not living every second in constant fear. I finally feel safe and even a little happy. I wish my mom knew how it felt to be safe and happy.

"Let's go, we're gonna be late for school," Reggie yells to me from downstairs. Picking up my phone, I try one more time to call her. Straight to voice mail. *Shit!* When she told me I needed to leave, I didn't think that meant she was cutting off all contact with me. I can't just pretend she doesn't exist. Leaving her behind was hard enough, that would be impossible.

I shove my phone into the pocket of my jeans and grab my backpack. Another good thing about living with Reggie is he has his own car. No more riding on that noisy ass school bus every day. The whole ride to school, I'm consumed with thoughts of my mom. Does she want me to stay away from her completely? Is she ignoring my calls, hoping I'll get the hint and eventually stop? The bag she handed me had a note and twenty-thousand dollars in cash. I've read the note so many times, I have it memorized.

Dear Paul,

I started saving this money the day your father hit me the first time, over twenty years ago. If the day ever came when I found the courage to leave, I knew I'd need cash to do it. After you were born, I no longer saved it for me. I knew you would need to get away from him and I wanted to make sure I could make that happen for you. Please remember how much I love you. Take this money and start a life for yourself that makes you happy. As long as I know you're safe and happy, I'll be okay.
Love always and forever,
Mom

She never says not to contact her ever again. Even if she did, I can't abandon her. I've always tried to protect her and I can't stop now. "Hey, Reg, can you drive me by my parents' house after school? I'm worried about my mom and I want to check on her."

"Yeah, sure. No problem," Reggie answers with a forced smile. Aside from my mom, he's the only person who knows everything that went on inside those walls. I know he's worried about me going anywhere near that house.

"I just need to make sure she's okay."

"You don't have to explain. I get it. But I'm sure he's pissed that you left. What will he do if he sees you? You've finally gotten away and I hate to see him do anything to you again." His tone is one of concern. I didn't plan on seeing my dad. I also never really thought about how he'd feel about me leaving. Why would he even care? I was always just in his way. What does worry me is whether he found out mom helped me leave. He would surely punish her for that.

"It's not me I'm worried about. After the last time, I don't think he'll ever touch me again. My mom is a different story. She won't fight back," I tell him.

The day went by so slowly, I thought I would go crazy. I couldn't focus on anything the teachers were saying. The closer we get to my house, the more nervous I become. I have this gnawing feeling that something's wrong. I don't know which worries me more: the things my father could've done to her in my absence or that she won't want to see me.

As we turn the corner and my house comes into view, the hairs on the back of my neck stand up. His truck is in the driveway. In my sixteen years, I've never once known my dad to be home before five o'clock on a workday. This isn't a good sign. Wiping my sweaty palms on my jeans, I try to calm my nerves. Reggie and I both look at each other and then the truck parked in the driveway next to my mom's car. Neither of us know what to do or say. Should I chance going in there and facing his wrath? I have no choice. There's no way I can leave without making sure she's okay.

"I know you have to go in there, but do you want me to go with you, just in case things get out of hand?" Reggie asks nervously. I appreciate that he's willing to do this for me, but I can't let him go in there. It's one thing to tell him about the things that have gone on in that house, but experiencing it firsthand is a whole other thing. I won't put my best friend through the same hell I've dealt with all these years.

"I better go by myself. Just keep an eye and ear out. If I need help, you'll know." Giving him a reassuring smile, I open the car door. As I stand, my legs are unbalanced. "I can do this," I whisper to myself as I steady my nerves. Walking slowly to the door, I ring the bell and wait. When there's no answer, I walk over to the living room window. The house is trashed. Chairs are tipped over, broken glass strewn about, a large amount of blood on the wall. I rush back to the door and turn the handle. Locked. I try again, slamming myself against the door. That's when I remember my mom put a spare key under a rock in the planter along the driveway.

Frantically grabbing the key, I steady my hand to unlock the door. Slowly and quietly, I walk into the house. Several walls have holes in them about this size of a fist. Plants are knocked over on the floor. The farther into the house I get, the worse the destruction is. In the dining room, food is spilled all over the table, floor, and splattered on the walls. All these years of witnessing the abuse from my father, never have I seen anything like this. The knot in the pit of my stomach becomes painful and I'm trembling from head to toe, petrified to keep searching the house.

I climb the stairs, silently praying my mom is okay. By the looks of this house, I'm scared I might be too late. When I see more blood along the stairs, I start to get nauseous. Following the trail, I end up in front of the door to my bedroom and fall to my knees right there in the doorway. "No, no, no," I repeat, over and over again. Lying on the floor, side by side, are my parents. Both dead. My mom is covered in blood, bruises, and cuts. This is what I've always been afraid of. My bastard father killing her and himself. The only difference is…I was always the one lying next to my mother when I had this nightmare. I never should've left her alone with him. I had finally fought back. He wouldn't have been able to do this if I was here. I might as well have been the one to pull the fucking trigger myself. This is all on me. I should be over there on that floor bleeding next to my mom. I don't deserve to live after running from here and leaving her alone. I'm a coward. She always called me her protector, even though he kicked the shit out of me every time. I still took some of the beating off of her, but not this time.

I glance at my father's hand, see the gun resting beside it on the cold wood floor, and my chest tightens. My father's voice taunts me. *"Pick up the gun, you selfish, weak coward. Go ahead. Be a man for once in your pathetic life. Pick it up and do what I would have if you hadn't run away like a little pussy."* He's right, I belong there with them. This is where I should've been. That's why he did this here, in my room. To show me I was meant to be a part of this, too. It's the way it's supposed to be.

Hands grip my shoulders, lifting me from the floor. "Paul! Let's go outside. You don't to see this," Reggie commands as he guides me out of my room and down the stairs. The minute we're outside, I break. Sixteen years of hurt, anger, guilt, and love pour out of me. I collapse on my front steps, my knees giving out, sobbing so hard, I can't breathe. Even being the monster he was, I loved my dad. I couldn't help it. I tried not to...I really did. We had some really good times together when he was happy and sober. I know he truly loved my mom and I, he just became a different person when he drank.

Sirens scream down the road and stop in front of the house. There's so much commotion all around me. Police officers try to ask me questions, but all I can do is sit here and cry uncontrollably. When a male officer resembling my father puts his hand on my shoulder to calm me, I'm thrown into a full-blown panic attack. I can't breathe, sweat pours off my face, and everything around me starts to spin. In a flash, I'm being lifted onto a gurney and loaded into the back of an ambulance.

I only spent twenty-four hours in the hospital then was able to go back home to Reggie's house. His parents told the police if they wanted to talk to me, they would have to do it there not at the police station. They felt I had been through enough. I was told my parents had only been dead a couple hours before I got there. If only I had checked on them sooner.

I didn't have an elaborate funeral service for them, because really, who'd show up? No one wants to be associated with the guy who beats his wife and son for years and then kills her. This town is too small for me to deal with any longer — everyone either giving me sympathetic looks or ones of disgust. I just can't take it any longer.

I bought a car a month ago and became emancipated. I knew I couldn't stay in this town for two more years. Just as I put the last bag into my car, Reggie walks out. He's pretty pissed I'm leaving him. We always planned on getting out of here together, taking off to L.A. and starting a band.

"I understand why you have to leave, it just sucks," Reggie states as he stares at the ground. "By the time I graduate and make it out to L.A., you'll be settled and have forgotten all about me. Things will never be the same, never be like we planned." I wish I could argue with him, but he's probably right. Things changed the minute I walked into my house and saw my parents dead on the floor. I changed. Something inside me broke. I failed to protect the one person I loved most in this world because I was a selfish bastard. For that, I don't deserve anything good and I sure as hell won't bring anything but misery to anyone who thinks they care about me. So, I lie to my best friend, hoping to avoid a drawn out scene or witnessing the pain me being lost for good will cause, truly earning my selfish bastard title. I smile wide and bring him in for a brotherly hug.

"Don't be a stupid fuck. It will just give me time to find a job and an apartment for us. We are still sticking to our plans," I say before getting into my car and driving away from the last person I will ever let myself care about. The last person I'll ever let care about me.

CHAPTER
Three

Paul

I OPEN MY eyes and glance around the room, not recognizing my surroundings. I'm a little scared to look over at the woman snoring softly beside me. Usually, I try to choose the girl I'm going home with before I drink myself into a stupor. Just because I like to party and never with the same woman more than once, doesn't mean I don't have standards. There have been a couple times I've woken up next to girls so fucking ugly, they'd scare the stripes off a tiger. The body next to me stirs, her arm slowly making its way around my waist. I hate this part. When I have to explain I don't cuddle. I don't kiss. I don't do anything that can be confused as more than just a fun night of meaningless sex. The only feelings involved are pleasure, nothing more. Of course, I tell them all of this upfront, but sometimes they still think they have the magical pussy that will make me fall head over heels. Not gonna happen.

"How about some breakfast, handsome?" she asks in a voice I can only describe as annoying, but I bet she thinks it sounds sexy. Carefully, I roll over in just a way that it causes her arm to fall off me. I'm relieved to see she's a very pretty girl. A blonde. I haven't been with a blonde in a while. Too bad I don't remember whether the carpet matches the drapes. I kinda like women who stick with their natural hair color. Maybe it's because they're not trying to be something they're not. Like it really matters. I won't be seeing them again. Over the last five years, I've lost track of the number of women I've slept with. But, since I've never been with the same woman more than once, the numbers are high.

"Thanks, but I have to get home and take care of some stuff before work," I explain as I get out of the bed and search for my clothes. Damn! I wish I could remember last night. By the way our clothes are spread out all over the apartment and chairs are knocked over, I would guess it was one hell of a night. One I probably enjoyed a great deal. And by the smile on....shit! I don't even know her name. Anyway, by the smile on *her* face and the googly eyes she keeps giving me, I'd say she also had a good night. Even wasted I don't disappoint.

After I find my clothes and explain again to Isabella — she told me her name after giving me the death glare for twenty minutes — that we would not be seeing each other again, I head home. I'm sure most of the girls I've been with are great. For once, the "it's not you, it's me" line is not a lie. It really is me. I don't deserve love or happiness. I left. Left her all alone with him, knowing he would kill her someday. It's all my fault. I killed her the second I walked away. I'm nothing but a coward and a selfish bastard — just like him. What if I'm like him in other ways? I don't think I could ever strike a woman, but I'm sure he thought the same at some point. As long as I don't ever put myself in the position to find out, everything will be fine. I'll be just fine.

I throw my keys on the granite counter and plop down on my brown leather sofa. I love this apartment. A two bedroom, two and a half bath, with a large eat-in kitchen. I also have a soundproof music room where my drum kit is set up, along with a few guitars and a mic. There's also a game room with a few old school video games, a dartboard, and a pool table. With it just being me, it gets a little lonely at times, but this is the best way. I never bring any of my hook-ups here, just in case they can't take no for an answer. This way, they won't know where I live. I have friends, but no one close. Not since I lost Reggie.

Three years ago, I decided it was time to move on. Reggie had just graduated and was calling me, ready to follow through with our plans. I missed my best friend, so I told him to get his ass in his car and get out here. We were gonna follow our dreams and start a band — me on the drums, Reggie singing and playing guitar. We would just need to find a lead guitarist and a bass player and we would be good to go. Reggie was halfway here when a guy driving an eighteen-wheeler fell asleep at the wheel. He drove right into Reggie's lane and hit him head on. Reggie was killed instantly.

Just another sign that I'm supposed to be alone. Reggie was the last person left who cared about me and now, he's gone. Just like my mom. People who love me die. My decision to move on was short lived. I can't have another person's death on my hands. So, when I get lonely, I like the three B's: booze, blow, and boobs. Not particularly in that order. It's been working out just fine for the last three years. Looking at the clock, I realize I need to move my ass to get ready for work. A quick shower, a sandwich, and I'm out the door.

I park in the back parking lot of Last Call. I've been working here since I first came to L.A. five years ago. I started out cleaning and fetching things for the bands or the owner because of my age. Now, I'm bartending. It's a great gig; lots of hot chicks to flirt with and I get to listen to all of the hottest bands. The club itself isn't anything special, but it's packed every single night. I'd like to think it's due to the exceptional bartender, but it's probably the awesome live bands here every night of the week. Tonight, Deuce, a local band, is playing. They've played here a few times before and they're really talented. These guys will make it big someday.

Tonight is crazy busy. Deuce drew in a bigger crowd than usual. A commotion at the far end of the bar gets my attention. A young guy is trying to sit at one of the stools and he's clearly had too much to drink. He had to have come here that way. He looks a few years younger than me and I know I didn't serve him. Something about him reminds me of Reggie. I make my way to the other side of the bar as a group of assholes start hassling him. They've obviously had way more to drink than this dumbass guy who has no fear and doesn't know when to shut his big mouth. It's almost like he's trying to get the shit beat out of him. Not only does it remind me of the time I saved Reggie from getting beat up, but I see something in this guy. Something I see in myself when I look in the mirror. He's broken, too. He wants these guys to hurt him so it takes away whatever pain he's running from. He wants to feel anything other than what he normally feels on a daily basis. I know that feeling all too well.

I nod to the bouncers at the door and they are quickly by my side. Things have escalated and the biggest guy in the group shoves the guy sitting by himself. I grab the big guy's shoulder and spin him around so he's facing me. The three bouncers hold off the rest of the group. "Do we have a problem here?" I ask. Luckily, the guy is a foot shorter than me and so drunk, he couldn't hit the broad side of a barn. "We don't. This guy does," he slurs as he tries to wiggle from my grip to get to the younger guy. "He spilled my beer and when I told him to apologize, he told me to fuck off." I couldn't stop the laugh that escapes my mouth. The kid is ballsy, I'll give him that. Not too smart for running his mouth like that when he's alone against five other guys who are clearly looking for a fight, but ballsy.

"I think it's time you all went home. There's not going to be any trouble in here tonight. Forget about your tab and walk out the door." They all look at each other and then at me and the bouncers.

"Fine. Fuck it. He wouldn't have been much of a challenge anyway," he sputters and they all turn to leave. The kid looks pretty pissed at me for ruining his chance at a fight. I have to agree with the other guy though; this kid wouldn't be much of a challenge. I don't think all the alcohol in his system would have even been the factor. I honestly don't think he would've fought back.

"Thanks, man, but I had that," the kid says.

"If by had that you mean had a major ass kicking coming your way then, yeah you had that," I joke. To my surprise, he bursts out laughing. I put my hand out and introduce myself. "I'm Paul." He shakes my hand.

"Kyle. Thanks again. I didn't mean to start any trouble for ya."

"No problem, but I think you've probably had enough to drink tonight. And I have a feeling I won't be able to serve you anyway, so it might be a good time for you to call it a night as well." He seems like a nice guy and I hate having to kick him out, but I really have no choice. He smiles and nods his head.

"Yeah, I think calling it a night is a good idea. I've caused enough trouble for one night. It was nice meeting ya, Paul. Thanks again for the save," Kyle responds.

"Anytime. Have a good night," I tell him as the bouncers follow him to the door. I still can't believe how much he reminds me of Reggie. Right down to meeting him in basically the same way I met Reggie — saving him from getting an ass whooping. I shake the thoughts from my head and laugh. I sure do miss Reggie. I miss having a close friend, but I know it's not a good idea for the poor soul who chooses to be my friend.

The rest of the night goes by smoothly. By the time I finish cleaning up after we close, it's three in the morning. I lock the back door and start walking to my car. There's a car parked in the back of the lot that shouldn't be there. I walk over to take a closer look. A shadow glaring from the streetlight shows someone is reclined in the front seat. When I get up next to the window, I immediately recognize the person as Kyle, the guy from earlier. The inside of the car is trashed. Various wrappers from fast food joints are strewn all over the front seat and the floor. Clothes are scattered around the backseat. It looks as if he might be living in his car. Not really a smart thing to do in this neighborhood, but not really my problem. I turn and start to walk back to my own car. About halfway there, I see Reggie's face and can imagine him telling me I can't leave this guy alone like this.

"Ah shit!" I hiss. I can't believe I'm gonna do this. I go back over and lightly tap on his window. He jumps up. Once he recognizes me, he opens his door and steps out of the car.

"Hey, man. I can move the car. I didn't see any signs that said no parking or anything, so I figured I was okay for the night," he stammers. I feel bad for the guy. The Florida plates show he's a long way from home and I can't help but wonder what it is he's running from.

"Look, I know it's none of my business, but it looks like you're living in your car. If you need a place to crash, I have an extra bedroom. You're welcome to it until you find a place." He seems taken aback by my offer. I guess I don't blame him. I would be too if some guy I just met offered me a place to stay.

"You do like women, right?" he jokes as he starts to laugh, breaking the tension. At least he has a sense of humor.

"Oh, so you're a funny fucker. You gonna follow me or not?" I ask as I start walking to my car. I'm kinda hoping he says yes. I think I could get along well with this guy.

"Yeah, I'll follow you, as long as you promise not to put the moves on me." He laughs and gets into his car.

Paul

THIS LAST year has been a whirlwind. So much changed after meeting

Kyle. We hit it off right away. I really tried to fight against becoming close friends with him, but it was no use. He is so much like Reggie… it's a little freaky at times. It's almost as if Reggie sent him to me to get my ass back to enjoying life. Whatever the reason and however he got here, I'm thankful for it. I didn't like being so alone. I still haven't, nor will I, changed my mind when it comes to a romantic relationship, but it's nice to have a good friend again. Besides, Kyle is broken like me. His girl tore his heart out, threw it on the ground, and then stopped the fucker into dust. That boy was a mess for a long time. He still is, even though he'll never admit it.

I was able to get him a job at the club and he moved into the guest room permanently. After we both admitted our dream was to play music, we decided to put a band together. Kyle had a name already picked out. Inspired by the girl who so brutally dusted his heart, he wanted to name the band Bleeding Hearts. It was fine with me. Chicks would eat it up. A few auditions later and we had found the perfect guys: Marcus Winters, who plays bass, and Angel Walker, our lead guitarist. The four of us have been inseparable over the last year, living the typical rock and roll lifestyle of sex, drugs, and booze. We've also become pretty well known here in L.A. Life has been good.

So, why am I sitting at the end of the bar by myself while my bandmates are celebrating? We were just offered a recording contract. This is what we've all always said we wanted. A shot at the big time. A chance to be rich and famous. Play sold out stadiums and tour the world. Problem is…I don't think it's what I want anymore. The rocker lifestyle is starting to get to me and the real shit hasn't even begun. I'm not enjoying it as much as I used to. My drug and alcohol consumption will only increase and it's already out of control. I just don't want to ruin it for the other guys. This is their dream, too. I still love playing music. I was happiest when we first started playing at Last Call a couple nights a week. I actually enjoy being a bar manager slash bartender.

"What's up? I thought you'd be more excited than anyone. Something wrong? " Kyle questions as he slides a shot in front of me. He sits on the stool next to me and waits for my answer. He knows something's up, but do I really want to tell him the truth? I've never lied to him before, so there's no sense in starting now. I grab the shot and down it. Maybe it will help ease the sting when my friend laughs at me for being a moron. Who would choose to be a bartender over a rock star?

"I don't think I really want this recording deal. I like playing the small clubs and bars when we feel like it," I spit out. Taking a deep breath, I look up to gauge his reaction. He's just nodding his head. He knows there's more and he's letting me get it all out before he chimes in. "I already feel like I'm out of control with the partying all the time. It would only get worse and that scares me. Right now, I can control it. I can stop the drugs and slow the drinking. Mix in touring, fame, and groupies…I think I'd be too far gone to ever stop it," I confess. There's no expression on his face to give away what he's thinking. With shaky hands, I pick up my beer and take a long pull. I wish he'd say something already.

Finally, he turns to face me with a small smirk on his face. Great. He's gonna laugh his ass off at me. Just like I thought. "Do you know what it is I've always wanted to do?" he asks. Now he's gonna put a guilt trip on me? I shake my head no and he continues. "If you laugh at me, I'll punch you in the face," he says sternly. "I've always wanted to open my own bar and grille. A cool place to hang out and see live bands. A place where I can play whenever I want. As long as we're being honest, I hate L.A. I want to go back to Oakville. I really miss small town living." That sounds nice. Perfect, actually. A small town that's quiet and peaceful.

"Do you need a bartender? That sounds like the kind of place I'd like to work at."

After talking for a few more minutes about his ideas for a bar, we decide to talk to Marcus and Angel. To everyone's surprise, none of us want to sign that deal. We were all just doing it for each other.

"A small quiet town sounds like the perfect place to raise a family. I proposed to Taryn last night and we both want children soon. I'm up for getting the hell out of L.A.," Marcus announces with a shy smile. *Wow.* I knew they were serious, but I never saw this coming so soon. It's great, though. If he's happy, then I'm happy for him. After we all congratulate Marcus on his engagement, everyone turns to Angel. I can't see him ever leaving here. Especially not for some sleepy town in the middle of nowhere. He'd run out of women to sleep with in the first twenty-four hours. He's worse than me when it comes to sleeping around, plus he's not as picky.

"What the fuck are you all looking at? Like I'd stay here if you all left. Besides, I've gone through all of the available women in Los Angeles, along with some who weren't technically available. A change of scenery might not be so bad," Angel quips before heading off after his latest conquest. We watch him, all of us stunned silent. I'm not sure whether it's his cockiness or the fact that he would go just to be with the three of us that has us so surprised. The four of us have grown close over the last year; it's inevitable when you spend so much time together. Kyle and I have become the closest, though. Marcus opens up very little about himself or his past and when he does share, it's never in great detail. Angel is very closed up. All we know is he was born and raised in L.A. and has no family. He's never tried to open up to us and we've never pushed him. The four of us are all broken or damaged in one way or another. We all fight demons from our past every day, and some of us, like Marcus, deal with them better than the rest of us. We don't need to pour our souls out to each other to know we have one another's back, no matter what the situation. Kyle is the only one who has a good family, or any at all, left, so that is what we've become to each other — family. These guys are like brothers to me, and all of us wanting to go to Florida to help Kyle start his dream seems to have somehow strengthened that bond.

Three months later, our four-vehicle caravan is pulling into Oakville. Angel and I both traded in our classic muscle cars for large SUV's, in order to haul all of our gear around. Marcus and Kyle traded their little crappy cars in for big four-door trucks. I always knew Kyle had a little cowboy in him because of those old cowboy boots he always wears, but Marcus buying a pick 'em up truck was a surprise. At least with the bigger vehicles we had no problem bringing everything we needed with us.

Kyle wasn't exaggerating when he said this was a very small town. I've only seen one stop light. Suddenly, Kyle hits his brakes and pulls into the parking lot of a restaurant. We all follow because we have no clue as to where we're going. The place looks old and like it's been closed for years. As soon as I come to a stop, I notice the "For Sale" sign in the front of the building with a "sold" sticker across it. This can't be the place he bought. It looks like a shit hole. He said the place he bought needed a little fixing up. This place looks like it needs a bulldozer and a fresh start.

We all get out of our cars. Marcus, Angel, and I are just looking at each other with 'what the fuck?' looks on our faces as Kyle rushes to the front door. Shrugging my shoulders at the guys, I slowly follow. When Kyle turns around, I see a sparkle in his eyes I've never seen before. The excitement is pouring out of him so rapidly, I can't help but be excited with him. He's like a kid on Christmas morning showing off all of his new toys. Talking a mile a minute, he's pointing out everything about this place that holds special memories for him. And now it all makes perfect sense. This is where he used to hang out with his girl. The one who crushed him. The one he's still in love with. He's still holding out hope that she'll come back to him someday. I don't see that happening, but who am I to say? I don't know anything about this girl. There's this little pain in my heart when I think about how much he must love her. I'm a little envious of the fact that I'll never be able to feel that. Even if my heart were whole enough to allow it, my head certainly wouldn't.

"So, what do you think?" Kyle questions, breaking me from my pity party. Luckily, I heard most of his ideas for renovations. I didn't see it at first but after hearing him explain it, I do.

"It's perfect. This place is going to be awesome," I tell him as he smiles wide. This is truly making him happy, which makes me happy. I think we're all going to like it here.

CHAPTER
Four

Holly

"Holly!" Ray barks as he searches for me. His footsteps are getting closer and his voice angrier. My heart is beating so fucking hard, I'm afraid he's gonna hear it and find my hiding place. When he's like this, he won't stop until he passes out or gets bored. The last time I locked myself in the bathroom, I figured he'd bang on the door for a while then go to bed. No such luck. It infuriated him more and he kicked and punched the door until he broke right through it.

A few weeks ago, I loosened the screws in the air conditioning vent along the wall in the hallway. I knew it would be easy for me to fit into and one place he wouldn't think to look. It's a trick I learned over my eighteen years of being tossed around from one foster home to another — the next always worse than the last. I learned quickly to never show how I was feeling about anything. No matter what was being done to me, I never gave them the satisfaction of knowing it affected me in anyway.

"You are going to be sorry when I find you. The more I have to search, the harder it's going to be on you," he hisses as he stops right in front of the vent. Through the slats in the vent, I can see Ray clenching his fists tightly. Silently, he stands there, waiting for me to make the slightest noise and clue him in on where to find me. He'll get what he wants if I don't get my damn breathing under control. My chest is tightening, making it even harder to calm down and control the fear and panic surging through me.

I should reveal myself. He's right. My punishment will be worse when he does get a hold of me. Normally, I would take the beating without a single tear being shed. Waterworks, as he calls them, only infuriated him more. This time is different than all the other times he's used me as his personal punching bag. For once, I have a reason to want to protect myself. For the first time in my life, I have the one thing I've always wanted. For someone to love me, no matter what, which is something I've yet to experience. For the longest time, I thought Ray was that person. But his true feelings became crystal clear the first time he introduced his fist to my face.

Oddly enough, telling Ray I'm pregnant is what caused his rage. Here I was thinking it would be happy news. How stupid of me to think my husband would be overjoyed, or at least excited, that he's going to be a father.

How the hell did I get here? How did this man, who I once loved so fiercely, turn into the monster searching for me now? And when did I become the weak woman who hides? We weren't always the people we are now. He was the sweetest, most romantic guy there was. I was a tough girl who wouldn't take an ounce of shit from anyone. He wasn't the type of guy who would beat on a woman and I sure as hell wasn't the kind of woman to sit back and take it. This is not how I envisioned my life turning out.

But, really, what the hell did I know? We dated all through high school. He was the only real boyfriend I ever had. Every girl in school wanted to be with him. He had it all. Quarterback of the football team, looks, a well-to-do family, the sweetest personality…I felt so honored that he even looked my way. Never in a million years did I think I was good enough to be with someone like him. I realize now I must have had chump stamped on my forehead. He knew a girl like me would do anything to be with him. And with my low self-esteem issues, no family, and no money, I could easily be controlled. It's just too bad I couldn't read him as easily as he could me.

"I'm quickly running out of patience. You don't really think this will be forgotten do you? Come out now and I'll show some mercy. Keep hiding and I will hurt you so badly, you'll be begging me to put you out of your misery." The vicious tone in his voice causes my body to shake. The smallest of gasps slips past my lips before I can stop it. Suddenly, I can't breathe. For the first time in six years, I can feel tears pooling in my eyes. When I see him turn around and start walking toward me, my entire body begins to shake uncontrollably.

He walks slowly, drawing my fate out for as long as he can, knowing it's terrifying me. The small space that was my safe haven only minutes ago, feels as if it's closing in on me. Abruptly, the vent cover is pulled away. Ray leans down and looks me in the eyes with such an evil expression on his face, I'm afraid I went too far. He might actually kill me this time.

I don't have a chance to think about it because he grips my ankles and yanks them hard. The force slams me to my back as he pulls me from the vent. I gasp for the air knocked from my lungs. My head is spinning while the wheels are turning in his. He's planning my punishment. My first offense was getting pregnant without permission. The second was running and hiding when he began to hit me. How can I stop him? He wouldn't actually want to hurt his own child, would he?

"I've told you over and over again, Holly, I will not share you with anyone. That includes some needy baby. You would no longer have time to take care of me the way you should. That's just not acceptable," he explains as he snatches me off the hallway floor by my hair, sending a blinding pain through my head. I squeeze my eyes shut, praying I can keep the tears at bay as he drags me to our bedroom. Even though I'm probably going to make him even angrier, I have to try. My baby's life may depend on it. I take a deep breath to try to calm myself as much as possible.

"Ray, please don't hurt our baby. I swear, I didn't do this on purpose," I plead. Swiftly, he spins around and kicks me right in the face. The force snaps my head to the side so hard, my tooth flies across the room and lands just in front of the dresser. The coppery taste of blood fills my mouth, making me nauseous. I swallow it down, too afraid spitting it out will only anger him further. I pray it doesn't come back up.

"Now you're gonna start back talking me? Listen, bitch, you do what I tell you. You owe me. No one else wanted you. Your own mother threw you away. I rescued you. I give you a beautiful home, take you to nice places, and give you purpose," he rants. My stomach rolls with every word passing through his lips. He truly believes the shit spewing from his mouth. At one point, I suppose I did, too. Not anymore, though. My mother's choice to put me up for adoption had nothing to do with me. I was an infant. I don't care if he lavishes me with jewels, he doesn't have the right to lay his hands on me.

"Of course, it won't look good if I send my wife to get an abortion. So, this is something I'm going to have to take care of myself. I was going to do it quickly, but since you hid from me and opened your mouth, I've decided to make it hurt like hell," he sneers. He walks away and I hear the closet door open. In this moment, something inside me changes. No longer do I want to curl into a ball and hide. I want to stand up and fight back. Show him I won't allow this to happen any longer. I need to protect my baby.

Slowly, I pick myself up off the floor. The room feels as if it's spinning and it takes a minute to steady myself. Once I have my balance, I turn to face Ray. Honestly, I shouldn't be surprised that he's graduated from his fists to the wooden bat gripped tightly in his hands. A slight snicker escapes me. Not because I think this is funny, this is just the way my luck works. I finally find the courage I need to stand up to him and it's too late. Tears begin to slide down my face and I let them. My poor baby never stood a chance. "I'm so sorry, my sweet baby. I wish I could protect you. I love you," I whisper as I rub my belly where I imagine him to be. 'I'm sorry' keeps repeating in my head, over and over. *Why couldn't I be stronger?* That's the last thought that crosses my mind before I feel the hard wood of the bat slam into the side of my head with a loud crack.

Holly

THIS TIME when I come to in a hospital bed, it's not my doting husband by my side. It's a police officer. Who called the cops? I was in no shape to call them and the neighbors have never called them over the years. When Tanya walks into the room, I have my answer. I met her a year or so ago when I went back to volunteering at Worthington House. Ray had become a pro at beating me without leaving marks on my face and I was getting much better at hiding them. Tanya is a social worker at Worthington House and we became friends quickly. Just by looking at me, she knew what my story was. Normally I would've tried to deny it, but there was something about her that made me trust her completely. I soon found out she too had gone through the same hell I lived every day.

She helped me create an escape plan, but I should've used it sooner. He killed my baby because I was too scared to leave him. I actually thought becoming a father could change him. How stupid of me to think that was even possible. Well, not anymore.

Since Ray is not the kind of man to let me go if I just up and disappear one day, Tanya came up with a plan that gave me leverage against him. Something to allow me to walk away without worry. I'll never be able to walk away and not spend every second looking over my shoulder wondering if this is the day he comes for me, but it's better than wondering when I'll be beat next.

"Damn, girl, you look like you went a few rounds with Tyson," Tanya jokes as she squeezes my hand. The poor policeman looks appalled by her remark. He doesn't realize it's the only way I can deal with the things Ray has done to me. I give him a reassuring smile to let him know it's okay.

"I'll be right outside the door if you ladies need anything," he says before walking out of the room.

I wait until he closes the door behind him. "How did I get here? Why is there a policeman keeping watch over me?" She holds up her hand, putting a stop to my questions.

"Ray called the police after setting up the house to look like someone broke in. He told them he came home and found you beaten and unconscious on the bedroom floor. Joe out there was my idea. I didn't want Ray anywhere near you. He's helped me in situations like this before," she explains. It sounds like something Ray would do in order to cover his ass.

"So? Did you meet with Ray?" I ask Tanya. I need this to work the way we hoped it would. I have to get away from him. When I try to sit up a little straighter, I let out a yelp from the sharp pain that radiates through my abdomen. Just another reminder of how much I've lost.

"Yes, I did. He was more than furious to know you've been recording every beating for the last year. He was really pissed when I showed him the photos of all the bruises with date and time stamps," she explains as she takes a seat next to me. She smiles brightly at me and hands me a big manila envelope. "He was more than happy to find out what it was we wanted in order to make sure none of this got out. I think he's more worried about his daddy finding out than the cops. So, on my way back here I stopped by the courthouse and saw a friend of mine who happens to be a judge. You, my dear, are officially a free woman." Slowly, I open the envelope and pull out the papers. When I read the words "Divorce Decree", tears spill from my eyes, but for the first time in a very long time, they're happy tears. I forgot what being happy felt like. Reality hits me, wiping away the happiness as quickly as it came.

"But…I have no way to get out of here. No money. No car. I'm sorry this was all for nothing." I lower my head, trying to hide the tears from Tanya. The butterflies dancing in my stomach just seconds ago have turned into painful twisting knots. Now, this is a feeling I know all too well.

Laughing, Tanya sits next to me on the bed. "Give me a little credit. Do you really think I'd get you this far to leave you hanging?" When I look up, she's just staring at me. "I've made sure you have enough money to get you by for a while, until you can find a job. I've also managed to get you a car — a piece of shit car, mind you — but it should get you far away from here." And once again, those butterflies are back.

"I'll pay you back. I promise. As soon as I can," I swear to her.

"No, you won't. First of all, it's too dangerous to send me anything that'll give away where you are. And second, someone did this for me once and made me promise that if I ever found someone who needed the same help, I would pay it forward," she says. With tears in her eyes, she tells me she'll be back tomorrow with clothes and everything I'll need to leave. She assures me the police will be guarding my room at all times. As I drift off to sleep, I try to think of where I'd like to call home. The last thing I remember is a vision of beaches and palm trees.

The next morning, Tanya is here bright and early. True to her word, she has a suitcase full of new clothes and a bag with toiletries. She also has a pre-paid cell phone and a new driver's license for me. Holly Anders is my new name. She says keeping the same first name makes it a lot easier for me to keep straight. I have no idea how she thought of all this or how she was able to get a new license for me, but I'm so grateful. Once I'm dressed and all checked out, the policeman walks with us out to the parking lot. For some reason, he's not in uniform today. Maybe it's his day off and he's just doing Tanya a favor.

She seems to know everyone. As soon as I step out into the open, my throat tightens and my heart begins to beat at such a rapid pace, I think it might explode. My eyes are scanning every inch of the huge parking lot. Joe, the police officer, grabs my hand.

"Holly, calm down. You're safe. I promise. We do this for women like you all the time." He looks down at me to make sure I comprehend what he's telling me. "There will be three of us following you until you reach the place you decide is right for you. We'll make sure you're safe, okay?"

"It's time to go. Take care of yourself, Holly. Please, try to be happy. I know it doesn't always come easy for you, but you deserve it." My cheeks heat from her words. "I wouldn't lie to you. You're a smart, beautiful, and strong woman. Make a great life for yourself," she demands as she hugs me so tight, I'm finding it hard to breathe. She holds me for a few more minutes. I thank her and get into my car. She definitely wasn't kidding. The car is a piece of shit, but I'm still smiling bigger than ever before. For once, it's my piece of shit — the first thing I've ever been able to call mine.

The Florida Keys is the destination I keep picturing over and over, so that's where I'm heading. We stop in this tiny little town called Oakville, somewhere around the Everglades, for gas and something about this place catches my attention. It's small, quiet, and everyone seems to know everyone else. This is the type of place you read about in books and magazines. I walk over to Joe and the others.

"This is it, Joe. I'm staying here," I tell him, and I can't help the smile that creeps across my face. "This is my new home." *That sounds really good.*

"I don't blame you. This is a beautiful little town. A perfect choice. Good luck, Holly. I hope you find happiness here," he says as he puts his hand out waiting for me to shake it. Taking him totally by surprise, I reach up and hug him. This man basically saved me and made me feel safe and protected for days, I'm not shaking his hand.

"Thank you so much. You have no idea how much this means to me. Thank you for everything you've done, I'll never forget you," I sob. After a few moments, I take a deep breath and center myself. No more being weak. No more crying over my past. This is my new start and no one will ever make the mistake of thinking I'm a weak woman who can be pushed around again. Joe breaks our hug, looks into my eyes, and grins.

"There it is. The fire I knew you've been hiding. You're a lot tougher than you think. Don't you let anybody push you around" He kisses the top of my head. "Now, go start your new life." I wave bye to the others as I get into my car. Taking one last look at the three of them, I say goodbye to Ray, my past, and most of all, the old Holly. "Hello, Holly Anders! Welcome to Oakville," I shout as I drive in search of a hotel.

CHAPTER
Five

Holly

FOR THE last two months, I've been staying at this little motel, but today, I move into my new apartment. Actually, it's my first apartment. I've never lived alone before. I've never had anything I could call my own until now. It's a small place, but it's very nice and comes furnished. There are four apartments in the building. The landlord said a young couple who just got married lives in the one directly upstairs from me. The other two apartments are occupied by hot, single guys around my age. Poor lady, she thinks she's being nice and doing me a favor by pointing out the available hot men. A normal twenty-three year old would be thrilled by the idea of two hot guys living in the same building, but men, romance, and dating are the last things on my mind. After what I've been through, I honestly don't know if I'll ever be ready for any kind of relationship again.

A month ago, I was hired as a waitress at KC's Bar & Grille. Kyle, the owner, really seems like he'll be a descent boss. He just bought the place and is remodeling. There's about a month left before the place is ready to open. It's actually turned out to be a good thing. I was able to use the time to find the apartment and get myself adjusted to being in this new town.

One night, a couple weeks ago, I found the plastic bag from the hospital that held my belongings from the night I was brought in. Tanya must have stuffed it in the duffel bag when she was helping me get ready to leave. As I pulled the clothes out and noticed the enormous bloodstains, I almost got sick. The memories of that night hit me full force. The blood stains a reminder of how brutal his beating was. He had two objectives that night: cause me as much pain as possible and kill our baby. Sadly, I allowed him to succeed in doing both. No longer will I be that weak woman who doesn't stand up and protect herself or the ones she loves. I may have learned that lesson the hard way, but at least I learned it.

I was surprised to also find my wedding ring in there. I didn't want anything that belonged to Ray. Not anything he bought, owned, or gave me. Which is why I left with nothing but the signed divorce papers. I couldn't very well send it back to him and I sure as hell didn't want it for sentimental reasons, so I drove to the nearest pawn shop and sold it. At least now I'll have a nice little savings to fall back on if I need it. I also splurged a little and bought some new clothes and things I needed for the apartment.

Pulling into the parking lot of the apartment building, I can't help the smile that spreads across my face. My first apartment. *Wow.* I still can't believe it. I quickly park as close to the building as I can and prop open the front door of the building so I can easily get in while carrying boxes and bags. As I open my trunk, I'm overwhelmed by fluttering sensations in my stomach. I can't wait to get the car unloaded so I can set up my new place. I want to know what it feels like to be able to hang a picture where I want it, or place the glasses in the cabinet next to the sink because that's where I like them. Never have I been in control over anything in my life. Ray told me what to wear, cook, how to clean, and pretty much anything else he could give me instructions on. It's a miserable way to live, always wondering whether you're doing everything correctly, never having the freedom to do anything the way you enjoy. From now on, everything is going to be done the way I want.

Loading my arms so full that I can't see in front of me, I make my way to the door. Thankfully, I have the downstairs apartment. If I were upstairs, I could just see it now...me tripping with all this shit in my arms, falling down the stairs, and breaking my damn neck. Yeah, that's how my luck usually works. Maybe this is a new start in more ways than one. Suddenly, I collide with a wall. I'm thrown backwards, everything in my arms flying into the air as I fall flat on my back, hitting my head on the hard concrete sidewalk. *Then again, maybe my luck hasn't changed at all.*

I lay there for a minute with my eyes closed, trying to will away the throbbing radiating through my skull. Slowly, I open my eyes, praying there's nobody else around. How embarrassing would *that* be? The vision that appears before me makes me think I'm either dreaming or I hit that wall really fucking hard and I'm dead. The face moving toward mine is that of an angel. A gorgeous angel whose beautiful green eyes seem to be looking right into my soul. A chill runs up my spine and my heart is about to beat right out of my chest. Then, he smiles. I've heard some of the girls at Worthington House mention panty melting smiles before and I always thought it was the stupidest saying. No longer do I feel that way. This man's smile awakens thoughts and desires I thought were long gone. When his smile widens to show a set of very lickable dimples, I realize I'm just staring at him with my mouth wide open. Then, he lets out a small, sexy chuckle. *My God!*

"Are you okay? You really should be more careful and watch where you're walking," he jokes as he bends so his eyes are level with mine. I'm still in a daze. Not only from the blow to the head, but from this beautiful specimen of a man standing in front of me. His hand moves toward my face and when his skin makes contact with mine, every nerve in my body begins to spark. Gently, he pushes up on my chin, closing my gaping mouth. "Seriously, are you okay? Should I take you to a hospital?" His smile fades, replaced with a genuinely concerned look.

Jesus, Holly, get it together! This is not like me. What is it about this guy that has me acting like an idiot? I mentally shake off my stupid behavior and get myself together. The last thing I need is to start thinking with my meat wallet. I probably wouldn't remember how it works anyway. I'm an idiot. That's all this is. It's been so long since I've been satisfied correctly and I see this very attractive guy and my hormones go crazy. I was a little nervous thinking there might be this weird spark of feelings between us. That's not something I want to deal with. But out of control hormones? That, I can handle. That's why they make vibrators. After making a mental note to go online and order one, I decide it's time to get up off the ground. If I stay here any longer in silence, the poor guy is gonna call an ambulance.

"I'm okay," I squeak out, attempting to stand. Once I straighten myself up, my vision gets blurry and I wobble on my legs. Before I tumble back to the ground again, strong arms scoop me up off the ground. Again, the instant our bodies touch, my pulse picks up, my skin is on fire, and my lady parts are tingling. Damn, is it really possible to be this horny? I've never experienced feelings like this before. Not even as a teenager when I first met Ray, before I knew the evil he hid so well. He starts walking toward the front door of the apartment building and I can't help but wonder where the hell he's taking me.

"I assume you're the new tenant in 2A?" he questions with a distressed look on his face. Is he really that worried about me? There's something about him that's so sad. It's in his eyes as clear as day, the pain he carries with him. He's been hurt badly. "Are you still with me, doll-face?" His voice makes me realize that I've been zoning out again. Being around this guy flips the stupid switch on in my brain.

"Uh. Yeah. I am," I mumble. He stares at me like he's waiting for something more, but I don't have a fucking clue as to what it could be.

"Do you have your keys? It would make it a whole lot easier to get in your door," he teases with a laugh and that sexy as hell smile.

"I see not only do you make a good wall but you're also an aspiring comedian," I tease back. Oddly, I feel very comfortable around this stranger… well, aside from the raging hormones. That's a little disconcerting. He's tall, six-two, maybe six-three, and very muscular. Not overly so, just enough to make you want to lick every one of them very slowly. Then, there's the tattoos. For some reason those always make people think trouble, but not me. Done right, tats can not only be sexy on a man, but also tell you a lot about him. Nothing about this man screams danger to me. It's those eyes of his. They seem to speak to me. Telling me he's kind and gentle. That he loves fiercely and he protects those he loves. The broken and sad part of him that shows through is what makes me so curious about him, though. What could possibly have happened to him to leave such a haunting look in those beautiful eyes?

"Are you always such a smartass or is this a result of the head injury?" he retorts. I pull my keys from the front pocket of my jeans. I'm expecting him to put me down so I can unlock my door, but he's still holding me securely against his chest. I look at him and then to the ground, thinking he'll get the hint. He does, he's just not going for it. Still holding me tight, he somehow removes one arm, grabs my keys, and unlocks my front door. *How the hell…?* "What can I say? I'm a very talented guy," he says with a smirk when he sees the confused look on my face.

"And full of yourself. Don't forget that one," I reply as he gently sets me down on my sofa. My pulse picks up when he sits close to me and places his hands on both sides of my face. He's staring right into my eyes. Is he going to try to kiss me? Shit. What do I do? The last thing I want or need is any kind of romantic or sexual relationship. Plus, we don't even know each other's names.

"Seems like you might like to be filled with me, by the way you're looking at me," he boasts with a laugh, then turns my head so he can examine the back for any cuts or bumps. Did he really just say that out loud? Worse yet, have I really been looking at him like I want him to jump me? Heat flames my cheeks and my eyes are probably as big as serving trays. Thankfully, I'm not facing him. God knows I don't need him to see my reaction. I just don't know if I'm more angry or embarrassed. Probably a little of both. That is, until he opens his mouth.

"Don't be embarrassed doll-face. I have that effect on most women. It's not your fault." I turn so I can see whether he's teasing or serious. Sure enough, he's fucking serious. He really thinks he's every woman's fantasy. Well, not this woman. There's no way I'm going to stroke his ego…or anything else, for that matter.

"Don't flatter yourself. That's the last thing I'm interested in. Even if I were, I wouldn't want it from you. No offense, but you're just not my type." He laughs and comes closer to me. He brings his lips as close to my ear as he can get without touching me. The instant his hot breath touches my earlobe, goose bumps cover every inch of me. My breathing becomes rapid and I silently curse my body for reacting to him.

"I'm every woman's type," he whispers in my ear. Before I can respond, he stands up and walks to the door. "You should put some ice on that nasty bump you have. I'll go grab the guys and we'll get your boxes brought in for you." Again, he doesn't give me a chance to respond or protest before the door closes behind him.

While I'm getting some ice for my head, I can't help but laugh. I still don't even know this man's name, yet I feel like I've known him my entire life. I have an awfully strong feeling he will test every ounce of willpower I possess. Thank God I'll be busy working and won't have too much time to be running into him.

Paul

WHILE I walk upstairs to get Marcus and Angel, I realize I never got the name of the beautiful redhead. I'm not shy or nervous when it comes to women. I have no reason to be. I'm not out to impress them. I'll never even see them again. But…there's something about this woman. There was this spark that ran through my body the second our skin touched. Just being close to her causes my stomach to flip flop and my palms to sweat. Then, when she opened her smartass little mouth, I was instantly hard. Never have I been turned on from just hearing a woman talk. Unfortunately, I can't let these feelings go anywhere. Even though I'd love to know what it would feel like to be with her, especially if just grazing her causes me to feel like I've been electrocuted, I just can't.

I gather the guys and tell them about the girl downstairs. To my surprise, I even end up spilling how it felt when I touched her. After they get the jokes out of their systems, they are understanding.

"Well, since you're not going for it, does that mean I can?" Angel asks. Clenching my fists, I slowly step up close to Angel.

"Don't even fucking think about it," I snarl while jabbing my finger into his chest. When he bursts out laughing, I get the strong urge to knock him on his ass.

"Yeah, that's what I thought. This may possibly be the one to break your whole no relationship rule. And since you already look like you want to throttle me, let me add that I think it will be a good thing. You are not your dad and the sooner you realize it, the happier you'll be," he states and quickly moves away in case I decide to swing. What the fuck does he know about any of it? Absolutely nothing.

"Keep your mouth shut about shit you know nothing about," I tell him as I start to walk toward the stairs. "Now, let's go and help this girl get her shit into her apartment." They both nod and follow behind. I know Angel means well, but he doesn't understand the hell my mother went through. I watched the man who loved her beat her, over and over again. Though my dad was a monster, there's no doubt in my mind that he loved my mom. The monster in him was just stronger than the instinct to protect her. Maybe I'm not like him. I don't think

I'm capable of hurting a woman like that, but he may have thought the same thing at some point, too. I'll be damned if it takes hurting someone I love to find out whether or not I really am like him.

With our arms full of boxes, we walk to her door. I lightly bang on it with my foot so she'll open up. I really need to find out her name. I wonder if it's as beautiful as she is. I shake my head, trying to will the thoughts away. I cannot allow myself to fall for this girl. I need to control it. Just… don't think about her. Easy enough. Sure. I'm snapped out of my thoughts when she opens the door holding a Ziploc bag filled with ice to the back of her head. It physically hurts me to think she's in pain. But…why do I care? I just met this girl, but it feels like I've known her my whole life. This isn't good. Marcus nudges me in the back, forcing me to realize I've just been standing here like an ass staring at her. I'm so glad Kyle's opening the bar soon. I'll be much safer at work.

"Ya going to introduce us to our new neighbor?" Angel jokes.

"Mr. Thinks-every-woman-on-the-planet-wants-him doesn't need introductions," she says with a smirk. The second the smartass comment comes out of her mouth, I'm left in great need of readjusting myself, which is impossible with a hand full of boxes. "I'm Holly. Why don't you all come in and put those down? Over there against the wall is fine. Thank you, by the way, for getting them." I look up just in time to see the shy smile grace her blushed face. She's cute when she looks shy and embarrassed. We all empty our arms and Angel strides right up to her with his hand out. When he gets close to her, she flinches and fear quickly flash in her eyes. I don't think the guys notice, but it's a look I'm all too familiar with. I used to see it in my mother's eyes all the time.

"Hi, I'm Angel. He thinks every woman on the planet wants him, but I know they all want me," Angel tells her with a wink and a small chuckle. Holly throws her head back and lets out the sexiest laugh I've ever heard. This woman is gonna wreck me. I just know it.

"I'm Marcus. My fiancé, Taryn, and I live right above you. Don't mind these two. They both think their God's gift to women," Marcus says as he shakes her hand. "Let's go get the rest of her things, dipshits." We go and grab the rest of the stuff from her car. I can't help but notice she doesn't have a whole lot and pretty much everything she does have is brand new. I wonder what her story is. The twisting in the pit of my stomach tells me I already have a pretty good idea. When I see a bag full of new deadbolts, I know I'm probably right. Here I was being a bit of an ass earlier and it's the last thing this girl needs right now — especially if she's running from someone.

As soon as we walk through the doorway to her apartment, a delicious scent assaults my nose. She must be cooking. She sees us come in and stops putting the dishes into her cabinet.

"Would you all, and Taryn, like to stay for dinner? I'd love to thank you for all your help. I prepared lasagna last night so I could just throw it in the oven. I figured I'd be exhausted from lugging boxes in. I have plenty here for everyone," she offers shyly. Definitely cute when she's being shy. Marcus and Angel look to me as if they're asking my permission. *Geez, just because I said I didn't want to get involved doesn't mean I won't be friends with her.* I give them a slight nod to let them know I'm fine with it.

"Sounds good to us. Taryn is at work, though. She'll be sorry she missed it," Marcus explains.

"Would you like us to put these on for you while you cook?" I ask, holding up the bag of locks. There's that look again. Someone has hurt her and she hasn't been away from him for long. Luckily, she seems to know she's safe with us. Even though we've all just met her, the three of us wouldn't let the asshole hurt her if he showed up.

"That would be really great. Thank you," she says, giving me the most beautiful smile I've ever seen. How could anyone hurt someone so beautiful and sweet? Just like my mother, Holly hides all of her pain so well, nobody would ever know.

"Angel and I will go get my tools," Marcus says while ushering Angel out the door. Angel has a confused look on his face until Marcus gives him a wink. I don't know what these two think they'll accomplish by leaving me alone with her. My mind is made on the subject of relationships and it's not going to change for anyone. And even if I wanted to change it, I couldn't. Not with her. I know she's been hurt. There's no way in hell I'd chance putting her through that again.

I shove my left hand in the front pocket of my jeans and pick up one of the new locks with the right. I pretend to read the instructions on the back because, honestly, I have no idea what else to do. My heart is racing and my hands are a sweaty mess. What is it about this girl that makes me feel like a thirteen year old whose never been laid? I sneak a glance her way and smile when she's doing the same.

"Would you like something to drink?" she asks while poking her head into the fridge. When she bends down to reach something on the bottom shelf, I notice how perfect her ass is and I can't stop staring at it. Then, I have this image of the two of us. We're both naked in bed and I'm holding her. What the fuck is that all about? When did I turn into such a pussy? Holly loudly clears her throat and I realize I'm still staring. Slowly, I lift my eyes to meet hers. "If you need some privacy to finish, the bathroom is over there. Just make sure you clean it all up with tissues, not a hand towel," she says then hands me a beer and goes back to making a salad.

"That won't be necessary. Don't get me wrong, it's a nice ass, but why do manual labor when there are so many willing women to do it for me?" I shoot back. If I keep saying stupid shit like that, I'll have no problem keeping my distance from her. She'll think I'm a grade A asshole and want nothing to do with me. When I hear her giggle, I wonder whether I need to rethink the trip to the bathroom. I know I want her to be repulsed, but at the same time, the fact that she found that remark funny turns me on. With all of these back and forth feelings I'm having, I'm going to end up with fucking whiplash.

When the boys get back, we install the three deadbolts and the latch lock for her. I honestly thought she bought extras. When she said she wanted them all on, it took everything I had not to bombard her with questions. There's definitely someone she's afraid of. Hopefully she'll tell us who it is so we can help keep an eye out.

Dinner is excellent. The girl can cook. I'll have to move boxes for her more often. We've all tried asking different questions to find out where she's from and why she moved to Oakville, but she's smart enough to evade them or quickly find a way to change the subject. I'm even more convinced now that she's running from someone. And since she doesn't strike me as the outlaw type, I would say an ex-boyfriend or husband. I have so many questions I'd like answered, but pushing her to talk to a total stranger would do more harm than good. I'll just have to tell the boys so they can help me make sure whoever he is, he doesn't get to her.

CHAPTER
Six

Holly

$\mathcal{T}$HIS LAST month has been sweet torture. Every time I see Paul, my stomach fills with butterflies and my lady parts tingle like never before. I'm not used to these feelings. The torture of it all is knowing the last thing I need is a relationship. And even if I were ready, who would want someone who comes with the kind of baggage I bring? As bad for each other as I think we are, being near him is like a drug. A drug I can't seem to stay away from, no matter how hard I try.

Every time I need my fix, I make up an excuse to ask Paul for help. By now, he must think I'm completely incapable of doing anything on my own. Once he finishes the task I ask him to help with, I tell myself I'm not going to call him again. But...a day or two later, I need help hanging a picture, fixing a leaky faucet, or moving a heavy piece of furniture. If I run out of things to fix or move, I invite everyone over for dinner.

This small group has quickly become my only friends. All of them are great. Not once have they pushed me to talk about my past. They've asked questions here and there, but if I don't want to answer, that's okay with them. Paul sometimes looks at me as if he knows all I've been through and I keep telling myself it's not possible. How could he have any idea?

Today is my first day working at KC's and I finally have the distraction I need to keep me off the crack that is Paul. I have to admit, I'm a little nervous. This is the first time I've ever been a waitress before and the fact that I'll be the only one for now doesn't help. Hopefully I'll catch on quickly. How difficult can it be? At least the dress code is something I can live with. Jeans and a KC's Bar & Grille t-shirt. After checking my appearance for the tenth time, I figure it's time to get going. I don't want to be late on my first day.

As I walk by Paul's apartment door, I'm so tempted to knock. There's no reason why. At least, not one I'm aware of. Something about him just draws me to him. Makes me want to be around him. Even though I know how bad the idea is, I can't seem to stay away. I force myself to keep walking past his door and to my car. Working is just what I need. If I'm busy, I won't have time to spend thinking about him. Maybe at night I'll be so tired from being on my feet for hours, I won't dream about him anymore either. Which reminds me, I need to pick up more batteries for the Paul stand-in I keep in the top drawer of my bedside table. Since I've met Paul, that poor thing gets one hell of a workout.

Pulling into the parking lot of KC's, my hands begin to shake and my mouth goes dry. "Pull it together. You've been to hell and back more than once, you can handle a job. Stop being a baby," I tell myself as I check my face one more time in the rearview mirror. "You can do this. This is the last piece of your new life puzzle." Smiling to myself, I exit my car. I'm ready. Once I get that first paycheck, I'll be officially taking care of myself. That's gonna be one hell of a feeling.

Walking into the bar, I'm pleasantly surprised at how much nicer it looks now that all the renovations are finished. The last owner let the place fall apart, but Kyle brought it back to life. He's updated it while keeping the original vibe. It has a fun, casual feel to it. The bar is u-shaped, located prominently in the center of the room. It has a gorgeous carved, dark wood base with a black granite countertop. Off to the right is a raised stage area with a dance floor. Behind the bar is a long rectangle window with a counter leading back to the kitchen. To the left, all along the walls, booths are set up and tables rest in the center of the floor. Two neon signs hang on the far, back, left corner above an arched doorway. One sign reads: POOL TABLES. The other brightly announces: RESTROOMS.

Kyle greets me with a huge smile when he sees me standing there, admiring the changes. "Well? What do you think?" he asks, handing me an apron, order ticket book, and a pen. The dry lump in my throat returns. This is it. My first job.

"It looks great, definitely the kind of place where I'd like to hang out," I tell him honestly. It really is somewhere I can see myself hanging out, even when my shift is over. I have a feeling this is going to be a very popular place. There's nothing else like it in this sleepy little town.

"Thank you. Let me show you around. My buddy will be bartending and helping you out. He should be here soon. Walt is a really nice guy, but I feel like should warn you...he's been through a lot of shit that has left some pretty deep scars. He believes it's better for him and any woman he might care for not to ever have a relationship that goes beyond being friends. He won't be friends with girls he's slept with and he won't sleep with a girl he's friends with. Does that make sense?" he asks. All I can do is nod my head yes. I feel bad for this poor guy. I, too, know how it feels to think you're so broken and damaged you'll destroy anyone who loves you.

"I don't want you to fall for him or anything and think it can go anywhere. He's the kind of guy who plays one-night only performances, with no returns. " When he looks up and sees me glaring at him in disbelief, he starts to back pedal. Why would he assume I'd fall all over this guy? "Not that I think you'd be into him, it's just most women are. I think you're a nice girl and I don't want to see you get hurt, so I just wanted to make sure I said something. He's been this way for years and I don't see it ever changing."

"I get it. Don't worry. The last thing on my mind is a relationship of any kind. I just left a really bad one and I'm happy being on my own. Thanks for looking out for me, though," I tell Kyle. I'm thankful when he doesn't press me for details. I'm just not ready to share my past with anyone yet, especially my new boss. He brings me to the kitchen and introduces me to Marty and Clark, the cooks. Both men seem very nice. Quiet, but nice. Kyle shows me how to run the registers and how he wants the close down process to go. He leaves me to fill salt and pepper shakers while he checks to see if Walt is here yet. So far, the job doesn't seem to be too complicated. But...we still haven't opened yet either.

Just as I'm putting the cap on the last shaker, Kyle yells for me. I finish what I'm doing and head out of the storage room. Legs are hanging out from under the bar and Kyle is standing next to them. Kyle's talking about the keg the legs are hooking up to the taps. That must be Walt. There's something strangely familiar about those legs... well, more so, the pair of combat boots. I stop dead in my tracks when the pair of legs speaks. The lump in my throat comes back and if I could see myself, I'd bet I'm as white as a ghost. I know that voice. At least...I think I do. It sounds just like Paul, but Kyle called his friend Walt. Am I imagining the similarities because I'm wanting to be around Paul? Holy shit! Do I miss him? No, that can't be it. We're just friends. There is nothing more than that possible for us. I can see it on his face when he looks at me. He doesn't want to be more and neither do I. Or, at least, that's what I keep telling myself.

"Hey, man, come out and meet our waitress," Kyle says. As soon as my name leaves his lips, the pair of legs moves to sit up and smacks his head on the wooden cabinet, forgetting where he is. A few curse words fly before the man emerges from underneath the counter. When I see his face, my knees begin to buckle. I quickly sit on a stool before I fall to the floor. Paul looks just as shocked to see as I am. Well, I hope its shock and not anger. It's kind of hard to tell. Kyle keeps looking from me to Paul and Paul to me. If he doesn't stop, he'll make himself dizzy.

"What is it? Do you two already know each other?" he questions as he looks to me for an answer. I'm still too stunned to form the words, so I just nod my head yes. "What am I missing? How do yo...oh, wait. How did I not catch this? Holly, you're the redhead who just moved into the apartment next to Paul." Again, I nod, still unable to catch my breath. How the hell am I going to distract myself away from Paul if I have to work with him twelve to fourteen hours a day? This is not going to be easy. Kyle has a sly grin on his face, as if he's enjoying the discomfort Paul and I are obviously sharing.

"Why didn't you tell me this was where you were working?" Paul asks me. His tone is a little harsh, which surprises me.

"I don't know. It never came up. Plus, I didn't know you worked here either. Kyle kept calling you Walt. Why is that, by the way?" My voice is a little shakier than I want it to be. I shouldn't have to explain myself to anyone, especially him. Kyle must start to feel the tension, so he speaks up.

"I call him Walt because the club we used to work at had two guys named Paul and it got confusing. So I came up with Walt. Ya know, from Walters," Kyle explains. When no one says anything, he continues, trying to ease the tension. "I thought you guys got along? Haven't you been hanging out together for the last month?" Clearly, Kyle is as confused as I am by Paul's tone.

"I wouldn't call it hanging out. I've helped her out a few times and gone over for dinner with Angel, Marcus, and Taryn," Paul states. Something about his words stings and my defenses go up.

"Don't worry, *Walt*. I'll stay out of your way. There's no reason we can't work around each other. According to you, it's not like we're even really friends or anything, right," I tell him with a shrug of my shoulders. He looks almost hurt, but why? He basically just said the same thing to me.

"Yeah, there won't be a problem," Paul says before turning back to hook up the keg. *Well, that was weird.* Whatever. I shouldn't care anyway. Keeping him at a distance is what I wanted to begin with. Knowing he's on the same page makes it that much easier. At least… it should.

The bar stays busy all afternoon until closing time. I'm catching on quickly and actually enjoying myself. All the people in this town seem so nice and friendly. They were all so welcoming. This town could be the subject of a Norman Rockwell painting. I now know where to go to have my hair done. Pat, one of the owners of the only salon in town, thought my hair was beautiful and couldn't wait to get her hands on it. I also now know where to buy meat, get flowers, take my car for service, and have my dry cleaning needs met. I seemed to be the center of attention today. Everyone wanted to check out Kyle's new place as well as meet Oakville's newest resident. I guess not too many new people ever move here. Most people will leave when they're young and come back when they're ready to settle down and start their families. I can see the appeal in that. It appears to be a quiet, friendly, and safe place to live. Except for one resident, everyone has made me feel at home and welcome.

I can't help but steal glimpses of Paul throughout my shift. I don't understand this man at all. A few times, I notice him doing the same to me. The mixed signals this man throws off are so fucking confusing. Remembering the warning Kyle had given me about *Walt*, I wonder what it is Paul has been through to make him so closed off. Is that why one minute he seems to care for me and the next acts like I have a deadly disease? I can understand not wanting a heavy romantic involvement with someone. I get that. I do. I feel the same way. It's the last thing I want in my life right now, maybe ever. But I thought we had a connection. Like...somehow we understood the pain and how broken we are without ever having to say a word. Looks like I imagined that, along with thinking he was my friend. Just thinking about not having him as a friend makes me nauseous. If it were another time, another place, I probably would've wanted to be more than a friend, but it's not and I was happy just to spend time with him. He is the only person I've been around who has made me feel completely safe. I was starting to enjoy that feeling.

Finally, at three a.m., we have everything shut down, put away, and cleaned up. Exhausted, I walk into the storage room to get my purse from my locker, ready to go home and fall into bed. I'm so wiped out, I don't think I'll have enough energy to change. When I turn around to leave, I slam into a hard, warm chest. The instant his cologne hits my nostrils, I know it's Paul's muscular chest I'm currently pressed up against. I stay there a few seconds longer than I should, enjoying how good it feels. To my surprise, he makes no effort to move either. The beat of his heart picks up to a rapid speed, one that matches my own. When his hands snake around my waist, my knees buckle and I wobble, almost falling. His grip tightens to hold me up. Snapping out of this lust-filled daze, I try to pull away, but his grip just gets tighter. Normally, I'd be panicked by now, but, like always, I'm not feeling threatened. At least not physically. My heart is a different story. He pulls me even closer to him, hugging me. My insides explode like fireworks on the Fourth of July. My skin heats and it's taking everything I have not to lean into him a little more and run my tongue along those delicious biceps staring me in the face. He rests his chin on the top of my head and when he nuzzles my hair and let's a low, "Mmm", I just can't take anymore. With all the strength I have, I break away from his embrace. Immediately, I feel a loss.

"What the hell?" I yell as I back away from him. He has a pained look on his face. I wonder whether it's from me yelling or the enormous hard-on he's sporting? *Holy hell!* I know how he feels. How can a man turn me on this much from just hugging me? His eyes follow the path mine took. When he sees what I did, he looks at me and smirks. The cocky SOB. "I don't understand you at all. One minute, you act like you want to be my friend and protector." His eyes widen. He must not have thought it was obvious. "Yes, I got a strong protective vibe from you all month. But then, tonight, you act like you hate me and you're pissed that we work at the same place. Which, by the way, I knew nothing about." He tries to interrupt me but I put my hand up, stopping his words. "And just now, you held me like you never wanted to let go. Don't get me wrong, part of me didn't want you to—" I stop, feeling my face heat with embarrassment. Did that really just leave my mouth? He looks like I just kicked him in the balls.

"Look, I just—" he starts, but I stop him. I don't want to hear him reject me. I have no idea what kind of game he's playing or why he's messing with me, but it stops here.

"No, you look. If you want to be friends…fine, I can do that. If you want to just be neighbors and coworkers, that's fine, too. Those are the only choices. There can't and won't be anything else between us," I state, thinking that will be the end of it.

"Are you saying you didn't feel anything from me being so close to you? You seemed to at least be a little turned on," he says as he moves closer to me. Knowing I have very little control over myself when it comes to him, I step back. He closes in on me, until my back is against the row of lockers. Putting my hands on his chest to stop him from coming any closer, my mind scrambles for what to say. My damn body is going to contradict any protesting my mouth does. My rapid breathing and dilated pupils probably give away my attraction to him. I'm so glad he has no idea about the wetness he's causing to pool between my legs.

"Not for the reason you think. You're a very attractive man, but of course you already know that." He shrugs his shoulders and smiles. He's still too close. His hot breath pulses against my lips with every exhale, hindering my ability to think. Pushing on his chest, I'm able to create some distance between us. "It's been a really long time since I've been with a man. To be completely honest…I'm just horny. At this point, if the wind blows the wrong way, I get turned on. Don't let it go to your head. I just need to get laid. It's that simple." Again, he has that cocky smirk on his face, as if he's the perfect man to give me what I need. As much as I want him to be, it's not a good idea. "With us being neighbors and working together, I don't think you're the right man for the job." Slowly, he nods his head. Disappointment is clear on his face, but it's quickly covered with his cockiness.

"Yeah, that's a good point. One time would never be enough for you and seeing me would make it difficult to stay away," he states. I want to punch him in the junk for being such a cocky ass, but I'm getting what I want, so I'll let it go. Well…almost.

"I'm glad you understand. Besides, I already have someone in mind to help me take care of my little problem. So, after tonight, I promise there will be no more feelings coming from me," I tell him. Quickly, I grab my purse and leave him standing there with his mouth gaping and nostrils flaring. I've managed to both shock and piss him off at the same time. I know staying away from him his the right thing to do. He has the power to destroy me completely, and I get the feeling I might hold the power to do the same to him.

Paul

My mouth hangs open in disbelief as I watch her walk away. Did she really just fucking tell me she has someone in mind to take care of her problem? So, in other words, she has someone in mind to fuck the horny out of her system. Before I can control the emotions flooding through me, I'm hurling my fist into the wall. A sharp, stinging pain radiates through my hand and up my arm.

"FUCK!" I roar in pain. Who is it? She doesn't know anyone outside of my friends. It can't be Marcus. He wouldn't do that to Taryn. That leaves Kyle and Angel. If I were to guess, I'd say it's Angel. So help me, I'll kill that motherfucker if he lays a finger on Holly. *Holy shit!* Am I actually jealous of the fact that someone else will be with her? A strong wave of nausea to hits me. I've never been jealous before. Of course I'm attracted to Holly, who wouldn't be? But that's all it is. Completely physical. Nothing more.

"Yeah keep telling yourself that, douchebag. You know you have feelings for her, you just refuse to admit it." Kyle sits down across from me and nods to the huge fist-shaped hole in the wall. "And you will be paying for that."

"Whatever. Take it out of my check and mind your own damn business," I growl as I get up and make my way to the door.

"You aren't your father, Paul. You are nothing like him. You'd never hurt a woman --- especially one you loved."

"You don't know a fucking thing. And who said anything about love?"

"Just don't let something epic slip through your fingers because you're a stubborn douche. Now, go home and put some ice on that hand. It's gonna hurt like a bitch in the morning." Kyle laughs as he locks the door behind me. Asshole. I know he's right about letting her slip away, but it still doesn't change anything. I can't be with her. It's for her own good.

When I pull into the parking lot of the apartment building, the nausea returns full force. Just thinking that Angel or some other guy is in there with her right now makes me want to hurl. Quickly, I get out of the car. I need a drink to calm myself before I do something stupid. Walking into my apartment and straight to the liquor cabinet, I grab a bottle of whiskey. I twist off the cap and guzzle right from the bottle, welcoming the burn. I bring the bottle with me to my room and set it on the nightstand. After pulling off my shirt, boots, and socks, I turn out the light and sit in my bed. I take another drink from my bottle. Before I can swallow it, I hear a noise from next door that causes me to spit a mouthful of whiskey everywhere. "Please don't let that be what I think it is." I forgot how thin these walls are. Kyle had the apartment next door before he had the one above the bar finished. I could hear every little moan from the women he brought home. I used to think it was funny back then. It's anything but funny right now. I have to know who she's with, even if it kills me…or him.

I scoot closer to the wall and rest my ear against it, trying to hear what's going on. There aren't any voices, but I can hear Holly breathing heavily. Another pleasurable moan slips from her lips, leaving me as hard as stone. How I wish I were the one making her moan like that. The moans get louder and the panting heavier. I know she's getting close. I know she's in there with another guy, but hearing her and imagining being with her has me so turned on, I can't help myself.

I slide my hand down my chest to the button of my jeans. As soon as I have my cock in my hand, something hits the wall right where my ear is resting. I jump back, my heart beating a mile a minute. *Shit!* That scared the hell out of me. Quickly, I put my ear back to the wall. I hear Holly cursing like a sailor. Something's definitely pissed her off. Did this guy do something to her? I'll kill him. It's then when I realize I haven't yet heard any voice other than Holly's. Relief washes over me. Maybe there isn't anyone in there with her after all. Then, it's confirmed. "Fucking batteries. Always going dead just when you need them. That's what I get for not finding the real thing," Holly shouts from her room. Obviously, she has no idea just how thin these walls are. She's about to find out. I pull my phone from my back pocket and begin to type a text message.

> *Our walls are pretty thin, doll face. Why don't you let me come over and finish what that battery operated imposter couldn't?*

I hit send and wait. If I can have sex with women I don't know, why couldn't I handle a purely sexual relationship with a woman I kinda like? So, maybe I more than kinda like her, but I can still keep the feelings out of it. When I hear the ding from my phone telling me she's responded, my heart drops to my stomach, worried over what her response might be.

> *Are you out of your fucking mind! You embarrass the hell out of me and then invite yourself over to fuck me?*

I wasn't even thinking that I might embarrass her. *Shit!* I'm an idiot. Quickly, I try to type a reply that will remove my foot from my mouth.

> *You have nothing to be embarrassed about. That was the hottest fucking thing I've ever heard. You had me so hard, I had no choice but to take matters into my own hands. If you know what I mean ;)*

Again, I sit here anxiously waiting for her reply. I feel like a teenager again, trying to get the hot girl in school to talk to me. God, this woman twists me in knots, but in a good way. I put my ear up to the wall. I can hear footsteps on the hardwood floor, as if she's pacing back and forth. After about five minutes pass with no response, I can no longer wait. Jumping up from my bed, I take another gulp of whiskey for courage. Stopping in my bathroom, I brush my teeth and use some mouthwash to get rid of the whiskey breath. I'm nowhere near drunk and I don't want Holly thinking I am because she can smell it on me. Once I'm sure the evidence of my liquid courage is gone, I make my way to Holly's door. I take a deep breath, trying to calm my rapidly beating heart. I don't want to startle her, so I type out a message on my phone.

Open your front door.

I can hear her giggle when she receives my text. Within a few minutes, I can hear the clicks of her many locks being unlocked. Slowly, the door opens and my jaw hits the floor. Her long, silky legs are on display, thanks to the very short flannel shorts she's wearing. As my eyes travel up past her flat stomach, I feel myself begin to strain against my zipper. Her tits look perfect in the tight tank top she's wearing. The hottest part is how she's looking at me. Her eyes scan every inch of me, as if she is starving and I'm a feast set in front of her. I've never had anyone look at me the way she is. And when she licks her lips, I just about blow in my jeans. Getting myself under control, I step closer to her. Her face instantly flushes and her breathing becomes faster.

"Are you gonna let me in, doll face?" I ask as I lazily run my finger from her shoulder down her arm. Goose bumps form all over her body from the contact. I love how the littlest touch or softest words cause her body to react.

"If you think I'm letting you in here just so you can fuck me you are sadly mistaken," she says, her voice shaky. She's just as turned on as I am, but she's nervous. I'm getting the feeling she has only been with one guy, maybe two at the most. She's not the type of girl who sleeps around. For the first time in my life, I'm ashamed of how many women I've slept with. Right now, is about her, though. I'm not here for me and I need her to know that.

"I never said anything about fucking you. I said I would give you what that toy couldn't. There are several ways to accomplish that without fucking you. Can I at least come in to talk about it? I'll tell you what I have in mind and you can decide if you're up for it. I would never do anything you don't want me to. If you tell me to leave, I'm gone." She eyes me carefully, considering my offer. She steps back and opens the door, allowing me to step inside. I walk past her and it takes every ounce of will power I have not to take her in my arms and show her how turned on I am. I can't do that though, as much as I want to. She's nervous, maybe even a little scared. I have to be very careful with her. Move very slowly. Make her see she can trust me. That I would never hurt her. Someone has really done a number on her and if I'm ever face to face with the bastard, he'll be sorry. I sit on the couch and wait for her to sit next to me. When she sits, she makes sure there's an appropriate amount of space between us.

"Neither of us is in a place where we want a relationship, but we both have needs and wants, right?" I pause to make sure she's with me so far. When she nods her head yes, I continue. "I won't lie. I'm attracted to you, more than I've ever been to any other woman. I get the feeling you're attracted to me as well." Again, she nods yes. "We're both adults who know what we want and what we don't. Since we're attracted to each other, why not meet each other's needs and wants together? And before you ask, no, this isn't something I've ever done before." She looks surprised.

"If you've never done this before, why now? Why with me?" she questions. And a damn good question it is. How do I answer that when I really don't know myself? I can only be honest. It's what she deserves. If she punches me in the face and thinks I'm a dick, so be it.

"Honestly, I'm not sure. There's something about you that makes me want to be around you. No matter how hard I try to stay away, I can't. The thought of another man with you makes my blood boil. Which is another new thing for me." She smiles a shy smile and inches a little closer to me. I can tell she wants to say something, but she's choosing her words carefully.

"Can you tell me what turned you against relationships?" she asks as she stares at her lap. Clearly, she's afraid I'll be upset with her for asking that question. Knowing she's feeling even an ounce of fear pains me.

"To my surprise, I do want to tell you about my past. I also want to hear about yours, but not tonight. Tonight is all about you. I want you to see that you can trust me. My intention was to come over here and bury my head between your legs until you begged me to stop." Her face flushes. It's cute that she's embarrassed by my boldness, but I also notice her squeeze her legs tightly together. The idea obviously turns her on as much as it does me. "But I don't think we're ready for that just yet. Instead, I'll spend the night and hold you while you sleep. This way, you can see how safe you are in my arms," I state. I watch her eyes bug out and her mouth fall open, but she snaps out of it quickly. When she stands up and starts to walk away, I get a little worried. What if she tells me to fuck off? I never really thought that was a possibility.

"You invited yourself, so I know it's not an invitation you're waiting for," she says as she glances at me over her shoulder. "Oh, and lock the door on your way." Then she disappears into her bedroom. That smart mouth of hers has me wishing I followed through with my original plan. I have a feeling this might be more difficult than I thought.

After locking up, I walk into the bedroom. Deciding to leave my jeans on, I turn off the light and climb into the bed next to her. Immediately, she snuggles up to me. Her head resting on my chest allows me to breathe in the fruity scent of her shampoo. Her arm wraps tightly around my waist as she lays her leg over mine. I wrap both of my arms securely around her and she lets out a contented sigh. This feels so much better than I imagined, but it also scares the living shit out of me. I swore I'd never allow myself to fall for a woman. Looks like I had no choice in that matter.

CHAPTER
Seven

Holly

SLOWLY OPENING my eyes, I glance over at the clock. To my amazement, it's already nine o'clock. I haven't slept past six in the morning in years. I don't usually sleep well and I constantly toss and turn. By morning, my bed is a tangled mess of sheets, but not today. We are in the exact same positions as when we fell asleep. Paul was right when he said I'd feel safe in his arms.

I tilt my head so I can see his face. He looks as peaceful as I feel right now. Maybe having me in his arms makes him feel safe. I have a feeling his demons hinder his sleep as well. As I watch him, I realize I'm fighting a battle I have no chance in winning. No matter what I do, I can't stay away from him. This feels wonderful, lying here safe and secure in his strong arms. At the same time, I'm also terrified because I can feel myself falling for him. Falling so fast and hard that if he's not there to catch me, my heart will be beyond repair.

Carefully, I slip out of bed, stopping in the doorway to take one more look at the tantalizing man. As I make my way to the kitchen, I feel lighter. Almost like one of the many weights holding me down has been taken away. Paul has taken it away. One night of making me feel safe and protected is making me want something I wasn't sure I'd ever want again. I could easily get used to falling asleep and waking up in his strong arms.

I start brewing a pot of coffee while I gather what I need to make French toast. It's so nice to get up and cook breakfast for someone because I want to. Not because it's expected of me or out of fear of what will happen if I don't. Remembering some of the beatings I've endured causes my body to tremble. Will I ever not be afraid? Is there ever going to be a time I'm not looking over my shoulder? Trying to shake off those thoughts, I get back to cooking.

"Something smells awfully good, doll face," Paul says. When I turn around, he's leaning in the doorway. One look at him and I've got an instant lady boner. What a sight. His arms are crossed and resting on his bare chest. The worn out blue jeans he's wearing are riding low on his hips, just enough to make you want to see what's hiding underneath. The sexiest thing of all is the crooked smirk on his face. One that tells me he knows I'm checking him out and enjoying every inch of what I see. He's eyeing me just as intently. We both stand there, staring at one another. Both of us memorized. Before I know it's happening, I'm in his arms with his lips gently brushing against mine. The kiss starts off soft and sweet. Just as it starts to heat up, a loud, ear-piercing beeping interrupts us. It takes a moment to realize what the sound is, but when I begin to smell smoke, I snap out of it immediately.

"Oh shit!" I scream and run to the stove. Grabbing the handle of the pan, I remove it from the stove and place it in the sink. Then I turn off the stove and open the window. Paul is standing on a chair, removing the batteries from the smoke detector. I'm thankful when the deafening beeping stops. The kitchen is completely filled with smoke. I hand Paul a towel and the two of us try to fan the smoke out the open window. Looking over at the sink, I can't believe my French toast is burnt to a blackened crisp. So much for the nice breakfast I had planned. I feel like an idiot.

Hopefully he's not upset with me for ruining his food. I should've been paying attention. With that thought, my heart starts to race. The paralyzing fear sets in. The fear I used to have when I knew I did something Ray wouldn't be happy about. All control I have over myself is gone. Struggling to swallow, I find myself slowly backing away from Paul and cowering down on the kitchen floor. My entire body is shaking. I watch Paul like a hawk, waiting for him to blow up and punish me for ruining our meal. He turns his head, noticing for the first time I'm no longer by his side. When he starts to walk toward me, my eyes immediately fall to the floor. My body stiffens to prepare for the blows I'm expecting him to deliver.

"Holly?" Paul whispers. I look up to see he's stopped moving in my direction. His hands are raised in a surrender pose and the look on his face...the emotions playing across his face is what snaps me out of whatever this is. It's a combination of pity, anger, sadness, and terror. The terror is what throws me. What does he have to be scared of? I'm the one on the floor acting like I belong in a strait jacket. "Holly, did I do something to frighten you? If I did, I'm so fucking sorry. I would never hurt you."

Oh, God. He thinks my behavior is because of something he's done. How do I explain to him that I didn't really think he was going to hurt me, but it's just habit? This is the type of thing I've been afraid of. I have so much baggage, how can I expect anyone to put up with shit like this? Something so small has turned into a major ordeal because of my fucked up past.

"It wasn't you. I'm so sorry. I've spent so many years feeling the wrath of my ex-husband when I did something wrong, or at least, something he thought was wrong..." I pause for a second, trying to gather my thoughts. Do I really want to go into this right now? After that incredible kiss this morning, I could see us having something. For the first time in a long time, I had hope that I might find happiness. Once he hears about all my demons and my screwed up past, he'll surely run the other way. Who wouldn't? The feel of his arms scooping me off the floor pulls my attention from my emotional struggle to his handsome face. His eyes are staring straight into mine, a look of understanding on his face; as if he knows the battle I'm fighting. He carries me into the living room and sits down on the couch, leaving me in his arms resting on his lap. Normally, I would find this ridiculous, but with him, there's something comforting about it. Still gazing into my eyes, he brushes a loose strand of hair away from my eyes.

"You don't have to explain anything to me that you don't want to. But you can tell me anything and I can promise you there will be nothing from me but understanding and support," Paul says with so much sincerity in his voice, I feel the walls I've built around my heart start to crack. What is it about this man that makes me feel like I can trust him?

"I want to. You have this way of making me want to open up to you, but it's so hard for me," I tell him while burying my head into his shoulder. He holds me a little tighter. I lift my head and look into his comforting eyes. "Trusting has never come easy for me."

"Just know that I'm here to listen whenever you're ready," he says, lightly kissing me on the forehead. "I understand more than you think. The look you had on your face, I've seen that same look on my mother's face more times than I can count. My father was a monster," he says, looking away, trying to hide the pain that's so evident in his eyes. He begins to breathe faster, most likely from the memories haunting him. My heart hurts for him. I can just imagine the things his father did to cause the pain he's fighting so hard to hide. I'm no stranger to that kind of pain or the difficulties of trying to keep it hidden from the rest of the world. When he looks back at me, he reminds me of a frightened child. A child who's seen horrors no child should ever have to witness. Reaching up, he wipes a tear that just dropped from my eye.

"Ever since I can remember, my father beat my mother. At first, it was every now and then. Usually when he had a really stressful day or had a little too much to drink." His voice is shaky. It's easy to see this is difficult for him. Taking his hand in mine, I gently squeeze it, hoping the gesture comforts him. "As I got older, the beatings became more frequent and more brutal. I would butt in to try to stop him, but it never did. It only turned his focus to me. I was okay with that, though. As long as he left my mother alone."

His entire body is trembling. Still on his lap, I wrap my arms around him, letting him know he's safe here with me. This urge to protect him, to keep him safe, is so overwhelming. I don't say a word, I just hold him close, hoping he feels comfortable enough to keep going. I know it's not easy for him to talk about, but I want him to be able to open up to me. Maybe then, I'll find the strength to do the same.

"When I was fifteen, I'd finally had enough. After years of abuse and begging my mom to take me and leave him, I just couldn't take anymore. Somehow, someway, I found the courage I needed to fight back. After that, I swore he'd never hit me again. I also couldn't sit back and watch her take it anymore. Again, I begged her to go. Instead, she gave me a packed bag and money. She told me to run and never look back, that she wanted me to be free and happy. I ran for my life that day," he tells me, his voice sad. I'm so glad he can't see my face because the tears are flowing and I don't think I'll be able to stop them. How could she not go with her son? How could a mother just send her son away on his own, not knowing where he was going or if he'd be safe? "After a while, I went to check on her. I was getting worried. She wasn't answering any of my calls. When I got there, the house was trashed. It looked like a tornado had come through it. I found them in my bedroom. My father had killed my mother and then himself." Paul's body shudders. I lift my head from his chest. When I see the tears falling from his eyes, I want so badly to take them away. I can't even begin to imagine the hell he went through at such a young age. I wipe the tears from his handsome face.

"I'm so sorry you had to go through any of that," I tell him sincerely. I know it must have taken a lot for him to tell me about his painful past. And now, he's going to want to hear about mine. It's selfish and unfair of me, but I just don't think I'm ready yet. What if he thinks less of me? He was a child and had no choice but to stay and suffer through the abuse. I was an adult. I had a choice. I was weak and afraid. I stayed and allowed Ray to do unspeakable things to me. I'm so ashamed of myself for not leaving Ray the first time he raised his hand to me.

Paul takes a deep breath and gazes into my eyes. He's giving me the opportunity to open up to him. To tell him all about the horrors that caused me to act like a complete nut case. The more I think about how he might react or what he'll think of me, the more nervous I become. I'm just going to tell him I need more time and pray he understands. When he flashes that sexy ass smile, I know he will.

"I have an idea. Let's get dressed and I'll take you out for breakfast," he says while removing me from his lap and placing me on my feet.

"Sounds great. Give me twenty minutes to get ready," I yell over my shoulder on my way to the bathroom. He comes up behind me, wrapping his arms around my waist. His lips are close to my ear, so close I can feel his warm breath move across it.

"You don't have to tell me anything until you're completely comfortable. I promise, I'll never pressure you into anything," he whispers. After kissing my neck and sending goose bumps all over my body, he releases his grip on me and is out the door.

I really hope he's truly the man he seems to be. God knows I'm obviously not the best judge of character. Whatever it is that tells me whether a guy is good or bad is broken. After all, I thought Ray was a wonderful man I'd spend the rest of my life with. Eventually, I know he'll need to know about my past, but thankfully, today is not that day.

Paul

CONCENTRATING ON making drinks is proving to be difficult tonight. Holly seems to be the only thing capturing my attention. I'm actually afraid she's capturing more than just my attention. There's something about this woman that draws me to her, no matter how hard I fight it. Honestly, I'm not sure I want to fight it any longer. I always promised myself I'd never fall in love. Looks like that's one promise I won't be keeping. Just the fact that I was able to tell Holly about my past says I trust her in a way I haven't trusted many. Reggie and Kyle have been the only two people I've ever trusted enough to open up to.

Spending the night with Holly was amazing. One of the best nights I've had in a very long time and there wasn't even any sex involved. Sex was the last thing on my mind. The only thing I could think of was holding her close and making her feel safe. She's going to need some time before she can trust me. Someone in her life has hurt her. It's so obvious to me. She's already let me in more than I imagined she would so soon. I need to make her see that I would never hurt her. Protecting her and keeping her safe is my only desire right now.

"Earth to Paul," Angel says while snapping his fingers in front of my face. When I look over to him and Marcus, they're both smiling. "Must be some hot piece of ass to have you zoning out," Angel says with a grin. Normally, I'd laugh right along with them, but Holly was not just some hot piece of ass to me. Just then, Holly turns around and the guys see who had my attention. They're no longer laughing. Actually, they both looked aggravated.

Marcus speaks up first. "Paul, you do know she's not like the girls you're usually with." I should be pissed. He's jumping to the conclusion that I want her for nothing more than a one-night roll in the hay, but I know he's just trying to protect her. And really, my reputation doesn't help. Before I can explain anything to them, Angel starts one of his rants.

"Don't you wonder if maybe the universe is trying to tell you something?" I open my mouth to speak, but he holds his hand up to shut me up. "Let's look at the facts. The two of you actually collide into one another. She lives in the apartment right next to yours, the one you have only because you won a coin toss, which you never win. Now, you both work in the same place. Do you need a fucking sledge hammer to the face to make you realize it's time you had more than just one night stands?"

"Are you finished, numb nuts?" I ask Angel. He plays it off like he's thinking about it.

"Yeah. For now," he says with a laugh.

"From the minute I saw her, I knew she was different. She just may be the one who changes how I feel about relationships," I tell them honestly. The shocked expressions on their faces are priceless, but no one is as shocked as I am. After spending so many years trying to avoid any kind of relationship, it's hard to wrap my head around the idea of actually wanting one. I'm still worried that I may have inherited my father's temper, but I can't imagine ever being capable of hurting Holly. If there comes a time when I think that's a possibility, I'll leave to make sure she's safe from me. It would probably be the hardest thing I'd ever have to do, but I'd do it for her.

"Well, it's about damn time I'm not the only one in a relationship!" Marcus says with a huge smile on his face. I know he's felt a little out of place being the only one of us with a girlfriend.

"There's no relationship yet. It's gonna take some time for her to trust me. I can tell she's been through some bad shit. Trust doesn't come easy to her right now," I explain. They both slowly nod, understanding more than most about the damage people we love can inflict on us.

I glance across the bar at Holly. When she notices me looking at her, she smiles shyly, taking my breath away. Once I can breathe again, I smile back and add in a little wink. She giggles and I can see from here that she's blushing. Holly quickly composes herself and turns her attention back to her customers. I hope she'll allow me to fall asleep next to her again tonight. I don't want to pressure her, but after last night, I don't think I can stay away. I'm hooked. Never before have I wanted just to hold a woman so badly. It's always been sex and nothing more, but with Holly, it's the total opposite. With her, I want so much more than a purely physical connection can give me.

"Hey, lover boy, there are other people in this place," Angel teases and nods toward a blonde at the end of the bar waiting to be served. After I flip Angel the bird for being such a smartass, I make my way to the end of the bar. The closer I get to her, the easier it is to see the way she's looking at me. I used to see that look all the time in L.A. The look that says she wants a whole lot more from me than just a drink. Before Holly, I'd have no reservations about taking her home for a night of meaningless sex. Now, I just want to make her drink, send her on her way, and get back to watching Holly.

"What can I get for you?" I ask as I try to look and sound as disinterested as possible.

"You can start with your phone number," she purrs while placing her hand on top of mine. I slowly slide my hand away, trying not to be rude, but I don't want her to get the wrong idea either.

"Sorry, but the only thing you'll get from me is a drink. What will it be?" I ask, sounding a little annoyed. Why have I never noticed before how annoying these girls can be?

"Hmm, what do I want? Sex on the Beach sounds good. Don't ya think?" she replies in what she thinks is a sexy tone. There's nothing sexy about it. It sounds more like someone dragging their fingernails down a chalkboard. Without warning, she leans over the bar and plants her lips on mine. Gripping her shoulders, I push her away. This girl is really grating on my nerves. She obviously can't take no for an answer and to make matters worse, Holly is standing next to Angel and Marcus. The expression on her angelic face is a mixture of anger and hurt. The anger I fully understand. This bitch is aggravating. But the hurt I see sends a stabbing ache straight to my heart. She has to know I didn't want this girl's lips on mine. I can't stand seeing her hurt. Even from the first day when I ran into her, seeing her in pain caused me pain. In that moment, I knew she was going to change my life.

"It does sound good. Just not with you," I state and watch the sly smirk on her face quickly turn into a sneer.

"Just give me three shots of tequila," she snaps. Happy that she's finally gotten the message, I quickly pour her shots and send her on her way. I make my way back over to Angel and Marcus, who are laughing it up.

"That was painful to watch. Have you ever turned a woman down before? There are nicer ways to do it ya know," Angel Laughs.

"No, I guess I haven't. I've never really wanted or had a reason to, until now."

"You mean, until Holly," Marcus adds with a sly smile on his face. He's enjoying all of this.

"That's exactly what I mean," I state proudly. I don't care if my best friends know. I'm falling for her and falling hard. The boys hang around a little longer to tease me. Marcus is the first to leave, saying he misses Taryn. This earns him some ribbing from Angel. And Angel, in his true manwhore fashion, leaves shortly after with the blonde who was trying to pick me up only an hour earlier. As I watch them walk out of the bar with Angel's hand on her ass, I can't help but laugh. Typical Angel. He doesn't care who he goes home with, just as long as he has someone to go home with.

"Hey," Holly says as she walks up behind me. I turn to face her and I'm concerned something is wrong. She doesn't look like her normal, happy self. She looks tired and worried. "Do you mind if I take off a little early? I'm not feeling well." Not once does she make eye contact with me, which has me wondering what's gotten her so upset she has to leave.

"Of course you can. Is there anything I can do to help?" I ask, hoping she'll invite me over after I'm done tonight.

"Thank you, but I just need some rest." I can tell she's in a hurry to leave.

"Can I stop by when I finish so I can check on you? Maybe even hold you again all night?" I ask, hopeful. I've been daydreaming about falling asleep with her in my arms again all day. My hopes are shattered when I see the tears start to form in her eyes.

"I need to be alone. I have some things I need to figure out," she says. Before I can argue my point, she plants a swift kiss on my cheek, grabs her purse from under the counter, and makes her escape out the door. She's having doubts about me. Everything was going smoothly until that bitch came along tonight. If Holly was watching, she had to see how annoyed I was at this woman and how much her lips on mine repulsed me. I'll give her tonight alone, even though it may kill me to stay away from her, but first thing in the morning, I'm going to explain what happened here tonight.

The last three hours have gone by painfully slow. I've done nothing but worry about Holly, replaying the look on her face in my mind, over and over again. I promised myself I wouldn't go to her tonight and I won't, but being home in my bed is the next best thing. The walls are so thin between us, I can usually hear her soft snoring and imagine myself lying next to her.

"Hey, man. Where's Holly?" Kyle asks, breaking me from my thoughts. Just like Angel and Marcus, Kyle has become attached to Holly. They all treat her like a little sister. Like me, they can see the damaged and frightened girl hiding under the badass attitude.

"It's a long story. She left a few hours early," I tell him. "Do you mind closing up for me? I need to get home so I can make sure she's okay."

"No problem," Kyle says, making his way behind the bar. I give him a smile and a pat on the back, then turn to leave. Just as I get to the door, he stops me. "Hey! You're my best friend, but if you hurt her in any way, I will kick your ass," he says with a laugh.

"If I ever hurt her, I'll help you kick my ass," I tell him honestly, and make my way to my truck. In the pit of my soul, I know I'd never do anything to intentionally hurt this woman. I couldn't bear it if I did. I love her too much. Stopping dead in my tracks, I realize what just happened. A huge smile spreads across my face when I say it out load to myself for the first time. "I love her." It feels like a weight has been lifted off my heart and shoulders. Now, hopefully, I can keep myself from going to her apartment and really scaring her away by proclaiming my love for her.

When I walk into our building, I'm so tempted to knock on her door. Maybe telling her how I feel is what she needs to hear. If she knows I love her then she will see how much I want her and no one else. Or it could scare the shit out of her and send her running. Yeah, this is going to require some more thought and patience on my part. I glance at her door one last time before making my way to mine and going into my apartment.

Anxious to be as close to her as I can, I go straight to bed. After pulling off my shirt and throwing it on the chair in the corner, I sit on the edge of my bed and take off my boots and socks. I lay down and slide as close to the wall as I can. Laying on my side, I put my ear up against the cool wall, just wanting to hear her breathe. I stay like that for several minutes before I begin to doze off.

My eyes fly open and my body stiffens when I hear a loud scream. I hold my breath because my heart is beating so frantically, it's the only thing I can hear. Another scream comes from Holly's bedroom along with a rustling sound. This time, I don't wait for what comes next. I fly to my feet and rush to my front door. The wood floor is cold under my feet as I run to Holly's apartment. I grab the doorknob and turn it only to find it locked. *Shit!* Of course it's locked, along with the many deadbolts I installed for her. Again, she screams and I can hear her pleading with someone to stop. Without thinking, I back up and slam my body as hard as I can into her door. I hear the wood crack under the force. I back up a little farther this time. When my body meets the hard wood of the door, it buckles and I fall with it. I land on her floor with a loud, painful thud.

More screams come from her room followed by something that sounds like a struggle. My blood runs cold at the thought of someone in there hurting her. Getting to my feet and ignoring the stabbing pain in my shoulder, I rush to her bedroom. I'm terrified to see what's behind the door. Slowly, I open it and fall to my knees from the sight before me. Holly is alone, curled up in a ball in the corner of her bed. Her arms are covering her midsection. Tears are streaming down her face like a waterfall and her body is shaking. I'm so disturbed by the helpless and frightened woman before me, I'm frozen in place. Her ear-piercing scream followed by her begging someone to "stop" and "please don't hurt our baby" gets me moving again.

I get into the bed next to her. I lay my hand on her shoulder and get a fist in my eye. She's still sound asleep, stuck deep in this nightmare. Realizing this isn't going to be easy and very painful, I just go for it. Fighting off her punches and kicks, I eventually get my arms wrapped around her. I hold her as close and tight to me as I can. Slowly, she begins to calm herself. She stops fighting back and the actions are replaced with the most heart wrenching sobs I've ever heard.

I have no idea what the hell to do. When she opens her eyes and sees that I'm holding her, an embarrassed blush graces her face and the sobs get louder as she buries her head into my chest. I scoop her into my arms, still holding her to my chest, and start off to my apartment. She no longer has a front door so she won't feel safe here. Besides, there's no way in hell I'm letting her out of my arms tonight. If she hates me for it, then so be it. I can't leave her, especially now that my suspicions have been confirmed. It sounds worse than I imagined.

When I get to the front door, Angel is standing there. He's as white as fresh snow, looking from me to the splintered door laying on the floor. When he sees the sobbing Holly clinging to me, his face contorts in pain. I don't know his story, but I do know he's had some serious nightmares. I've witnessed a lot of them and they put this one to shame. There's understanding in his eyes when he finally looks away from Holly to me.

"Go. I'll take care of the door. Help her, please," he whispers before moving to the broken door. As much as he needs someone, she needs me more. As I get to my door, I pass Marcus carrying his tool box. He looks at Holly then to me, his eyes pleading with me to do something. How in the hell did our broken and damaged souls find each other? I nod to him as he goes to help Angel fix the door.

Locking my door behind me, I walk directly to my room. Still holding her tight, I lay us both on the bed. Bringing my mouth to her ear, I whisper, "You don't have to say a word. No explanations are needed. I just want you to know you are safe with me. Cry, scream, throw things, or hit me. Anything you need to do to get it out, do it. I'm here. I won't let you go, I promise." Her arms tighten around my waist and she allows herself to cry softly into my chest. I just hold her tighter and allow her to get it all out.

I rub my hand soothingly up and down her back, telling her everything will be okay eventually. "Thank you," she whispers once her crying subsides. Within minutes, she finally falls into a peaceful sleep. Shortly after, I'm able to drift off, praying she'll let me in.

CHAPTER
Eight

Holly

I'VE BEEN lying awake still wrapped in Paul's arms for over an hour. I'm so embarrassed he saw me that way last night. I remember the nightmare I was having clear as day. It's one I have often. I have no idea what he heard, so how do I explain it? I know he cares for me, but just how much? He doesn't do relationships, so how long would it take before he was off with some skank like the one hitting on him last night? How long before I'm a heartbroken mess because I allowed myself to trust another man?

I turn my head slowly so I can see his face. With his eyes still closed and his chest rising and falling at a steady pace, he looks so handsome. And even with all of the questions and doubt swirling around in my head, I still feel safe and peaceful. At least, I do before he scares the crap out of me.

"Stop over thinking it, doll face. Tell me what you want when you want. I'm not going to push you. Just know I'm here for you and I will be for however long it takes for you to see we're made for each other," he states in a sleepy voice that makes my heart race. This time when I look up at his face, he's wearing a sexy smile. Slowly, his eyes open. He gives me a wink and pulls me closer to him. "I hope bringing you here was okay. I couldn't leave you alone last night and… well, your door was a mess."

"There's no place I'd rather be. Thank you for saving me from my nightmare. I can't usually sleep after I have one, but, for some reason, I can if I'm in your arms," I tell him. What is it about this man that makes me feel safe? Is it the way he never pushes me to talk or the look in his eyes that says he knows what I've been through and would never allow it to happen again? I feel like I did when I was a kid taking swimming lessons and it was time to jump from the diving board for the first time. Deep down, you know you'll be okay when you jump, but there's still this one part of you that is playing the "what if" game, over and over. Deep down, I know Paul cares for me. The scary part of taking this plunge with him is how he'll react to the things I have to tell him. He's told me about begging his mother to leave for years and how angry it made him when she didn't. What is he going to think of me when he finds out how long I stayed with Ray before leaving? Or when he finds out I am the reason my baby is dead? I knew what Ray was capable of and I stayed. If I would've left, my baby would still be alive.

"You're thinking too much again. I have an idea. What would you say to a picnic at the lake?" he asks.

"It sounds great, but it's time for me to tell you about my nightmares and why I have them."

"I'll be happy to listen, but let's have our picnic first. I want you to have a chance to relax before you have to dredge up all the bad memories. At least for a few hours anyway." I nod, agreeing. It would be nice to have a normal day. Depending on how he feels about me after I tell him everything, it may be our last day together. "Go get in the shower and I'll go get you a change of clothes," he says and gives me a sweet kiss on my forehead. He sits us both up in the bed. Before he stands, he gives me a longing look and runs his hand along my cheek. "I promise I'd never do anything to intentionally hurt you. I'll prove it… no matter how long it takes. I'll make you see how much I care for you." With that said, he gets up and walks out the door.

As I slip under the hot spray of the shower, I try to let it wash away the anxiety I feel about telling Paul of my past. What if he can't forgive me for allowing my baby to die? It's not like I could blame him. I still haven't forgiven myself. If he can't handle it, then I guess it's just not meant to be. Better to tell him now, before I fall for him even harder. Who am I trying to fool? I've already fallen for him pretty damn hard. I was trying to avoid one thing and what do I go and do? Fall in love with the first guy I run into...literally. The creaking of the bathroom door pulls me from my thoughts. For a few seconds, it's quiet and I wonder whether Paul's going to get in with me.

"I, uh...I'll set your clothes here on the counter. Take your time. I'll be in the kitchen getting our picnic ready," Paul says nervously. When I hear the door close behind him, I realize I'm a little disappointed he didn't try to come in here with me. If he turns me away after I tell him the truth, it's going to break me. I quickly finish my shower and get dressed. I need to get this day moving and to the point where I tell Paul the truth. If it doesn't happen soon, I may lose my nerve.

As I walk into the kitchen, I'm blown away by the scene before me. There's a large picnic basket on the table with wine, cheese, crackers, sandwiches, and even chocolate covered strawberries lying next it. This surprises me in itself, but hearing him singing *Step by Step* by New Kids on the Block while he packs the basket really has me smiling. What grown man knows that song, let alone dances around the kitchen singing it? He has a sexy singing voice, but the way he moves his hips to the beat is even sexier. He dances around some more, gathering up things for our basket. He spins around with his arms spread out in this big huge gesture. When he sees me leaning against the wall, he freezes, arms spread out, and mouth gaping open in shock. I can't stop the laugh that escapes my lips. Quickly, I slap my hand over my mouth to muffle the laughter.

"Something funny, doll face?" he asks with a smile and a laugh of his own.

"No, not funny. I thought you looked cute," I tell him. He places his hand over his chest and feigns injured.

"Cute? You know that was hot." Of course it was hot, but I'm not admitting that to him. "Come on. Tell the truth," he jokes as he stalks toward me very slowly. He's looking at me like he's a predator and I'm his prey. If I thought his little song and dance was hot, then the look he's giving me is scorching. His intense gaze is lighting fires all over my body.

"I am telling the truth. It was cute. If hot is what you were aiming for, skip songs by boy bands who were popular twenty years ago," I say, trying to keep a straight face. A lopsided grin spreads across his face as he continues to inch closer to me. Every step he takes causes my heart to beat faster. Now, he's so close, I can feel his breath on my face.

Bringing his lips to my ear, he whispers, "I thought girls go crazy over boy bands. " He takes his finger and runs it from my shoulder slowly down my arm, leaving goose bumps in its wake. Between him being so close and him touching me, I feel like I might explode. I want him so much. He kisses my neck gently and I can't control the whimper that escapes my lips. He knows he's got me all hot and bothered. I'm sure he also knows he could take me right now without protest. Truth be told, I want him to.

"Son of a...what the hell was that for?" I scream as I try to get the cube of ice to fall out of my t-shirt. How did he do that without me noticing? When I finally get the cube to fall, I look over to Paul, waiting for his explanation. He's laughing so hard, I can see tears in his eyes.

"I thought maybe you needed to cool down a little," he says in between his laughter. "I'm sorry, doll face." *Sorry my ass.* The shit-eating grin on his face contradicts his apology. "I'm gonna take a shower. Then we can go." He kisses my cheek on his way to the bedroom and I finish packing the basket. When I hear the shower turn on, I quickly fill the biggest pot I can find with ice and cold water. Payback's a bitch, buddy. I creep into the bathroom and immediately become distracted by his impressive silhouette. After a few seconds, I remember my mission and climb on the toilet as quietly as possible. I lift the pot and dump the ice-cold water over the top of the shower doors. The second it hits him, he lets out an extremely girly scream.

"Sorry. I thought maybe you needed to cool down some," I tell him and haul ass out of there before he has a chance to retaliate.

"Well played, doll face," he yells to me while chuckling.

We ride to the spot Paul is taking me for our picnic without speaking much. It's a comfortable silence. The windows are down and a warm breeze is flowing through the truck. The radio is cranked up just right and set on a really good classic rock station. *Carry on my Wayward Son* comes through the speakers and I smile. I love this song. Obviously, so does Paul. He turns the volume even louder while tapping his hand on the steering wheel to the beat. At the same time, we both start singing along. I can't help it. There's just something about this song. Paul smiles at me when he notices he's not the only one singing along. It's hard for me to believe how comfortable I feel around him. This would never have happened with Ray. For the first time in a long time, I feel alive. I feel happy.

Before long, we're turning onto a dirt road. When we reach the end, I see a small lake. It's beautiful. There are cattails and majestic Oak trees surrounding the lake, making it very secluded. There are wild flowers growing along the grassy banks. I'm in awe of this spot. It's like something you'd see in a movie. I wonder how Paul knows about it. That thought makes my stomach turn. What if he brings all his women here to seduce them? Am I just going to end up as one of many notches on his bedpost? As soon as the truck is stopped, I grab for the door handle. I need some fresh air before my thoughts choke me. Before I can make my escape, Paul takes a hold of my arm.

"Stop it, doll face," he says sternly. I can feel him looking at me, but I keep my face turned away. I'm afraid I'll lose it if I have to look into his eyes.

"Stop what?" I ask, confused. There's no way he knows what I'm thinking.

"I've never been here before, let alone brought another woman here." How the hell did he know what I was thinking? I turn to look at him. His green eyes plead with me to believe him. To trust him. Haven't I learned by now that he's one of the good ones? He's not just trying to get in my pants then kick me to the curb. When I don't say anything, he continues. "This is the first time I've ever seen this place. Kyle told me about it." He releases me. "Kyle thought you'd like it and I wanted to take you somewhere quiet." I feel terrible for jumping to conclusions. I'm such a bitch. I wouldn't blame him if he dumped my ass off here and left. If I were him, I'd make my sorry ass hoof it back home.

"I'm sorry. I know I need to work on the whole trusting thing. I promise I'll try harder." A sly smirk crosses his face and makes me think he's up to something. "You didn't bring me here to dump my body did you?" I joke, hoping to lighten the mood and take the spotlight off my massive bout of idiocy.

"Hardly," he says in almost a whisper as he inches closer to me. He places his hand on the nape of my neck, causing goose bumps to spread all over my flesh. Gently and ever so slowly, he guides my head closer to his and before I know it, his lips are on mine. I'm instantly on fire from the connection, but when I feel his tongue slip through my lips, I think I might combust on the spot. The kiss is the most intense kiss I've ever had. So intense, I'm getting light headed. Abruptly, he pulls away with a chuckle. What the hell?

"This is your punishment for jumping to conclusions." Punishment?

If kissing me like that is punishment, I'm going to be jumping to a whole lotta conclusions. "Leaving you all hot and bothered. If you're nice, I might do it longer next time," he laughs and hops out of the truck, leaving me a hot puddle of desire. If his kisses bring on sparks like that, I wonder what sex with him would be like. Just the thought has me all tingly. I follow him out of the truck, hoping next time happens before I have to tell him my story.

Paul

FOR THE last hour, I have not been able to get that kiss out of my head. Not only was it just plain fucking hot, I felt this connection to her. I've never felt that before with anyone. It was amazing and frightening at the same time. I most definitely have to do that again. I'm not sure why but the longer we sit here, the more nervous and fidgety she gets. Is it because I kissed her? Maybe she didn't like it as much as I did. Or maybe she's not ready to be intimate with me. Those thoughts never crossed my mind until now. She always seems to get as worked up as I do when I'm around her.

"Paul, before we take whatever is going on between us any further, I need to tell you about my past," she says, nervously. Her eyes are everywhere but on me. What is she so afraid to tell me? I've told her my demons. Could she have been through worse? Just the idea of someone hurting or mistreating her makes me want to find them and kick their ass.

"As long as you're ready. I don't want you to think you have to."

"I do need to, but it's more because I need you to know everything. If there is going to be anything between us, I won't have secrets." She's still looking down, avoiding my eyes. I can see the fear all over her beautiful face. What has her so worried? What can be worse than the things I've confessed to her? My past is beyond fucked up. I put the fucked in fucked up.

"Then, I'm all ears, as long as it's what you want." She nods and smiles nervously. Twisting a strand of hair around her finger, she begins. I sit quietly, holding her hand and listen. My heart aches at the shit she had to endure while being tossed around from one foster home to another. I will never understand how anyone can deliberately hurt a child. It's just impossible for me to fathom. The more she discloses, the more uncomfortable she looks. Honestly, there's nothing for her to be so nervous about. There isn't anything that could make me not want her. Well, that's not true exactly. Cheating on me and hurting children would cause me to walk away. I'd most likely still want her, but I would walk away.

"We were married right out of high school," she says, her voice becoming shakier with every word. Suddenly, I'm a little scared of what she's going to say. "Ray had me fooled. He had me thinking he was my Prince Charming, but he was more like a male masochist version of the evil queen." She continues on about Ray, her ex-husband. The more she tells me, the angrier I get. My jaw clenches and my free hand is balled into a fist. I'm in no way angry at her, but at this asshole who used her as a punching bag for so long. Not only did he beat her down physically, he also beat her down mentally. I can hear the guilt in her voice. She still thinks she's to blame for the way he treated her. That she deserved every put down. Every punch.

She looks up, her eyes widening when she notices the anger and disgust on my face. Swallowing hard, she continues warily. "I should've left him the first time he laid a hand on me. I need you to understand that I had no one and nowhere to go. I guess that's what made me the perfect target for him. It didn't take a whole lot of effort to isolate me from family and friends. Actually, it took no effort. I didn't have either." The sadness in her eyes makes me want to hold her and tell her it's all over. I will destroy anyone or anything that ever hurts her again. However, I let her continue. She needs to get this out.

With tears building in her eyes, she eyes me cautiously. "It's my fault. I stayed too long. The second I found out, I should've left and never looked back." Burying her face in her hands, I hear her softly sobbing. The sound breaks me in two. Reaching out and taking her face in my hands, I lift it so she's looking right at me.

"Do you need to stop? There's nothing you could tell me that will make me love you any less." The instant that four letter word leaves my mouth, I wish I could take it back. Not because I don't mean it. I know with everything I am that I'm in love with this amazing woman. This just isn't the right time to declare my love for her and besides, I'm not quite sure she's ready to hear it. The gasp that slips from her lips tells me I've shocked her with my declaration.

Slowly shaking her head, she gathers her composure and continues. The pain and agony combined with regret and guilt that's been plastered on her face intensifies. "I accidentally got pregnant. Ray didn't want to share me. Not even with his own child." She fidgets with the corner of the blanket we're sitting on. I think I know where this is headed and it makes me sick. Five minutes. Five minutes alone with this guy is all I need to show him how it feels to be beat on. If I ever lay eyes on him, he's going to wish he were dead.

"He said he couldn't allow people to find out he sent me for an abortion, so he'd have to take care of it himself." She's full on sobbing now. I'm livid. I jump up from my sitting position next to her. I have the strong urge to hit something hard. Preferably this Ray guy's fucking face. I'm pacing back and forth like a crazy man. I need to calm myself down. The last thing she needs is me scaring her. "I'm so sorry. It's all my fault. I killed my baby," she cries out. *What the fuck!* She's shouldering the blame for it all. When I turn around, she's up and starting to walk away. It hits me. She thinks I'm angry at her. Damn it, I'm such an ass.

"Wait, doll face!" I yell out to her, panicked it's too late to explain. She stops dead in her tracks, but doesn't turn around. Slowly, I ease closer to her. "I'm angry, but not at you." She turns around. When I see the tears steadily streaming from her face, I can't stop the ones building in my eyes. The pain she's feeling, I'm feeling for her. She has endured so much, but still, she goes on, smiling. She's stronger than she realizes.

I reach my hand out to her. I can feel her body shaking when she places her hand cautiously into mine. Guiding her back to the blanket, I sit, pulling her down with me and placing her between my legs so her back is resting against my chest. I encircle my arms around her waist, trying to make her feel safe and loved. "You did nothing wrong. Ray is the monster. You did not kill your baby. He did." Her shoulders begin to shake and I know she's once again sobbing.

"But...if...if I would have been strong enough to leave him earlier, it never would've happened," she says in between sobs. "I knew what he was capable of. I didn't protect my baby. What the hell kind of mother wouldn't do everything possible to protect her child?" The heartache in her voice rips me apart. It kills me to see her feel guilty for something she had no control over. She may have known what he was capable of, but even she probably never imagined he would go so far as to kill his own unborn child.

I lift her face so I can look into her beautiful green eyes. I need her to hear me and see that what I'm saying is the truth. "Not even you could have known he was capable of something so reprehensible. You are a good person. You would've been a great mother, and you will be someday. You need to stop blaming yourself." She sniffles and I notice the corners of her mouth lift into a small smile.

"How would you know whether I'm a good person? How do you know I would be a good mother? We hardly know each other. Even my own mother didn't want me," she says. How do I make her see how amazing she is? The truth. That's how. This is a something I never thought I'd be doing. Hearing the way she feels, I can see we are one in the same. I never felt I deserved anything good in my life either. That is, until she came along.

"I knew the instant we collided you were something special. I had this feeling you would somehow change my life. You already have even in the short amount of time we've known each other. I vowed never to fall in love with anyone. Like you, I felt like I wasn't worthy of being happy, that I couldn't possibly make anyone else happy. I've tried to fight it, but it's no use." Suddenly, she jumps to her feet and bolts toward the truck. I'm up and following close behind. When she's almost to the truck, we both stop in our tracks by a bolt of lightning that looks as if it stretches down from the sky and touches the ground. A crack of thunder so loud it vibrates through my body follows. I didn't even realize storm clouds had moved in. Although, I suppose with the conversation we've been having, it's fitting. I snatch up Holly's hand and lead her to the back of the truck, lowering the tailgate with my free hand. Grabbing her by the waist, I set her on the tailgate. I settle myself between her legs, forcing her to face me while also keeping her in one place.

"I need you to listen to me now. If you don't feel the same way, I'll take you home, but at least hear me out." Her eyes fill with tears and I'm scared they mean she doesn't feel the same. It's time to man the fuck up and take a chance. She nods her head, giving me the okay to continue.

"I've fallen so head over heels in love with you, doll face, that it terrifies me." My heart is pounding so hard in my chest, it's drowning out the booms of thunder in the sky. I've never told anyone but my parents that I love them. "When you knocked me on my ass that day, it was the best thing that's ever happened to me. You are the best thing to ever happen to me. I want to be with you, protect you, and love you for as long as you'll allow. If you'll allow me."

"You love me?" she questions, looking stunned.

"Yes, doll face. I love you." Taking my hand, I caress her soft cheek. "I never believed in all the 'love at first sight' bullshit or the 'you'll just know' garbage until the day I met you. I want you. All of you. And I promise, right here and now, if you give me a chance, I will do everything in my power to always keep you safe. I'll always make you feel special and loved. And I will never ever hurt you." Holy shit. That felt good to say out loud. She's just staring at me, her mouth gaping open and her eyes wide in disbelief. The longer she stays that way, the more my stomach churns. A tear slides down her cheek and she looks away. *Oh, God.* She's going to tell me to take a hike. She doesn't feel the same way. How could I have been so wrong? I really thought she felt it, too. This connection we have. The same spark I feel with even the slightest touch from her. Did I misread all of those looks that told me she wanted me in every way?

I start to back away from her, not wanting to hear her rejection. The pain will be unbearable. Before I lose the connection from her legs, she grabs my hands and pulls me back to her. Her soft, tiny hands reach for my face and she guides it until its mere inches from hers. The smile that appears on her lips has my heart doing backflips.

"Ray was the only man I've been with. Hell, he's the only man I've ever kissed." That statement disturbs me. He never deserved such an amazing woman and the thought of any man being with her, other than me, makes my skin crawl.

"Trust has always been an issue for me, but after I left him, I didn't think I would ever be able to trust anyone again, let alone another man. Then, I ran into you. Literally." A sweet giggle escapes her lips and its music to my ears. "For some reason, I trust you. I trust you with my life, but I have no idea why. I just do. Just like I know, without a doubt, that I'm in love with you, too," she declares before bringing her lips to mine. The kiss starts slow, her lips gently exploring mine. When her tongue pushes through my parted lips, I'm about to fucking explode. These feelings of intense lust, love, and need are so new to me. I've never needed to be close to a woman before. With Holly, I can't seem to get close enough. At least, not yet.

Telling me she loves me turned me on more than anything or anyone ever has and all I want to do is lay her out on the hood of this truck and worship every delicious inch of her body before I truly make her mine. However, she's going to have to set the pace. The last thing I want is to push her too far too fast. The look of pure want on her face causes my heart to thump against my ribs so wildly, I'm scared they might break.

"I want you, Paul. Right here and now. Make me yours," she whispers as she peppers light kisses along my neck, driving me insane. As hot and bothered as this woman has me, I'm going to embarrass the shit out of myself. I'll end up exploding the second she touches me. Just what I need...her thinking I'm a minute man. At least she doesn't have a lot to compare it to.

"Anything for you, doll face," I tell her before crashing my lips into hers. I intensify the kiss and she lets out a soft moan. It's the hottest fucking thing I've ever heard. Another loud crack of thunder sounds just as the sky opens up and cold rain pours down onto us. I start to pull away, but Holly grips my ass and pulls me back to her. I take that as a sign she doesn't care about the rain. Honestly, neither do I. Not when I have this beautiful woman pressed up against me.

As I move my lips to her neck, I kiss and suck gently. Her breathing suddenly picks up and another sexy moan leaves her. With her hands still on my ass, she pulls me in, grinding herself against my painfully hard cock. Gently, with my hand guiding her head, I lay her down in the bed of the truck. I begin to draw a path with my tongue from her neck to the top of her breasts, exposed thanks to the low cut tank top she's wearing. Reaching my hands to the bottom of the tank top, I slide it up very slowly. When her bare breasts come into view, I can't stop the guttural growl that escapes me. I want so badly to just rip her shorts right off and bury myself deep inside of her, but I won't. She deserves and needs slow and loving. At least, I thought that's what she'd need.

"I've spent so many years being told what to do, how to do it, and when to do it. For once, I want to be the one in control. Do you mind?" she asks shyly. *Hell no, I don't mind.*

"You have no idea what a turn on that is for me," I tell her honestly, shaking my head. "You tell me or show me what to do and I'll gladly do it. I'm all yours." Holly grabs my head and pulls it toward her chest until my lips are pressed against one of her pebbled, pink nipples. My jeans are so tight right now, I'm going to have a permanent zipper indent on my dick. Glancing up at her, I can only see desire in her eyes, which fuels my desire even more.

I take first one, then the other nipple into my mouth. With a combination of licking, sucking, and some light nibbling, I move back and forth between both breasts until she's squirming beneath me.

Holly grabs a hold of my hand and slides it down her stomach. When she reaches the waist of her shorts, she places my hand on the button. I flick open the four buttons with ease. Grabbing the belt loops, I roughly yank her shorts to her ankles and over her sandals. A breathy moan comes from her and it encourages me to keep going. Without hesitation, I rip the purple lace panties from her body and watch as goose bumps form all over her skin.

I groan, the sound deep and throaty, almost animalistic. "Shit, doll face, you're beautiful. Every piece of you is perfection. If you look this good, I can't help but wonder just how good you taste." Licking her lips, she smiles at me, obviously liking my train of thought.

"Why don't you find out?" she asks, almost sounding like a dare. One I'll gladly take and enjoy. I lean down and kiss her lips, then nibble on her earlobe.

"I plan to," I whisper in her ear, feeling her shiver. I kiss my way down her body until I reach her core. When I dip my tongue into her folds, she bucks her hips up, driving my tongue into her entrance. Her clit is swollen and she is soaking wet — and it has nothing to do with the rain. Sucking her clit into my mouth, I swirl my finger into the wetness around her entrance. She moans loudly, raising her hips, pushing me closer. I moan, letting the vibration wrap around her. Flattening my tongue, I swipe up her slit and thrust two fingers inside. She moans deeply as her wet heat wraps around my finger, making my cock swell even further.

"Holy hell...that...feels amazing," she pants, thrashing her head from side to side. Her hips buck harder, causing my fingers to push farther inside her. I curve my fingers and thrust harder. Using my thumb, I circle her clit slowly before adding more pressure. Keeping my pace, I stand and lean over, taking her lips with mine. The taste of her on my lips causes her to moan and she lifts her hips higher, grinding herself against my palm so beautifully. I move down and draw a slow circle around her nipple, blowing softly and then sucking before moving over to the other. I bite her nipple gently and release it with a pop before moving to swirl my tongue in her belly button. The sight of her, her head moving from side to side, the guttural moans escaping her lips, her hips undulating so perfectly, her pussy becoming tighter and tighter around my fingers, has my cock so painfully hard and ready to burst. She is absolutely breathtaking.

"God, Paul...I'm so close. Please don't stop," she begs. Like there's anything that would make me stop. I slow the thrust of my fingers, adding more concentration and pressure to that spot so deep within her. Removing my thumb, I swirl my tongue around her clit and suck forcefully, thrusting my fingers in shorter, faster bursts.

She tenses and her body jerks and shudders. A string of curse words flies from her lips and I remove my fingers, diving my tongue within her depths, tasting all of her. After one last, long swipe of my tongue, she sits up, takes hold of my t-shirt, and yanks my face up to meet hers. She crushes her lips against mine and our tongues find each other immediately. After a few intense seconds, she pulls away and runs her tongue across her lips, tasting herself once more. I groan, the small gesture more erotic than anything I've experienced.

Reaching between us, she unbuttons my jeans and pushes them down my legs. My cock springs free, causing her to gasp. She's not shy as she openly stares at my erection with lust-filled eyes. I allow her to look, waiting for her to make the next move. She slides toward the edge of the tailgate, reaches out, and takes my cock in her hand. I grab onto to the truck, trying to stop my legs from buckling and sending me to the ground. Her hand slides up and down my shaft, gripping with just the right pressure. I moan and breathe deeply, forcing my impending orgasm back. She feels incredible. Too good. Extending my arm, I take her perfect breast in my hand and squeeze slightly. Sparks of pleasure ignite at the base of my spine, moving lower. She builds the pace slowly as I run the pad of my thumb over her sensitive nipple. She moans breathily and reaches down between her legs. With her free hand, she slides two fingers into her wetness. A whimper escapes me, which only seems to fuel her intentions. She adds another finger and winks at me before throwing her head back and moaning. She moves her hips slowly, fucking her fingers while increasing the pressure of her hand wrapped around my cock. My entire body is shaking, trying to control the threatening release.

Removing her hand from between her legs, she moves it to my cock, coating it with her slick juices. Slowly, she strokes my shaft until it's completely covered with her arousal. Just as I'm hanging by the last thread of self-control, she hooks her ankles together and pulls me to her, until my cock is rubbing against her entrance. She wiggles her hips, rubbing her clit against the head of my cock. I groan, my cock so hard, it hurts.

With a small giggle, she positions herself just right. One thrust of her hips and my cock is sliding into perfection. Warm, wet perfection. If I died right now, right here, I would go happier than I've ever been. I snake my hand around her waist and bury myself fully inside her. She lets out a satisfied moan. "Mind if I take over from here, doll face? I really don't want to embarrass myself," I tell her.

Smiling at me, she lays back, resting on her elbows. "I'm all yours," she states, and that's all I need. I move almost completely out of her and slowly, so very slowly, slide back in. Her eyes flutter closed.

"Open those beautiful green eyes. I want you to see what you do to me," I grunt out as I slowly pump in and out of her. She's so beautiful, pure pleasure written across her face. Her eyes slowly drift open and I'm lost. My eyes never leave hers as I move in and out. Moans, heavy breaths, and the rain beating down are the only sounds I hear. I feel her start to tighten around me and I reach down, gliding my thumb over her clit and applying pressure. I pick up speed, her tightening heat making me lose all control. One more swirl of my thumb and a deep thrust, her body shudders and her walls spasm, gripping my cock tightly as she screams my name. I close my eyes, reveling in how sweet my name sounds coming from her mouth. I thrust once, twice more before the most intense orgasm I've ever had takes me over.

Our eyes are still locked on one another and she has a pleased and satisfied look on her face. A confidence I haven't seen before. I pull out of her and lift her into my lap as I sit on the wet, cold tailgate. She snuggles into my chest, letting out a content sigh. "As much as I want to stay like this, I better get you out of the rain before we both catch our death," I tell her.

"A hot shower does sound good. But only on one condition," she says with a wicked grin.

"And what would this condition be?" I ask.

"You have to join me. I'm up for round two," she states. And just like that, I'm hard as a fucking rock again. This woman just might kill me, but what a sweet fucking death it would be.

CHAPTER
Nine

Present

Holly

I'M PARALYZED by fear as I stand in the doorway, my mouth agape and my body shaking as I stare at my own version of the boogeyman. In my head, I'm screaming at myself to run, to get the hell away from the man who has caused me so much pain. I always feared he'd find me someday. Looks like today is that day.

"Holly, who is it?" Amber asks, walking up behind me and snapping me out of my frozen state. How do I explain him? More importantly, why is he here?

"Are you okay? You don't look so good."

My throat is so dry, the only reply I can give is to nod my head. Paul is the only one who knows everything about Ray. Everyone else knows I was married and it ended badly, but that's the only information I've shared.

Amber looks from me to Ray and back again, waiting for someone to speak. Ray being his usual charming self quickly extends his hand to an unsuspecting Amber. "Hi, I'm Ray." Not knowing any better, she makes a move to shake his hand. The thought of him laying a finger on Amber makes my skin crawl. Luckily, my brain wakes up. I grab Amber's arm and yank her behind me, yelling, "No!" This draws the attention of the four very protective men in the house. I feel Paul behind me before he grabs me by the waist and pulls me against him protectively. A sinister smile crosses Ray's face.

"What's going on, doll face? Who's this?" Paul questions. My head is spinning from the fact that Paul and Ray are face to face. He said once, after he found out about Ray, if he ever saw him, he'd kill him. I don't believe that was an empty threat. My pulse is racing and my lunch is dangerously close to reappearing. Paul's grip gets tighter. He knows something is wrong. I need to tell him before Ray does.

"Paul, this is Ray." He looks at me, his eyes questioning, wondering if this is *the* Ray. "My ex-husband," I announce. Five distinct and very protective growls sound behind me along with a gasp from Amber. Paul's arm is no longer around me. Instead, he has his hands around Ray's neck and is pushing him out of the doorway and down the steps to the porch then into the yard. Kyle, Angel, Marcus, and Clark are following closely behind. For the first time ever, I'm no longer afraid of little Ray Marconi. No longer is it just me against him. This has to stop before Ray isn't capable of speaking. I need to at least know why he's here, then they can do anything they want with monster.

My feet finally catch up with my brain and I begin to move. When I reach Paul, the anger radiating from him is so strong, it practically slaps me in the face. Seeing him so filled with rage is frightening. To my surprise, I'm also finding it pretty damn hot. Knowing he's doing this because he loves me and wants to keep me safe has me quite turned on. Shaking the inappropriate thoughts from my mind, I place my hand on his arm in hopes that my touch can calm him.

"As much as I want to see you rearrange his face, I need to know why he's here," I explain to a rather stunned Paul. I squeeze his arm gently and smile to let him know I'm okay. Paul tightens his grip on Ray and pulls him closer.

"You have five minutes to talk then I'm going to send you on your way via my fist. If you upset or hurt her in any way, you're fucking gator food," Paul threatens. The boys shake their heads slowly in agreement. If Ray has any brains, he'll do as he's told.

"I just want to apologize to her, to make my peace," Ray says. I don't buy it, though. Marconi men don't apologize, no matter what. To them, it's a sign of weakness. I know, without a doubt, he hasn't changed. He's the same mean and violent man he's always been. It's in his eyes. They're still as cold and threatening as ever. This realization causes bile to rise in my throat.

"Well, get to it, man. You have five minutes and the clock is ticking," Paul barks.

"Can I at least talk to her in private, over on the bench? You can stand here and watch me like a hawk. I give you my word that I'm not here to hurt her."

Uneasiness washes over Paul's handsome face. He doesn't like Ray being out of his reach. I point to the bench, indicating that Ray should sit down. Taking Paul's face in my hands, I kiss him softly on his lips. "It's okay. I'm okay. I'm not afraid of him anymore. You and our family give me courage I didn't have in the past. Besides, we are only fifteen feet away and as menacing as you boys look, he wouldn't dare try to hurt me," I tell him with a wink, trying to remove some of his worry.

"Fine, doll face, but if he hurts you in any way, he disappears and not even you'll be able to stop me," Paul states. For the first time, I really see just how much he loves me and how far he'd go to protect me. It's a reflection of how I feel. I love him more than anything. I would also do anything to protect him. Which is why I'm even hearing Ray out. I know he's not here to make amends. Ray is ruthless and will do anything necessary to get what he wants and he wants something. He wouldn't be here otherwise.

I take a seat on the bench as far away as it will allow from Ray. I can feel five pairs of watchful eyes on us both, just waiting for him to screw up so they can teach him a lesson. Not that I can blame them, especially Paul. If his parents were alive and just a few feet away, I'd feel the same way. We're protective of those we love. That's just the way it is.

I take a deep breath, hoping to calm my erratic heartbeat as I try not to notice the creepy way Ray is eyeing me up and down. Unfortunately, Paul has noticed and he looks like he's only seconds from ripping Ray apart.

"Why are you really here, Ray? What do you want?" I ask, getting straight to the point. I don't want to drag out this little reunion any longer than necessary. Being this close to him makes my skin crawl.

"Always so impatient. You don't believe I'm here to apologize?" I shake my head no. The condescending tone in his voice has me on edge. Even if he was here to apologize, he'll never find forgiveness from me. "Looks like you've smartened up some since you ran out on me. I'm surprised, however, that you returned to the slums. I don't want to be here anymore than you want me here, but I have no choice. I need you to do something and after walking out on me like you did, you owe me," he sneers. Chills race down my spine. What the hell does he need from me? Better yet, where does he get off thinking I owe him any fucking thing? I knew him being here couldn't be good.

"I don't owe you a damn thing, but I'll humor you long enough to tell me what you want." I'm proud of myself for putting on a strong confident front even though, on the inside, I'm anything but.

"Looks like the old man is about to kick the bucket," he says coldly. "There's only one way he'll leave me the inheritance I deserve and it involves you. He was under the impression that you are the perfect wife for me. The old man believes I've put in too much time and energy into molding you," Ray explains.

This whole family is fucking insane.

"Would you just get to the point, already? What is it that you need me for?" Ray lets out a small chuckle and shakes his head. I find myself imagining his head exploding and it makes me smile to myself. My patience, along with that of the angry group of men, is wearing quite thin right now.

"I figured it was obvious," he teases with a smirk. A smirk I'd like to wipe off his face via a Mack truck. "You're going to come home and tell the old man I took you back. We'll play the happily married couple until he kicks it, then you can return to your tattooed Neanderthal. Don't worry, I only want my money, not you — especially now that you've been tainted by him," he says, tipping his chin towards Paul. Sitting there with my mouth agape, I begin to laugh. Quickly, the laugh becomes uncontrollable. Tears are streaming down my face and my sides are beginning to hurt from laughing so hard.

Has he lost his ever loving mind? Does he honestly think I'd be alone with him, let alone go back and live with him? "That was funny. Really," I say, getting my laughter under control. "Have you had a head injury recently? Have you forgotten why I left you? If you think I'm going anywhere with you then you're a freaking loon." He turns his face back to me; his lips are pressed tightly together and his eyes look angry and cold. I've seen that look before. My body trembles as the reality of the situation hits me full force. Obviously laughing at him wasn't the right thing to do.

"I tried to ask you nicely. As nicely as I could anyway. But, you leave me no other choice," he sneers, still keeping his composure. "You will come with me or else I'm going to make all of your newfound friends and boyfriend disappear. Forever. You know what I'm capable of, Holly." Bile rises in my throat, causing it to burn. "In case that's not incentive enough, there is one more thing that will change your mind."

What else could he have that would be worse than threatening all of the people I love? There are no secrets between Paul and I he can try to hold over my head. The cocky look on his face tells me he has something he thinks he can use as leverage. Now, I'm curious.

"I've known where you were for a while. You've been so wrapped up in the bartender and all of his low-life friends, that you never noticed me watching you," he confesses without any remorse.

"Just spit it out already. What is it you think you have that could possibly make me go back to a monster like you?" I bark out. I'm tired of his head games. Giving him a one way ticket home on the end of Paul's size thirteen sounds really good right about now.

"Well, like I said, I've been watching you. I know things no one else knows yet." My throat is dry and I'm finding it very difficult to swallow. There's no possible way he can know. There's only one secret I have. One I haven't even shared with Amber yet. Hell, I've only known for two days. I planned on announcing it today, but Paul proposed and I got distracted. Then Ray showed up. He can't be the one to tell Paul about this. It has to come from me. Noticing the panicked look in my eyes, his face lights up and an evil grin appears.

"Don't worry you're pretty little red head, Holly. I won't tell your precious Paul about your pregnancy. I will, however, end it if you don't do what I want and keep your mouth shut," he snarls. Chills run up my spine and my stomach churns. I know he's capable of making good on that threat. There's no doubt in my mind. How do I do what he wants? I can't just tell Paul I'm going back to my ex-husband. If he believes I did it on my own accord without being forced, he'll be devastated. How do I destroy the man I love? But…do I really have a choice? I allowed Ray to take one child from me, I can't allow him to do it again. I won't allow it a second time. I have to protect my child. Paul's child. I look over at the handsome man who just asked me to be his wife and wonder whether he'll ever be able to forgive me when this is over. Will he understand I'm only doing this to protect him, our baby, and the ones we love?

I fight back the tears threatening to overtake me. I don't trust Ray at all. What if this is all a ploy to get me back and he hurts me and the baby anyway? "Why should I trust you? How do I know when this is over my baby and I can leave unharmed?" I question, wishing I could think of a way out of this without anyone getting hurt.

"I give you my word. You're yesterday's news to me. I have someone else now. You were so far beneath me, I don't know why I was with you in the first place. Just do as I say and as soon as I get what's mine, you're free to go," he says with a look that says I'm not worth the dirt on his shoes.

"Fine. But if you lay so much as a finger on me or anyone I love, I'll make you pay. I'm gonna need some time to figure out what to tell everyone."

"You have twenty-four hours and not a minute more. Remember, everyone has to believe you're coming back to me as my wife. My father will find out if even one person knows the truth. And if that happens, you won't be breathing long enough to make me pay for anything. I'll pick you up this time tomorrow." With that, he stands up, leans over, places a kiss on my cheek, and walks away. It's a gesture that makes me want to hurl as well as punch him in the fucking throat. I have twenty-four hours to decide how to break the love of my life, and just when he's finally found a way to heal from his past.

Paul

EVER SINCE that no-good prick showed up yesterday at the party, Holly has been acting strange. She's on edge and when she smiles, I can tell it's forced. Last night, this morning, and during the several times we made love today, it seemed as if she were holding on for dear life. As if she were afraid to let go because if she did we'd drift away from each other. With every glance, her eyes were trying to tell me something she couldn't. It's almost as if she's trying to say goodbye. But why? I tried to get her to tell me everything the bastard said to her, but she just says it was all empty apologies. "Nothing important," she repeats. For the first time since I've met her, I don't believe her. My gut is telling me our lives are about to change and it's not a change for the good.

"What are you thinking about, handsome?" Holly says in a sleepy voice. Again, there's that sad smile. I need her to tell me what's wrong, but how?

"Just thinking about how beautiful my fiancé is," I tell her with a forced smile of my own. She gets out of bed and quickly heads into the bathroom, closing the door behind her. When Holly finally exits the bathroom, she's fully dressed. "Where are you going, doll face?" I inquire. I need to know what the hell is going on. The pit in my stomach is getting larger by the minute. She can't or won't — I don't know which — make eye contact with me when she answers.

"Amber called. She needs me," she says nervously. Bending down, she kisses me with so much passion, it leaves me weak. My heart is racing, not because of the kiss itself, but because of what I'm afraid it means. She runs her lips along my ear and softly whispers, "I love you more than anything, Paul Walters. Please don't ever forget that." When she stands up, I can see tears in her beautiful green eyes. Before I can stop her, she turns and bolts out of the bedroom. By the time I can get myself to move to try to stop her, she's already getting in her car.

Running back to the bedroom, I fumble around, trying to get dressed. My clouded brain is making it difficult, but I have to go after her. I run into the bathroom to grab my pants and notice her phone on the counter. I know it's an invasion of privacy, but this is an emergency. Looking through her recent texts, I see one from Ray. It came in around the time she came in here. With shaky hands, I swipe the screen and open the message.

Ray: It's time. Meet me at the bar. Don't take anything with you. Not even this phone. I will make sure you have everything you need when we get home.

"What the FUCK!" I scream as I throw the phone across the room and watch it break into pieces against the wall. What the hell is going on? Why is she going with him? The man who beat her, who killed their unborn baby. She wouldn't go with him willingly.

When I pull up to the bar, I see them both there. He's holding the passenger door open, allowing her to get in. I skid to a stop inches from the asshole and I jump out of the truck, unsure whether I put it into park or not. My head is so fucked up, all I can think about is stopping her.

"Doll face? What are you doing?" I question, anger consuming me. But when the words leave my mouth, it sounds like the plea of a child.

"I know you don't want to go with him. Please tell me what's going on," I beg.

She looks so frightened. He's forcing her somehow. That's got to be it. It's the only explanation. Ray grabs a hold of her arm and pushes her toward the car. Him touching her sets me off. I rush him and take hold of his shirt collar, lifting him off the ground and slamming him against the back of the car. My entire body is shaking. If I'm not careful, I might just end up killing this fucker.

"Take it easy there, Hercules. She's going with me willingly. She's done slumming and ready to get back to her real life," Ray gloats. I pull my fist back, ready to knock his head clear off his shoulders, until Holly places her trembling hand on my shoulder. As always, her touch instantly calms me. I let go of Ray and turn to face her. Her eyes are filled with unshed tears, pleading with me to understand. But…what am I supposed to understand? That she would willingly go back to this ass when she fought so hard to get away from him? I just don't buy it. I can't. She wouldn't leave me for him.

"Please, Paul, you need to let me go. I know you don't understand why I'm doing this right now, but you will one day. I promise," she says before kissing my cheek and getting into the car. When she closes the door, I can see tears steadily streaming down her face. She doesn't want to go. I knew it. Whatever it is, I can fix it for her. As I go to grab the handle, the car begins to back out of the parking spot. I'm losing her. I can't protect her if she leaves with him. She never told me where she lived before coming here. She was always afraid I'd try to hunt Ray down.

I run along with the moving car, slamming my hands against it. "Doll face, I can protect you! Whatever he's holding over you, we can fix," I yell as the car switches into drive. Holly is no longer trying to hide her tears. Sadness and regret are so evident on her face, even through the tinted window. She mouths, "I'm sorry".

"Please, baby, don't go!" I cry before the car speeds away. I fall to my knees in the middle of the parking lot and cry. My entire life just drove off. This feels like my mom all over again. She's walking away from me, the one person who would die to protect her and into the arms of the man she's needs protection from. Why? Why would she go willingly back to him? Didn't she have enough faith in me to know I'd keep her safe? "Why are you doing this to me, God?" I cry out into my hands.

"I've had plenty of women scream out 'God' in my presence, but never a man," Angel says from behind me. I can't help but laugh. He can always lighten the mood, no matter how dark. Quickly trying to wipe the moisture from my face, I turn to see Angel, Marcus, Clark, and Kyle all standing behind me, concern showing on their faces. They all know how hard it was for me to open up enough to fall in love with Holly. Not that I really had a choice. The harder I fought against it, the harder I seemed to fall.

"Come on, man. Let's go get a drink. Maybe we can help you figure all this out," Kyle suggests, reaching his hand out to help me off the ground. Its times like this I'm so glad I have these guys. I grab Kyle's hand and he yanks me off the ground. I'm also thankful it's Sunday and the bar is closed.

"How did you know I was here?" I ask as we walk up to the front door. Kyle looks away from me and unlocks the door. He doesn't want to tell me how he knew, but he will.

"Holly called a while ago and told Amber she was leaving with Ray. She asked Amber to make sure I was here because you'd need me," he says sadly and opens the door. "I called the guys and we got here as soon as we could." I just don't understand. If she was so fucking worried about me and knew I'd need my friends, why did she leave?

"Did she tell Amber why she was going with him in the first place?"

"She told Amber she has to go, that she loves us all and because of that, she has to leave," Kyle says with a shrug of his shoulders. What the hell does that mean? Because she loves us she has to leave us? Kyle looks at me sympathetically. "I don't get it either. For now, let's drink. We can try to figure it all out later. Beasley is on his way," he says with a wink. Well if anyone can get to the bottom of what's going on, Lee Beasley will. Not only is he the Sheriff of Oakville, he's Amber's dad.

By the time Beasley arrives, I've put away a few beers and even more shots. I tell everyone all about Holly and Ray. Normally, I wouldn't tell anyone about the hell Holly's been through, but this situation calls for it. If Beasley is going to be able to help, he needs to know everything.

"I just don't know what he could possibly have used to threaten her with," I explain to Beasley when he asks why she'd go with him in the first place. "Even if he threatened to come after one of us, she had to have known we'd band together to keep everyone safe. It makes no sense." Taking another shot and slamming it back, I close my eyes. All I can see is the agony in her face as they drove away. If he hurts her, I will kill him. I'll be damned if I allow another abusive prick to take away a woman I care about.

"I'll get this info to my P.I. friend. I don't know how long it'll take to get a lead, but I promise you, Paul, I will do everything I can to find her. She's become a second daughter to me. I don't want her with this guy any more than you do," Beasley confesses. For such a bad ass, he sure is a softie when it comes to family.

"Well, since I can only wait for now, how about you boys get me good and drunk," I state, raising my shot glass for a refill. I can't do a damn thing to help her right now and that kills me. All I can do is pray that she's okay. The ache in my heart is threatening to tear me to shreds. Right now, numbing the pain is the only thing I can do.

CHAPTER
Ten

Holly

IT'S BEEN three weeks since I came back to this house — the house I swore I'd never set foot in again. Ray has played the part of the perfect gentleman so far. He's actually reminding me of the Ray I thought I married. The sweet and gentle man I intended to spend the rest of my life with until the monster inside him came to the surface. I'm beginning to question his motive for having me here. He said it was to prove to his dying father that we were back together, but I have yet to see his father, who's supposedly in the hospital. He also said he wasn't interested in me because he had found someone else, yet he barely ever leaves my side.

After the first week, I began falling into my old routine. I wake up early cook breakfast and then spend the rest of the day cleaning until it's time to cook dinner. How the hell did I get here? This is not where I want to be, not where I need to be. With Paul, that's where I should be. I'm just going to have to tell Ray I'm going home and pray I can get out of here without incident. He wants me to think he's changed, but there's no way someone like him can change. A man like him always has to be in control. The minute he believes he's losing control, he'll try to get it back the only way he knows how. Fear. Fear is what he uses to show he's in control. That he has the power.

The sound of his footsteps behind me causes me to jump in my chair. "What are you in such deep thought about?" Ray asks as he pours himself a cup of coffee before sitting across from me. I look down and notice my mug is empty. I laugh to myself. If that were Paul, he would have checked my coffee to see if I needed a refill before thinking of pouring his own. I guess I should be grateful that Ray even poured his own coffee. Before, he would have sat down then told me to get his coffee.

As I get up to refill my mug, I wonder if now is the time to bring up my concerns. I remember what used to happen to me when I'd question him and just the thought causes my pulse to quicken. My hands begin to shake and coffee spills over the top of my mug. This time when Ray speaks, I can hear the old Ray in his voice coming through.

"You're thinking about the wanna be rock star, aren't you?" he barks. My cheeks heat and I clench my fists. How dare he put Paul down. Paul is ten times the man Ray could ever dream of being.

"You need to stop putting him down in front of me. I love him. It's bad enough that you're forcing me to be here, I won't listen to you bad mouth him," I announce. At first, it feels good to stand up to him for the first time, but when I see the anger in his eyes, I wish I had just kept my mouth shut. The vein on his forehead is protruding; the first sign that he's angry. This is the point when his fists usually meet my face. What the hell was I thinking? I have to think about my baby, I can't be mouthing off to him, giving him an excuse to lash out. Not that it usually takes much of an excuse. He grips the coffee mug so tightly, I'm afraid it will shatter. When I hear his teeth grinding, I start to get a little nervous. Instinctively, I rest my hands on my stomach. Ray's eyes follow the motion. He pinches the bridge of his nose and takes a deep breath.

"I'm sorry, but he's not good enough for you. You deserve better," he sighs. He has to be kidding. He wouldn't know better if it slapped upside the head.

The words are out of my mouth before I even think about the consequences. "Better? If you are meaning someone like you, then you're clearly out of your mind," I challenge. He stands up so abruptly, his chair goes sliding across the floor and slams into the cabinet. The pounding of my heart is the only sound I hear.

"Are you trying to push me?" Ray bellows. I can tell he's really trying to rein in his temper and here I am, continuously poking the bear. "I'm trying to be nice. To change for you. Be the man you deserve. You constantly aggravating me isn't helping." He begins to pace around the kitchen. I don't fail to notice his fists clenched at his sides. A sane person would just shut the fuck up. But, of course, I'm not that girl.

"I'm not trying to provoke you, but you can't possibly expect there to be anything between us. The only reason I'm here with you is because you threatened the people I love and my baby," I squeak out. My mouth is dry and I'm finding it difficult to swallow. His face turns bright red as he stomps toward me. Covering my belly again, I brace myself for what's coming next. I can feel a gust of cool air on my face as his fist barely misses me and slams through the sheet rock wall behind me. The crack causes me to jump and a small whimper escapes my lips.

"Why do you push me?" he screams so close to my face, I can smell the coffee on his breath. "I'm willing to forgive you for leaving and shacking up that degenerate. Why won't you forgive me?" He slowly backs away from me, never taking his eyes off me. My body is still trembling with fear, yet I can't seem to control my words.

"There are a lot of things I can forgive. But you lost the right for forgiveness when you deliberately killed our baby," I cry. Even though I know tears anger him more than anything, they begin to fall and I don't try to stop them. I've never confronted him about this. I was always too afraid to do so. Now, I'm still afraid, but it's as if the dam that's held in all of the pain and anger bursts. "Do you honestly think you have a chance in hell at getting me back? Let me make it clear for you now, Ray. I will never be with you again. Why? Because I hate you. Nothing could make me love you again. Nothing."

Ray reaches down, picks up his coffee mug, and hurls it at the wall. "You've always been an ungrateful bitch!" he thunders as he grabs his car keys from the hook by the door. "By the time I get back, let's hope your attitude has had a major adjustment. If it hasn't, I'll just have to adjust it for you," he roars as he walks out the door, slamming it closed behind him.

When I hear the car pulling out of the driveway, I finally let out the breath I've been holding. He has changed some. If I had talked to him like that before, I'd be on the floor bleeding by now. I'm amazed he was able to walk away and control his temper. However, I don't think I'll be that lucky twice.

I need to get out of here. I should have known he was trying to get me back. This whole thing was a ploy from the get go. His father probably isn't sick at all. And if there was another woman, why has he not left my side once in three weeks until now? Getting up from the table, I start to search for a phone. It's time to get my friends involved and let them know why I left. I pray they will even give me the time of day. Paul is never going to understand why I did this. I can't say I really blame him, but I need to make him understand that I was only trying to protect him and our baby. This is not how I wanted to tell Paul he's going to be a daddy.

After I look through the kitchen with no luck, I move to the rest of the house. The living room, dining room, all four bedrooms, and now, his office. Nothing. Not one phone in the whole house. He's trying to keep all contact from me to Paul cut off. So far, he's done a brilliant job. What am I going to do? Paul has no idea how to find me, or even where to begin to look. I've never told him Ray's last name and when I left Ray, my last name was changed in hopes it would help keep me hidden from Ray. I don't even think I've ever told Paul where I lived before moving to Oakville.

When I see a sheet of stamps lying on his desk, it gives me the answer I need. If I can't call anyone, I'll send a letter. They have to know I'm not here because I want to be with Ray and the look on Paul's face the day I left told me that's exactly what he thinks. I just hope he hasn't written me off. I need him to get me out of this mess. Why didn't I go to him in the first place to ask for help? I should have known Ray was deceiving me.

I find a piece of paper, a pen, and an envelope. I sit and quickly begin to try explaining to Paul all of the reasons I left, and how, at the time, it seemed like the only way to keep him, our friends, and our baby safe. As I write it down now, I am starting to see how stupid a move it was for me to make. Why couldn't I see it at the time when it mattered the most? Rushing to get this finished before Ray comes back, I pray I'm making sense. I pray he will somehow understand why I thought this was what had to be done.

Quickly, I fold the letter, place it in the envelope, and seal it. I address it to Paul but leave off the return address, writing it in the letter instead. I don't want to risk this coming back here and Ray finding it. After placing the stamp on it, I put everything back exactly how it was when I came in here. I need to keep Ray calm and happy until Paul comes for me or I can find my own way out. I still believe Ray could hurt the people I love and I can't allow that to happen. So, until they know his threats and that he's capable of pulling them off, I need to play nice.

Looking out the window, I check to make sure Ray hasn't returned yet. If I remember correctly, there's a mailbox on the corner directly behind us. I slip on my shoes and head out the back door. I go through the gate located in the back corner of the enormous, fenced-in backyard. Thankfully, he doesn't keep it locked. After a minute or so trek through some light woods, I reach the street behind us. I'm thrilled to see the blue mailbox sitting on the corner. I rush up to it and drop my letter inside.

When I come through the gate and into Ray's backyard, my heart starts pounding and my legs go weak. Ray is standing in the center of the yard. His fists are clenched at his sides and his chest is rising and falling quickly. When he sees me come into the yard, a look of relief washes over him, but the anger hasn't left.

"Where were you, Holly?" Ray questions, trying not to sound irritated. I need to keep him happy. There's no way I can fight him off if he gets angry and my baby is the most important thing.

"I was just feeling a little cooped up so I decided to go for a walk," I answer with a smile. "Is that okay?" I add, letting him think he's in control. When he smiles, I know he's appeased.

"No, it's fine. Next time, just ask and I'll take you. I don't like you wandering around on your own, okay?" He caresses the side of my face with his hand. The gesture makes me want to vomit; instead, I smile and nod my head yes. "Let's go inside. I think I'll grill us some steaks for dinner," he says, placing his hand in the center of my back and guiding me toward the house. God, I hope that letter makes it to Paul quickly. I don't know how long I can keep this up.

Paul

"Are you planning on leaving this bar stool any time soon? You really need a shower," Kyle sternly says.

"Yeah, you fucking stink, dude," Angel chimes in.

"Way to kick a guy when he's down. If I go upstairs and take a shower will the two of you get off my back and leave me the fuck alone?" I bark. I'm in no mood for their teasing right now. Holly's been gone almost a month. No one has heard from her and I'm losing my shit. I can't figure out why she left. There had to be a reason she just up and took off. I need to know what it is because my mind keeps wandering to the possibility that she left me to go back to Ray. I don't want to believe it, but what choice do I have? If that's not the case, why would she up and leave without an explanation? There's nothing else I can think of that would make her go with him willingly. After all that man did to her, after all he took from her, how could she go with him?

"It will be a good start. Amber went by your house and grabbed you some clothes. They're in the bedroom upstairs. She didn't think you'd want to go home. She also said the mail is beginning to pile up and wanted to know if she should bring it here for you," Kyle states. I don't know what I'd do without such great friends in my life. Amber is right, I haven't wanted to go home. I went there the first night Holly left but couldn't handle being there without her. We've been living there together for over a year now, so the memories overwhelm me. Luckily, Kyle keeps the apartment above the bar empty just in case.

I know I'm being a dick to everyone, but I can't seem to control it right now. Thankfully, they all get it and aren't taking it personally. Even they can't seem to understand why Holly did this — especially after I told them everything Ray did to her. Just thinking about it pisses me off all over again.

"Fine. Anything to shut you assholes up. Please ask her to bring the mail here when she gets a chance. I can't go back to that house yet. Not without Holly," I grunt and wobble too my feet from my more than comfortable barstool. I sat here last night after my shift was over and began to drink away my anguish. This is where I woke this morning and began again. I haven't left since, so I suppose it's time I got up for a while. Before I make my way upstairs, I reach over the bar and grab a bottle of Jack Daniels. Kyle doesn't stop me, he just shakes his head. He's been here himself. He knows what I'm going through and the only way I'm not going to lose my mind is by keeping it as fuzzy as possible. There's no better way to do that than my buddy Jack.

I finally make it up the stairs after tripping, several times, and let myself into the apartment. Just as Kyle said, there's a pile of my clothes on the bed. I raise my arms to pull off my shirt and get a whiff of myself. The guys were right, I fucking reek. I make my way to the shower. I turn on the hot water as high as it will go, hoping it will wash away the ache in my heart from being without Holly. It doesn't work. Nothing does. I want her here with me, safe in my arms. He had to force her somehow. I have to believe there was a reason Holly would go with him and leave me alone. Tears begin to fall as I think back on all the times I've held her in my arms. I slide down the wall and let it all out. I need to get her back. If he harms her in any way, I'll never forgive myself and he'll no longer be breathing. When the water begins to run cold, I quickly wash up and get out.

Wrapping a towel around my waist, I go into the bedroom and lay down on the bed. I reach for my phone and check for messages, but there's nothing. I can't call her and she hasn't called me. I'm getting frustrated, but I'm not giving up hope that he has forced her to go with him. Not until I have something solid to prove it. I have to believe she still loves me. There hasn't been anything to solidly back that theory up either.

I forwarded all her calls to my phone, just in case she calls it. I know it's a long shot, but right now, that's all I have. As I scroll through the list of voicemails, there's a number I don't recognize, so that's the first one I listen to.

"Ms. Anders, this is Dr. Monty's office calling to let you know you missed your fifteen week prenatal appointment. Please call us to reschedule," a bubbly voice says as I drop the phone to the bed. My head is spinning and my heart aches. Holly is pregnant? I'm going to be a dad? Why wouldn't she tell me this? So many emotions are swirling around inside me, it makes it difficult to know what I'm really feeling. Fear. Fear is the biggest emotion. Knowing what that son of a bitch did to Holly's first baby, his own child, leaves me very afraid of what he'll do to ours. If he did all of this to get Holly back for himself, how is he going to handle finding out she's carrying another man's child?

The lump in my throat is so overpowering, I'm finding it hard to breathe. Quickly, I throw on a clean pair of jeans and a t-shirt and frantically dial Kyle downstairs. It takes three attempts because my hands are shaking so badly. He answers on the third ring.

"No, I'm not coming up to wash your back. You're on your own there, man," Kyle chuckles. Any other time, I could've seen the humor there, but now is not that time.

"No time for jokes, KC. I need you to call Beasley and Amber. Have them meet us here. Please. I'll be down in a minute," I stammer and hang up without giving him a chance to reply. It feel like my entire world is being ripped away from me. This is why I spent so many years not allowing myself to care about anyone. I don't like this helpless feeling. Knowing the two people I love more than anything are in danger and I'm sitting here with my thumb up my ass unable to do a damned thing. How is it that I'm already so in love with and protective of a child I just found out about? A child I've never seen, or held, yet I'm willing to die to protect it. Getting them back to me safely is my only concern. I won't let that bastard hurt another child...my child.

Sitting on the edge of the bed, I put on my socks. After slipping on my boots and lacing them up, I stand and glance back at the bed. Memories of all the time Holly and I have spent in this bed begin to flood my mind. Until Kyle gave Holly and I his mother's house, we lived here in this apartment. So many nights we've laid in this bed after making love, discussing what we both wanted our futures to look like. I remember the first time she brought up the idea of kids. I have to admit, I was a tad freaked out. After growing up the way I did, I was afraid I couldn't possibly be a good parent. But when she looked into my eyes and told me I'd be a great father, all my worries disappeared. Seeing how happy Kyle and Amber are with Cody helps, too. It's hard to believe I want this so badly now. I spent so much of my life telling myself I could never be any good for anyone, that I'd only cause pain for anyone who loved me, but Kyle and Holly showed me how wrong I was. I clear my head of all the memories swirling around my mind. I need to get downstairs.

As I walk up to the bar, everyone is already there waiting. Beasley, Kyle, Angel, and Amber all turn to look at me with curious expressions on their faces. Amber slides over, making room for me between her and Beasley. I walk over and slide onto the barstool. Beasley slaps me on the back as he gives me that fatherly look of concern. He may be Amber's real father, but he treats the rest of us misfits as if we are his children. It's something I needed even before I knew I did.

"What's up, Paul? Any new info that might help speed this along some?" Beasley questions as he hands me a fresh beer. I take a long pull and try to gather my thoughts into words.

"I'm not sure it will help us, but it makes this search a whole lot more urgent," I state and take another sip of my beer. "I was listening to Holly's messages and there was one from Dr. Monty's office." Amber and Kyle both look at each other in shock. They know Dr. Monty because he was their doctor through both of Amber's pregnancies. I look at Amber. If anyone other than Holly knew about the baby, it would be Amber. They tell each other everything. I can't imagine her telling anyone else before telling the two of us. "Did you know Holly's pregnant? According to the message, she missed her fifteenth week appointment."

"Paul, I swear, I had no idea. She did say she had some big news to announce at the party, but then Ray showed up and things got weird. She must've planned on telling us all that night. You didn't know either?" Amber asks. I shake my head no. I can't help but think of how happy I would've been if she'd had the chance to tell me in front of all our friends.

"After what you told us about Ray, this new information does change things. I'll call my buddy to see if he's gotten any closer to finding her. Meanwhile, I need you to guys to look through her things and see if there's anything that can point us in the right direction," Beasley orders.

"I can go look through her things at the house," Amber offers as she pulls a huge pile of mail from her even bigger purse. I take the pile from her and quickly flip through it, but it looks like nothing but bills.

"That would be great. I'll check the few boxes we still have in the closet upstairs. Thank you all for being here for me," I say awkwardly. I kiss Amber on the cheek and wave to the guys before heading back upstairs to the apartment. Please, God, let us come across something to help us find her. I can't lose them.

CHAPTER
Eleven

Holly

I DON'T KNOW how much more of this I can take. I'm nothing more than a prisoner in this house. Ray doesn't leave for any reason. He even has the groceries delivered to us. I'm going stir crazy. I thought for sure Paul would've come for me by now. Two weeks have gone by since I sent my letter to him. There's only one of two possible reasons. One, he hasn't gotten the letter, which means it's gotten lost and he won't get it. With Ray sticking around, there won't be another opportunity to send a new one. The second reason, the one I pray won't be the one, is that he's given up and has let me go. The thought of that happening has my chest tightening and bile creeping up my throat. What if he doesn't want me? What if he truly thinks I left him for Ray?

With each day that goes by, my belly gets a little bigger. Anyone could tell now that I'm pregnant. I keep having dreams of a baby girl. I would love to have a little girl. I wonder what Paul would prefer. Knowing how protective he is, I'm guessing he'll want a boy. I wish I could share all of these things with him. We should be discussing names and choosing items for a nursery. I hope we'll still have a chance to do those things together.

"Please tell me you aren't sitting here bellyaching about that putts you left back in redneckville," Ray says sarcastically. I've been trying to keep him calm and not start any arguments. Telling him I was thinking of Paul will only piss him off. So far, he hasn't laid a hand on me, but my luck will only go so far. I do, however, need him to understand that I need to see a doctor.

"No. I was actually thinking that it's past time to see a doctor. I need to make sure the baby is healthy," I tell him, hoping he understands instead of getting angry. Watching his face, I notice his features soften just a little at the mention of the baby. As much as I hate him, I can't help but be amazed at the changes I see in him. Not that these changes make any difference. I love Paul. I'm carrying Paul's baby. Ray had his chance to be my husband and the father of our child, but he threw that all away. Not me. I moved on, as difficult as it was. Somehow, I found a man just as broken as me. We helped each other put all of the pieces back together and the ones missing, we created along the way.

I'm afraid that by doing what I considered to be the only way I could keep my loved ones safe, I'm now the one who threw away my chance. Paul trusted me. Something that was almost impossible for him to accomplish. Now that he thinks I've broken that trust, it won't be possible to rebuild it. He won't even want to try. I know this because it's the same way I'd handle it. Wrong? Maybe, but it's the only way to guard yourself. We've learned if a person hurts you once, they'll do it over and over again, until you put a stop to it.

"I'm sorry, I wasn't even thinking. I'll get you an appointment with a doctor," Ray says. Inside, I'm jumping for joy. Not only do I get to make sure my baby is healthy, I may also have a chance of getting the hell out of here. Maybe in the doctor's office I can get to a phone and call Amber. After all of the things she's been through, she'll understand why I did this. "I know a great doctor who makes house calls." And just like that, my world shatters. Suddenly, I feel hopeless; a feeling I haven't had since the last time I was in this house. I need to get out. Get away from this man and back to Paul. My mouth takes over. I know I'll regret standing up to him, but I'm stronger now. A lot stronger than I was before.

"Ray, you can't keep me locked in this house. We had a deal. I'd stay here and pretend with you until you convinced your father we were still together, then you'd let me go back home. Is your father even sick?" I squeak out. My voice didn't sound as confident as I would've liked.

"I always thought you were a smart girl, but I'm seriously reconsidering. Of course he's not sick. He doesn't even like you. I want you back. I knew I could make you love me again, I just had to get you back here alone with me," he states as he takes my face in his hands. My stomach begins to churn. His touch repulses me. How could I have been so stupid? I begin to back away from him. I can see the anger appear in his eyes at my obvious rejection. There's the Ray I remember. The backs of my legs hit a chair and stop my escape. The sound of my heart thumping against my chest is deafening.

Ray lunges toward me, grabbing my shoulders. He begins to shake me. "Why won't you just forgive me? We can start over. I promise, I'll love this baby like it's my own," he pleads.

"Are you forgetting what you did to your baby, Ray?" I spit. For a second, remorse crosses his face, but it's quickly replaced with pure anger.

"Can't you see I'm trying to change? I'm sorry for the things I've done. At some point, you need to realize you are responsible for some of it, too," he fumes as his grip gets tighter. Even though my entire body is trembling, my mouth still won't stop.

"No one deserves to be beat, Ray. There's no excuse. But none of that matters any longer. You need to face the facts." I take his face into my trembling hands and look him straight in the eyes. He needs to understand. "I do not love you. I never will love you. We will never be back together. Those are the facts, Ray, and nothing you say or do will change them," I state and watch as a single tear falls from his eye. I follow its path down his cheek until it drips from his chin onto my wrist. Something about that single tear frightens me. My hands fall from his face to the ever-growing bump, covering the only thing I care about at this moment. To myself, I pray that my baby stays safe from the beating I'm about to take.

From the corner of my eye, I see Ray's hand close into a fist. Instead of closing my eyes and waiting for the blow, I keep my eyes fixed on his. His eyes darken until they're almost black. His jaw is clenched so tight, I can hear his teeth grinding together. I brace myself for what is coming next. Even when his powerful fist connects with my face, I keep my eyes open and trained on his, showing him I will no longer cower to him. He can beat me bloody, but I refuse to show fear. This bold move seems to anger him more, because the next blow is much harder, causing my eye to swell shut immediately.

"If you would just do what you're told, I wouldn't have to do this. I was doing so well, but you have to push and antagonize me to the point where I can't control it," he barks as he slams his fist into my face once more. I know he's split my bottom lip when I feel the blood trickling down my chin. I want to wipe it away, but I don't dare remove my hands from my belly. "You will love me again, Holly, even if I have to force you to."

"You can't make me love you. This tactic of yours is only going to make me hate you more than I already do," I say as I hold my belly even tighter. Only when I feel the fluttering do I take my eyes off Ray. A huge smile crosses my face as I look down at my belly. I'm so thrilled to have a sign that the baby's okay. I don't realize how Ray sees my smiling face. To him, it's me defying him yet again.

The punishing blows come harder and faster. One after another. He doesn't let up. I'm covered in blood and I can see it spattering against the wall. I should be hurting, but I'm not. Every time Ray delivers a blow to my face, my little angel moves and kicks, letting me know how strong she is. She's giving me the strength to hold on. Making me believe there's still hope of getting my life with Paul back.

My hands have not left my belly. No matter how hard the punch, I've kept my baby protected. Ray is out of breath and finally beginning to slow. My left eye is swollen completely shut and my right is close behind. I can barely make out Ray's face as he brings it so close to mine, I can feel the quick bursts of his breath hitting my face as he pants. The fact that I'm still conscious surprises us both.

"You will learn to love me again. Even if it's only because you fear otherwise. And if you don't, I'll just make sure you aren't around to love anyone else. If I can't have you, neither can he," he whispers before delivering one final blow that has me seeing nothing but black before I lose consciousness.

Paul

"Fuck!" I scream, throwing everything within my reach, including my cell phone. Amber just called and told me she and Becky couldn't find anything to help us find Holly. How could I not make her tell me Ray's last name. Not to hunt him down, but so I at least knew who to protect her from. I have this sick feeling in the pit of my stomach. It keeps telling me I need to find her. She needs me and so does our baby.

My every thought the past few weeks has been of Holly and now, our baby. I had a dream last night about them. Holly was sitting in a rocking chair in the middle of a nursery decorated in pink and black. She was rocking a bundle wrapped in a pink fuzzy blanket. As I approached, I could see the face of an angel peeking out from the blanket. Wisps of red hair were scattered on top of her little head. And when she opened her little eyes, I was blown away. She had the most beautiful sparkling green eyes I've ever seen. I never imagined myself being a father, but I've been excited ever since I found out about the baby. My dream that we're having a girl has shaken me a little. What the hell do I know about taking care of girls? As long as she doesn't start dating until she's forty, I'll probably be okay. One thing I do know is any boy interested in her better watch himself.

The sharp stabbing pain in my heart brings me back to reality. I need to find them. I grab the stack of mail and hurl it across the room. The frustration of being helpless is driving me mad. I watch the pieces of mail fly through the air. One envelope in particular catches my eye as it floats to the ground. I walk over to pick it up off the floor. When I recognize the handwriting, my knees become weak and I have to sit down before I fall down. It's from Holly. I'd know her perfect handwriting anywhere. There's no return address written on the envelope, but at least there's a postmark. Maybe it could help Beasley. My chest tightens when I see it was postmarked over two weeks ago. Damn it! She could've already been home, safe and sound in my arms. With shaky hands, I open it. My heart pounds loudly as I begin reading Holly's words.

> Dear Paul,
> I don't have much time to explain. I'm sorry you have to find out this way, but I'm pregnant. Yes, we are having a baby! Ray had been watching me for months and found out. He threatened to hurt you and our friends unless I came with him. When I told him no, he threatened to harm our baby the same way he harmed his. I'm so sorry, Paul. I didn't know what else to do. I panicked. I just wanted to keep you all and our baby

safe. He promised to let me come home as soon as his sick father thought we were back together. I don't believe his father is sick. I think it was all just a way to get me to go because he wants me back. I love you, Paul, and only you. Please believe I never left you, especially for a monster like Ray. I've left all the information you'll need to find me below. Please hurry. So far, he hasn't hurt me in any way, but I'm afraid that may change.
Love,
Holly
Ray Marconi
11218 Lincoln Rd.
Fern, CA

My doll face needs me now. I pick up what's left of my phone and haul ass downstairs to the bar. I'm so glad when I see everyone sitting around the bar. As I approach, I can't contain my excitement. I hold up the letter so they all can see it. "I know where she is. I have to go now," I yell as I reach the bar.

"Take it easy, man. You're gonna give yourself a fucking stroke," Angel teases. His voice sounds playful but his eyes are anything but. He's concerned about how I've been handling this whole mess. Everyone who knows me is concerned. Shit, even I'm worried. But now, my only mission is getting to my girls.

I fumble with my phone, trying to get the battery back on from where it was knocked off my phone when I threw it upstairs. "What are you trying to do?" Kyle questions.

"I need to search for flights going to California, but I need my phone to work first," I reply. Every time I think I've got it, the damn thing falls right off. Beyond aggravated, I throw the phone again. This time, it lands in several pieces on the floor. Great. Controlling my temper might be a good idea. Amber must think so, too. She places her hand on my arm and gently gives it a squeeze.

"Paul, Angel's right. You need to relax. Let me make a phone call and a plane will be fueled and ready to take us wherever she's is. First, please tell us what's going on and where she is," Amber says in her motherly tone, instantly calming me. I smile at her, trying to convey my appreciation. I didn't miss the "us" in her sentence, reminding me again how lucky I am to have them all in my life. How lucky we are to have them. They all love Holly and would do anything to help bring her home.

I sit, take the beer Kyle offers me, and hand the letter over to Amber. She gasps as she reads Holly's words then passes the letter to Beasley. He reads it quickly then pulls out his phone and reads off Ray's name and address to the voice on the other end.

"Call me as soon as you have any info," Beasley orders before hanging up. "I want to get all the information I can on this guy so I know what and who we're dealing with." He pinches the bridge of his nose and lets out a sigh. "We need to do this one by the book, boys. I have no jurisdiction in California. I won't be able to steer things our way if the authorities get involved." He looks at each one of us sternly, making sure we get what he's saying. I get what he's saying, I'm just not sure I like it. I want nothing more than to see Ray's face bloody and bruised as a result of blows from my fists. So help him, if he laid a finger on her...he'll no longer be breathing. "Is that going to be a problem? Believe me, I know how badly you want to flatten this S.O.B."

"I just want Holly in my arms and at least one good punch to that fucker's face," I say with a chuckle, only half joking. Beasley nods his head. He understands. After all, he shot the guy who took Amber. He knows what I'm feeling. I really do need to get one good punch in just to show the ass what it feels like to be hit by someone bigger and stronger. He deserves a real beating. One that has him begging me for mercy, but Holly and our baby's safety are more important. Me being locked up won't do them any good.

Angel is the last one to read the letter. Once he finishes, he hands it back to me. Amber ends her call and informs us we need to be at the small airport just outside of town in two hours. It seems too long to wait. The longer it takes us, the more time he has to hurt her. My fists are clenching at that thought. Again, it's Amber who calms me. She begins to spit out instructions like a drill sergeant. She's most definitely been around Holly for way too long.

"Becky and Clark are going to watch the bar. Taryn is staying with Cody," she states before turning to me. "Paul, you go upstairs and pack a bag. I'll run home and pack one for Kyle, Holly, and myself. Dad, Angel, you both go get your bags together then meet the three of us at the airport," she concludes with a nod. She gets off her stool and starts for the door. When she turns and sees none of us have moved, she places her hands on her hips. "Did I stutter? Why aren't you all moving your asses? I told you what you needed to do. Should I draw a damn map?" Her angry tone lights a fire under us and we all scatter, everyone except Kyle.

"You didn't tell me what to do," Kyle teases. Amber rolls her eyes and stomps out the door. He looks to me and laughs. Shaking my head at his taunting of Amber, I continue on to complete my task. I'm not messing with her.

Grabbing the duffel bag from the closet, I begin tossing clothes in. I have no idea what I'm packing. My mind is too focused on Holly. There's this twisting in the pit of my stomach, telling me something's wrong. Telling me I'm too late and Ray has already hurt her. If that's the case, I'm not sure if I'll be able to control the rage.

Too many years were spent watching my father brutalize my mother. The pain and embarrassment in her eyes were an exact match to the look I saw in Holly's eyes when she first told me about Ray. I made a promise to her that he'd never be able to hurt her again. The fact that I didn't keep that promise will haunt me until the day I take my last breath.

Even if it takes the rest of our lives, I will make her feel safe again. I'll make sure she knows I would die to protect her. That I'll destroy anyone or anything that tries to hurt her again.

THAT HAD to be the longest fucking flight in history. Or maybe I'm just anxious to get to my girls. We all exit the small plane and pile into a large SUV waiting for us. I would sure like to know how Beasley ended up so connected. I guess that's a question for another day. I can't lose focus on why I'm here. Holly and our baby. They are all I should be thinking about. No distractions.

Beasley opens the passenger side door, while Amber, Kyle, Angel, and I slide into the back. Driving is a huge muscled man with a military style haircut. I'd assume he's in his early thirties. He's dressed like the FBI or CIA agents you see in the movies. Again, this really makes me wonder about Beasley. The interaction between him and Beasley tells me they know each other. Beasley introduces him as Liam. I don't miss there's no last name given to us.

"I've called the State Police. They are on standby in case we need them. The town cops are too loyal to Marconi Senior," the big guy says to Beasley as he gets the SUV moving. The only thing I want to think about is getting Holly. All I need to know is where she is. I could give two fucks about State Police and town cops. Anyone gets in the way of me getting to Holly will be taken out. Plain and simple. I'm not letting anything stop me.

"I know how I'd feel if it was my girl in there Paul. I'd want to beat the mother fucker to death, but I need you to keep it together. We go in get your girl and get out. No trouble. Marconi Senior isn't a guy you want pissed at you. If we do this quietly he'll forget all about you and punish his son for bringing this on. Marconi Senior doesn't like eyes on him or people asking too many questions. He definitely doesn't want it to get out that he and his son beat women," the big guy says, staring at me from the rearview mirror, waiting for my confirmation.

"As long as she's okay and the ass doesn't get in my way, I'll be fine," I state honestly. I can forgo Ray's beating if it means Holly and our friends aren't harmed any more after this. "How long will it take us to get there?" I ask.

Liam responds, "About an hour or so. There shouldn't be any traffic this early in the day. I'd guess we'll be there around one o'clock." I want to scream. Another damn hour before I have her in my arms. Leaning my head back against the seat, I close my eyes and try to sleep. Anything to make the next hour go by faster.

CHAPTER
Twelve

Holly

I AWAKE WITH a scream, covered in a sticky sweat that causes goose bumps to spread over me when the sheet falls from my upper body. Taking deep breaths, I try to calm my racing heart. Once my one good eye adjusts, I notice I'm in my room. Ray must have carried me up here after I passed out. I lift my hand to my face and wince from the contact. Every part of my face I touch hurts. I'm afraid to look in a mirror. I know it's a swollen and bruised mess. My chest begins to tighten when I start to remember how it got that way.

Immediately, my hands go to my belly to hold and comfort my baby. I hold my breath, waiting to feel her move. Something to let me know she's okay, that he didn't harm her, too.

"Please, baby girl. Let momma know you're okay," I whisper to her. Tears sting my eyes and the air is knocked out of my chest when she delivers the strongest kick I've felt from her yet. "Thank God." I guess I should feel grateful that Ray was nice enough to concentrate his rage to my face. The bruises will heal and the pain will fade. The loss of another baby at his hands is something I'd never recover from.

I never thought it would be possible to recover the first time. But thanks to Paul, I was able to move on. He helped put all my broken pieces back together. I didn't realize until now that he did so much more than just help. He is the glue that holds all the broken parts of me together. Without him, I fall completely apart again. Here I am, right back in the place I fled from. The place I've tried so hard to put behind me. The place I swore I would never be again. I need him so much. To pick up my shattered heart and soul and put them back together once again.

I'm afraid this is a need that will never be met. If he hasn't come for me by now, he never will. He's had plenty of time to get my letter, but I think I've hurt him too much, leaving like I did and not telling him about the baby. Maybe this was all just a little too much for his fragile heart. I should have told him about Ray threatening me. But I didn't. I was a coward, giving Ray the power he needed in order to control me once again.

I need to think of my baby. I can't stay here with Ray, but honestly, where can I go? Ray has made it clear that he can and will find me anywhere. Yet, if I stay, my baby and I are in serious danger. What am I gonna do? I need to control my mouth around Ray. Go along with him long enough to get to a doctor so I can make sure my baby's okay, then I can figure out what to do next.

I ease myself off the bed and make my way to the bathroom. I need a shower. Hopefully it will help wash away more than the sweat my nightmare caused. I flip on the light. When I see my face in the mirror, it causes my stomach to roil. The tears sting as they slide down my swollen and sensitive cheeks. This isn't a view I thought I'd ever have to see again. In fact, I made a promise to myself that I would never have to see myself like this again. I allowed this to happen. It's no wonder Paul doesn't want me. I'm a weak pathetic woman. Willingly, I went back with a monster. Ray can't take all the blame for this. I allowed this to happen. I endangered my baby. If something happens to her, it's all my fault.

My realization causes my heart to ache as I enter the steaming shower. Sobs wrack my body as I slide down the cold tiles to rest on the floor. The burning hot water does nothing to take away the hate I have for myself right now. "I'm so sorry, sweet girl. I thought I was protecting you. Instead, I was walking us both into the lion's den," I cry quietly to my baby as I massage my belly to comfort her. I sit on the hard shower floor, holding my belly and crying, wishing I could think of a way to get us out of this mess.

Protect Me

I don't know how long I've been sitting here. The water is now freezing cold and my body is protesting the uncomfortable tile floor. Getting out of the shower, I notice the sun has come up. A new day is upon us. Another day of uncertainty. Of trying to keep my mouth shut, unknowing what will set him off next. And when I do set him off, will he be generous enough to stay away from my baby or will she pay the price for my stupidity?

A soft knocking on the bathroom door causes me to jump. I'm not ready to face him yet. "Holly?" Ray calls out softly. I don't answer right away. I can't. "Holly, honey. I'm so sorry. I've been trying so hard to change. I want you to love me, not fear me. I've made breakfast. Please come down when you're ready and join me," he pleads. When I hear his footsteps lead toward the bedroom door, then the sound of the door closing, I quickly get dressed.

T-shirts and sweatpants make up my wardrobe these days. Ray allowed me to order some clothes on-line when I could no longer fit into what I'd brought with me. He wasn't too thrilled with my choice of clothes, but he didn't fight me on it. I wasn't going to choose anything that made me look good in his eyes. I've worn no make-up since I've gotten here weeks ago. I keep my hair in a loose ponytail, which is something Ray hates. He always wanted me to wear my hair down. Besides, it's not like I'm allowed out of the house.

As I approach the kitchen, my stomach growls. Bacon, eggs, toast, coffee, and orange juice are scattered around the table. I didn't even know Ray could cook. I've never witnessed it before. He thinks these little things will make up for the brutal beatings. There's no way that will ever happen, but, in order to keep myself and my baby safe, he can't know that. I need to make him think I notice the changes he's trying to make. Make him believe that there are still feelings between us, other than the pure hate and loathing. Anything that will keep his filthy fucking hands to himself. I can't risk him harming the baby. And I don't think my face can take another pounding.

Ray turns to face me when he hears me approach. His eyes land on my battered face and his happy expression is replaced with one of sadness and regret. He may regret what he's done after the fact, but it still doesn't excuse that he did it. "I'm so sorry," he says while pulling out my chair. I sit and think about my response. Needing to control my mouth, I choose my words carefully.

"I know you're sorry and I can see you're trying to control it. Next

123

time, I'll try, too. I'll try harder to not provoke you," I say the words, hoping he believes them. The smile that crosses his face proves to me he does. He may be sorry and he may try not to lose his temper, but it changes nothing.

"I've managed to get you an appointment with a doctor this afternoon," Ray says with excitement. Butterflies dance in my stomach. I'll finally know for sure that my baby's okay. I'll also get out of this house, if only for a couple hours. The excitement is quickly knocked out of me. "He will be here at one o'clock, and he's bringing a portable ultrasound machine so we'll be able to see that beautiful baby of ours."

His words are like a knife through my already broken heart. This is not our baby. She's my and Paul's. Ray will never be her father. I won't allow it. In order to keep the peace and avoid another beating, I go along with him. With a false smile plastered on my face, I let him hear what he needs to. "I can't wait." His face lights up. Clearly, he likes that I'm as excited as he is.

We both continue to eat. I will say, the breakfast is tasty, and it's probably the nicest thing he's ever done for me. "Thank you for making me breakfast, Ray. It's really delicious," I tell him in hopes of keeping the good mood going. As long as it keeps him happy, I'll deal with it.

The rest of the day goes by slowly. With each hour that passes, I become more anxious. I want to see my baby, hear her heartbeat, but more importantly, I need to hear the doctor say she'll be okay. After we ate breakfast, I cleaned up the dishes and Ray went into his office to work. Now I'm just sitting here on the couch, trying to will the clock hands to move faster.

When one o'clock finally rolls around, I'm about to jump out of my skin. My stomach is filled with butterflies. I can't wait to see my little girl. Even though it hasn't yet been confirmed, the dreams I've been having along with a strong gut feeling tells me it's likely. Of course, I'll be happy either way. As long as it's healthy.

A white Mercedes pulls into the driveway and I'm all but bouncing up and down from the excitement. Ray comes out of his office and heads outside to meet the doctor. There's a woman with him, who I assume is his nurse. The nurse goes to the trunk and when she reappears, she's carrying a large white case. Ray leads the two into the house.

Ray introduces me to Dr. Northman and his nurse, Sonya. Both stare at my battered face and I wonder what excuse Ray used to explain this mess. Quickly, I have my answer. "Holly, Ray tells me you were in a pretty bad car accident and that you've been worried about the baby." I nod my head yes. Does he really buy that story? The only marks on me are to my face and it's so clear what caused them. How can people just ignore something so obvious? How can they live with themselves knowing they did nothing to help? I guess in this town, money and the name Marconi will keep anyone's mouth shut.

They begin to set up the ultrasound machine. "We'll hook it up to your large television screen so it's easier for you to see. Ray, once I'm all set up, can you please close the blinds and turn off all the lights? That will also make it easier to see," the doctor says while he and Sonya continue setting up. My heart is pounding in my chest like a jackhammer. The suspense is killing me.

Once they are all set up, the nurse has me lay down on the couch. She gently slides my shirt up so it's resting just below my boobs. She then eases my sweatpants down so they are resting below my baby bulge. Grabbing a bottle, she squeezes a cold jelly onto my belly, causing my body to break out in goose bumps. Dr. Northman pulls the footstool up to the couch. The living room is dark with the exception of a small glow coming from the ultrasound screen and Ray's big screen. He takes the wand thingy and moves it on my belly, spreading around the jelly.

My heart is beating a mile a minute. The excitement is building inside to the point I may explode. I just want to see her. Suddenly, I hear this loud fast-paced whooshing sound. My breath catches in my throat and tears form in my eyes. Looking over at the doctor I ask, "Is that the baby's heart beat?"

"It is. It sounds perfect and very healthy," he replies. It does sound perfect. The most beautiful sound I've ever heard. Then, I see the most beautiful sight ever. My baby. I can make her out perfectly. Her little hand keeps moving to her face. Her little legs kick out every few seconds. It's wild seeing her kicking on the screen and feeling it at the same time. I went with Amber a couple times to the doctor when she was having ultrasounds. It was amazing watching hers. But this…this is beyond words. Tears are streaming down my face and I can't stop smiling, even if I tried.

From the corner of my eye, I see Ray rush out of the dark living room. I'm so mesmerized by the screen and the loud whooshing of my baby's heartbeat, I don't give him much thought. I just assume he's tired of watching someone else's baby. It's fine with me. I don't want to be sharing this moment with him. Paul should be here with me. Oh, how I wish he were here, experiencing this right along with me.

I hear a commotion in the foyer, but I'm still too enamored with the sights and sounds of my baby. A hand grabs mine. At first, I assume it's Ray. As I start to pull my hand from his, I feel it. That spark of electricity I only feel when Paul touches me. My heart speeds up and the tears are flowing harder as I look up and catch sight of the man I've been praying will save me. His eyes are glued to the screen, watching in complete awe.

Softly, he whispers, "I'm here, doll face. Everything will be okay now. I promise," never taking his eyes off our beautiful baby.

Paul

SLEEP ISN'T possible. Every time I close my eyes, I see Holly. I try to imagine what she looks like with a swollen belly. Hot as shit, I assume. Kyle always said Amber was even sexier when she was pregnant. I'm guessing Holly will be the same. Her belly big and round because she's carrying our little girl.

I glance out the window just as we pass a *"Welcome to Fern"* sign. My heart starts to race in anticipation. I need to get that woman in my arms. It's hard to breathe without her. Needing and wanting her so much is something I never imagined possible. Every bit of pain I feel when I'm not with her is worth the enormous amount of pleasure and happiness I get when I am.

Liam pulls the van into a long driveway. The house is bigger than I had imagined, beautiful really. You never know what kind of horrors can be hidden inside a home that looks so normal and happy on the outside. My house as a child was that way. A beautiful house with a perfect lawn in a perfect neighborhood. No one would ever suspect the house belonged to a monster capable of beating his wife and child on a daily basis.

"Are you okay?" Amber questions, a worried expression on her face. Her question pulls me from the thoughts turning my stomach. I give her a tight smile and a nod.

"I'm okay. I'm just worried about what we'll find in that house.

What kind of shape Holly will be in." Taking a deep breath, I try to calm myself. Thinking about what he might've done to her infuriates me. "If he hurt her, it's all my fault. That letter sat for weeks because I was too busy moping around like a little fucking brat." Amber grabs my shoulders and turns me to face her. Her nostrils are flaring and her eyes are looking into mine.

"Now, you listen to me very carefully, Paul Walters. You are not to blame for any of this. She left with him. She didn't trust us enough to help her." She stops and looks around. Every eye in the SUV is on her. Is she really going to blame Holly? She holds her hand up, stopping me from speaking and continues. "She is not to blame either. She did what she thought was right. I may be upset and disagree with how she handled it, but I love her for wanting to protect us. The one to blame is Ray. One day, he'll pay for everything he's done to hurt her." I nod at her. I see what she's saying. I can't say I disagree. I wish Holly would have come to me instead of leaving with him. He is the one who frightened her so much she felt she had no other choice. Ray is the one to blame. I get some satisfaction from knowing I'm about to walk in that door and take her from him. Take her back to where she belongs: with me.

We all file out of the SUV. Before we can get to the door, it opens and a very angry Ray storms out. The second I see him, my fists begin to clench, just itching to beat the piss out of him. Liam whispers to me, "I'll take him. You go find your girl." He goes straight to Ray and takes hold of him. I run through the open front door, my need to get to Holly urgent.

Just outside of the living room, I'm stopped in my tracks by a sound. I remember hearing the same whooshing sound when we went to one of Amber's ultrasounds. My legs become weak as the realization of what I'm hearing hits me. That's my baby's heartbeat. Slowly, I move forward into the dark living room. Joyful tears fall from my eyes as I see my baby as clear as day on a huge seventy-inch screen. I pull my eyes from the screen long enough to see Holly laying on the couch. I go to her side, still unable to fully take my eyes off the screen. I crouch down next to her and whisper, "I'm here, doll face. Everything will be okay now. I promise." She reaches out, grabs my hand, and squeezes it. Both of us are silenced by the vision of our baby. Our beautiful baby.

"Would you like to know the sex?" The man, who I assume is a doctor, asks. He has a very confused look on his face as he watches our interaction. He says nothing, though. I suppose that's what you do when someone probably paid you a boat load of money and has the last name Marconi. Holly looks up to me, waiting to see what my answer will be.

"I do if you do, doll face. I know it's going to be a girl," I tell her. She giggles.

"I think so, too," she laughs, nodding her head to the doctor. He moves the wand along her belly a little more.

"Well, you're both correct. Congratulations. It's a girl," he says. He moves the wand some more and types something on the keypad. "All done. Sonya can you turn on the lights, please?" He hands me a small stack of photos of our baby girl as the lights come back on.

I turn to show them to Holly and as soon as I see her face, the air is knocked out of my lungs. My body is trembling. A sharp pain radiates through my chest. Her face is swollen and covered in bruises. Her eye is unable to open it's so swollen. The range of emotions I'm feeling threaten to break me. I'm angry, most of all. That son of a bitch.

"Paul, it's okay. I'm okay. Our baby girl is okay. That's all that matters right now. Please, just take us home," Holly pleads as she takes my hand and rubs it along her swollen belly. She knows me so well. Knows I'm about to explode. Knows if I get my hands on Ray, I won't stop until he takes his last breath.

I gently take her battered face in my hands. Softly, I place kisses on every cut and bruise I see. On her forehead, her nose, each eye, both cheeks, and finally her lips. As soon as my lips touch hers, both of our bodies' shudder, sobs overtaking us.

"I'm so sorry, doll face. I didn't protect you like I promised," I cry.

"No. You have nothing to apologize for. I didn't give you the chance to protect me," she says, looking into my eyes. She's silently pleading with me to forgive her. There's nothing to forgive. Just having her here in my arms is all I need to forget everything. "Please, just get me out of here. I want to go home," she begs.

"As you wish," I reply and pick her up off the couch. Cradling her in my arms, I carry her outside. As soon as we walk out, Amber sees Holly and gasps, throwing her hands over her mouth. The boys all follow Amber's gaze and I see the anger in their expressions. I glance around, looking for Ray. Liam has him pinned against a car by his throat. That explains why he's not running his mouth.

Amber opens the back door to the SUV, allowing me to put Holly inside. I kiss her lips gently. "There's one thing I need to do. I promise it will only take a second," I tell her, hoping this won't piss her off. I can't stop myself, though.

I walk over to where Liam has Ray pinned against the car. Liam sees me coming and when I get close, he lets him go. I really don't know what Holly saw in this guy. Compared to me, he's scrawny. Ray stands up straight and lunges toward me. Does he actually think he's gonna hurt me? I pull my arm back, ball my hand into a tight fist, and slam it right into his nose. There's a loud crack and blood goes everywhere. It looks like his nose explodes. A huge smile crosses my face. Damn, that felt good.

I walk over to where Ray landed. He's rolling around, moaning in pain, and holding his hand to his nose. I wish I had a camera. Reaching down, I grab him by his shirt. "You're lucky my girl wants to go home. I could use your face as a punching bag all day. You deserve it after what you did to Holly's face." I take a deep breath. Thinking about what he did and having him in my hands is making it difficult to walk away. "Stay away from Oakville and Holly. She doesn't want you. You're getting off easy this time, you won't be so lucky if you cross me again," I threaten. I stare him down until he looks away first, then I shove him. He bounces off the car and falls to the ground. I give him one hard kick to his ribs before walking back to the SUV. I couldn't help myself. He's getting off way too easily. But I have everything I want and need smiling at me from inside the car.

This time, the plane ride seems way too quick. Having my girl curled into me, as if that spot was made just for her body to fit against…I don't want this moment to end. She fell asleep the second we were in the air. She probably hasn't had a good night's sleep in weeks, worried about that asshole and what he might do if she let down her guard. I need to stop thinking about it if I want to keep my sanity.

I did, however, come up with a great idea while I watched the love of my life sleeping. Life is way too short. Anything can happen at any time. I realized something in those brief moments of watching her sleep peacefully with her hand resting on her swollen belly. I don't want to wait any longer to be her husband. I asked, she said yes. So, tomorrow, we're going to do it. I have it all planned out in my head. It'll be perfect and if by some chance it isn't up to her expectations, then we'll have another one anyway she wants — as long as we are husband and wife tomorrow.

I catch Amber's attention and motion her over. As quietly as I can, I whisper my plans in her ear. A huge smile spreads across her face as I finish. "Oh my God! That's perfect, Paul," Amber whispers excitedly.

"Can you make it happen? I'll keep her busy until tomorrow evening. I don't plan on leaving our bedroom," I say with a wink that makes her giggle.

"Leave it to me. It'll be perfect," Amber promises. I believe it will. If there's anyone who loves Holly as much as I do, it's Amber. She'll make this even better than I've pictured in my head. As she scurries over to tell Kyle our plans, I watch my wife-to-be sleep. I'm going to be a husband and a father. Two things I never imagined I'd be. I never wanted it. Now, I can't imagine how I could survive without it.

CHAPTER
Thirteen

Holly

WE'VE ONLY been home a couple hours and Paul is acting very strange. There are constant texts coming in and phone calls he has to take in another room. What is so important that it's taking him away from our time together? We've been apart for weeks, I didn't think anything would keep him away from me. Does he not want to be with me because he's angry with me? I wouldn't blame him. Even though I thought I was protecting him, our baby, and our friends, what I did was wrong. I put myself and, even worse, our baby in serious danger. The condition of my face is proof enough of that. I should have just told him right away about Ray's threats.

Paul walks back into our bedroom, his phone still in hand. "Doll face, Amber's gonna come over for a little while and visit. I need to go help Kyle down at the bar," he says with an apologetic look on his face. I can feel the heat move up my face. What the hell is going on? He's really going to leave me now, when we haven't spent any time together? He is trying to avoid me, just like I thought. Panic begins to set in from the thought that he may not be able to forgive me.

"What's so important that Kyle needs you right now?" I bark, realizing how nasty I sounded. Starting a fight will get me nowhere.

"I'm sorry. It's just…we've been apart for so long and we've only spent a couple hours together. Most of which you've been distracted with your phone." Paul smiles as he lays next to me on the bed. He holds his arm out, encouraging me to snuggle into him. Resting my head on his chest, he wraps his arm around me. I take a deep breath, inhaling his scent. I could stay like this forever, only getting up for food and bathroom breaks. Being here like this with him is my heaven. In here, we're protected from the world. Protected from anything or anyone who'd want to hurt us. Wrapped in his arms is like being wrapped in a safety blanket.

"Do you trust me, doll face?" Paul asks as he kisses the top of my head. Of course I trust him. What kind of question is that? I trust him with my life. That's not my issue. I'm being stingy. I want him all to myself. At least, for a little while. It's the only way I can find out whether he'll forgive me. Soon enough, we'll have to go back to the real world and back to me looking over my shoulder, wondering when, or if, Ray will come for me again.

"Yes, I do," I reply.

"I'm working on something with Kyle. You'll know all about it tomorrow and after that, I'm all yours. No interruptions. For now, I need you to trust me, okay?" I look up at him. Something in his eyes tells me that whatever this is, it's important to him. I put him through hell these last few weeks, I owe him this much. I run my hand along the slight stubble on his face, admiring how handsome he is.

"On one condition."

"And what might that be?" he asks and slides down the bed until we're face to face. When I feel his breath across my face, my heart skips a beat. How can someone affect me so much? So easily. He brushes his lips lightly against mine, causing goose bumps to spread all over my skin.

Closing my eyes, I try to gather my composure. One little touch of his lips and all thoughts fly right out of my head. Finally, I remember what I want to say. "After you finish helping Kyle, I get you all to myself. No phones, no televisions, and most importantly, no leaving this bed." A sexier than sin smile slowly spreads across his face.

"That can be arranged. There's nothing else I'd rather do," he says sweetly. Lightly, his lips kiss mine. Within seconds, the kiss heats up. His tongue passes through my lips, exploring my mouth furiously. I can feel it all the way down to my curling toes. But, this kiss seems different from all the other kisses he's ever given me. There's a need there. Like I'm a lifeline he's clinging to. Or…could it be that he's having a hard time saying goodbye?

When he breaks the kiss, I'm left breathless and wanting more. So much more. And judging by the lustful look in his eyes, so does he. That is, until he scans my battered face. The pain is so evident on his face. What is it that pains him so much? Is it that I was injured or the fact that I left him thinking I didn't want him? Whatever the cause, it doesn't change the fact that I hate myself for causing him the slightest amount of pain.

The doorbell sounds and Paul hops off the bed to go answer it. I'm assuming it's Amber. To avoid the look Paul just gave me coming from her, as well as the pity I'm sure will accompany it, I decide to go into the bathroom to try to cover some of this up. I can't stop the tears from falling when I see my gruesome reflection in the mirror. I'm not even halfway through my pregnancy and I'm already proving to be a terrible mother. I endangered our baby by going with Ray. How could I think I was actually protecting her? What made me think I was capable of this? I've had no role models. No mother to teach me what it takes to be a good mother. The tears are falling faster now. I don't buy into the bullshit of it all comes naturally. I've seen firsthand how some people are just not meant to be parents. What if I'm one of them? Even worse, what if Paul think I am?

The knock on the bathroom door startles me, causing me to jump. "Holly? You decent? I'm coming in," Amber yells through the door. As she walks through, there's a huge smile on her face, until she notices my tears. Within seconds, her arms are tightly wrapped around me, pulling me in for a comforting hug. "What's the matter, sweetie? Did Paul make you cry? I'll kick his firm little ass if he did," she jokes. Well, it's partly a joke. I don't doubt that she'd at least try to kick his ass if he hurt me. I smile into her shoulder, but start to cry even harder. "Talk to me, Holly. Now," she orders and I lose it even more.

Amber squeezes me tighter. My shoulders shudder from my sobbing. I keep trying to catch my breath so I can tell her why I'm so upset. She guides me out of the bathroom and pulls me down to sit on the bed. "Take a deep breath and tell me what has you so upset," Amber says in that calming, motherly tone of hers. She's one of those women who is meant to be a mother. She's going to be amazing at it. Cody is one lucky little man to have the parents he has.

"I'm going to be a horrible mother. Look at how badly I've screwed up already. I could've gotten us both killed. I have no idea how to be a mother, let alone a good one," I bawl. Amber begins to laugh. Seriously? She's going to laugh at me while I'm having a nervous fucking breakdown?

"Yes, what you did wasn't the smartest move. You should've come to us. But the fact that you left with a man who terrified you in order to protect your family and friends tells me a lot about the kind of mother you'll be. You're brave and caring, willing to put aside your fears for the safety of the ones you love. Hell, that's being a parent in a nutshell. You put their needs before your own. Nobody is perfect, Holly, and babies don't come with a manual. We learn as we go. Mistakes will be made. The most important thing is to love them unconditionally. I think that's something you'll be able to do without a doubt. You've got this and you have Paul to help. I have a feeling that together, the two of you will give that little girl so much love, it'll be coming out of her ears," she says, smiling brightly at me.

Instantly, I feel a little better. I'm also relieved that she doesn't seem to be too angry with me for my stupid choices. Losing her as a friend would be unbearable. She's the first best friend I've ever had. I need her in my life to keep my crazy ass sane and in check. "Thank you. What would I do without you?" I say, sincerely.

"Oh, I don't know. If I had to guess, you'd probably go bat shit crazy," she teases. "Besides, do you remember how many of these hormonal melt downs I had? It's perfectly normal to be freaking out and scared. I was. The important thing is that we are all here to help you through it." I grab her in my arms and hug her tight. When she pulls back, there's an enormous smile on her face. "Now, would you like to know what's been going on with your man since you got home?" Something about her smile and happy demeanor tells me I really want to know.

"Does a bear shit in the woods?" I ask, telling her to spill. Her smile widens, if that's even possible.

"Okay, girls, come on in," Amber yells toward the front of the house. Becky, Chelsie, and Taryn all walk in, wearing smiles that match Amber's. Now, I'm really curious as to what's up. "We are all here for a slumber-slash-bachelorette party," she squeals, clapping her hands. I'm confused. Whose bachelorette party are we having? Taryn and Marcus are already married. And as far as I know, Becky and Chelsie are single.

"What are you talking about? Whose bachelorette party? I wasn't gone that long, was I?" I question. Looking from girl to girl, they all have this sappy, doe-eyed look on their faces. I swear, if they don't tell me what the hell is going on, I'm gonna go postal on their asses.

Laughing, Amber finishes, "Your party. Paul is planning a surprise wedding for you. We're all here to help you celebrate your final night of freedom and get ready for tomorrow."

"He's what?" The range of emotions flowing through me right now is making me dizzy. I'm shocked that he's doing this. Here I was, not ten minutes ago, thinking he may not want me anymore. That's obviously not the case. Just when I thought I couldn't possibly love him more than I already do, he proves me wrong.

My heart is so full. Overflowing with love. Love... I never expected to have in my life. Friends and a family I thought would always be out of my reach. The tears start again, but this time, it's for a whole different reason. Suddenly, all my fears are gone. I know in my heart that no matter what, I have people who will be always have my back. With all of these people I love in my corner to help guide me, I know, without a doubt, I can do this.

"He's really doing this? I'm getting married tomorrow?" I ask nervously. My entire body is trembling from the excitement and anticipation of being Mrs. Paul Walters. The girls all burst into a chorus of congratulations mixed with some girly squeals. And so, the whirlwind begins.

Paul

SITTING IN Kyle's office behind his desk, I glare at the notebook with a mile-long to do list in front of me. The longer I stare at the scribble on the page, the more frustrated I become. I may have gotten myself in over my head with this whole wedding deal. I had no clue how much went into planning a wedding. No wonder people take months to plan them. What the hell was I thinking? There's no way I'll be able to pull this off. "Son of a bitch!" I yell as I throw the notebook across the room.

"Hey, now, let's not bring my mom into this," jokes Angel as he saunters in. I swear this guy doesn't have a care in the world. Always a smile on his face and a smartass remark on his lips. Right about now,

I'd like to smack that shit-eating grin off his ugly mug. "Why so pissy? Bite off a little more than you could chew?" he asks, ducking to dodge the pencil I throw at his head.

I pinch the bridge of my nose, hoping this pain in my head goes away. I could also do without the six-foot pain in the ass standing in front of me. "If you're not here to help me, get the fuck out." Angel throws his head back and lets out a deep laugh that makes me want to kick him right in the junk.

He grabs his chest. "Chill out before you hurt my feelings." I can feel the vein throbbing along the side of my head as he leisurely takes the seat across from me. That grin still plastered to his face. I don't think he realizes how close he is to leaving here with my foot up his ass. "I had a...I mean, I know a girl who is a wedding planner. She's waiting at the bar to help you put this shindig together in time," he says, his smile getting even cockier than before. I'm not going to admit it to him, but he may have just saved my ass.

"And the fact that you've slept with her won't be a problem?" I know I'm being an ass, but I can't help it. This has to be perfect. This is supposed to be the most magical and special day of her life. My job is to make sure that happens. Even if it kills me. With the way it's going so far, that's a very possible outcome.

"You know I never leave them anything but happy and wanting more. She's no exception, just a little clingy. So, I'll take one for the team to help make Holly's day perfect."

"I'm sure it's a major sacrifice for you," I laugh. Crap. He's never gonna let me forget this. I wish I didn't need his help so badly. "Okay. Bring her in," I sigh. When the leggy, big chested blonde walks in, I know for a fact this isn't a hardship on his part at all.

She bends down and picks up the list I threw earlier. I see her eyes scanning the page as she nods her head. Looking up at me, she gives me a wink and a smile. "No problem. I got it. I'll let you know when I need help from you strong men." Turning on her heels, she kisses Angel's cheek then walks out the door. What the? She didn't even introduce herself. Is this really what she does for a living? And if so, does she make any money?

"Trust me, Sasha is one of the best wedding planners in Miami. I promise you, Holly is going to love it."

"So help me, Angel, if just one little thing goes wrong, I will kick your ass all the way back to California."

"Yeah. Whatever. Now, get back to writing your sappy vows. You're whipped. You know that, right?" he throws over his shoulder as he quickly walks out, closing the door just in time to block himself from another flying notebook. One of these days, I'm not gonna miss.

I look up at the clock. Two hours have passed by since I started writing these vows. Looking at the pile of crumpled up papers on the floor next to me, I wonder why I decided to do this in the first place. There are so many things I want to say to her. I feel the emotions, I just can't seem to find the right words to describe them. Inspiration. That's what I need. I reach into my back pocket and pull out my cell phone. Scrolling through the photos, I look for one in particular. My heart rate picks up to a rapid pace once I come across the photo I am looking for. It's the first picture we took together. I was looking directly into the phone, but Holly was looking at me. We had just started dating and it's when I started to see her begin to let her guard down with me. It's so evident in her eyes. The trust. The love. They were both there long before this picture, but she wasn't allowing herself to feel them. Not that I can say I was either.

"Hey, what's got you so deep in thought?" Kyle asks while sitting on the couch in the corner.

"Trying to write my vows. It's not as easy as I thought it would be," I tell him as I sit back in the chair and close my eyes. My head is pounding. If it were up to me, we'd have already gone to the courthouse. No fuss. No muss.

"I have a feeling you're overthinking it all. Picture her walking toward you looking more beautiful than you've ever seen her. Then, think about that one moment you knew without a doubt that she was it," Kyle says with a sappy look on his face. It doesn't take a genius to know he's thinking about Amber. It's so hard to believe that at one point Kyle and I did nothing but party. Booze, drugs, women, and music. The last thing on our minds was a wife and kids. That's all we lived for. When Marcus settled down, we all called him a pussy, but now I get it.

"So, why don't you take a break for a little while? The guys are here for a little impromptu bachelor party," he says hopefully. Since Angel got the wedding planner, I do have more time and God knows I could use the break.

"Okay. But just for a little while." Getting up from my chair, I follow a smiling Kyle out the door. As soon as we get in view of the main bar, all the guys stand up and begin to whoop and holler. Everyone's here. Even Beasley. I'm really touched to have these guys here to celebrate our getting married. A pang of sadness hits me. I sure wish Reggie were here with me. He and Holly would've really liked each other.

As thankful and happy as I am to be hanging out with my friends, my only thought is still Holly. This time tomorrow, she'll be my wife. A few months after that, I'll be someone's dad. Strangely enough, though, I'm not nervous about either event. I can't say there's ever been anything I've ever wanted more.

CHAPTER
Fourteen

Holly

THE SUN peeking through the blinds warms my face and coaxes my eyes open. As I lay there, a smile slowly creeps across my face. I'm getting married today. It seems as if I'm finally getting everything I've always wanted. Is it even possible? I've spent so much of my life being disappointed. Every time I think I'm happy, it's ripped away from me. I'd be lying if I said I wasn't worried about that happening now. I'm terrified.

A soft knock sounds on the door before it slowly opens. Amber peeks over, checking to see whether I'm awake. "Good morning, almost Mrs. Walters," she giggles out as she comes bouncing over to the bed. Plopping down next to me, she looks over and smiles wide. "Are you ready for this?"

I'm more than ready to be Paul's wife. There's just one problem. Well, actually, there are a few. First, I have no idea where or when this is happening. Then, what about a dress? And even if I did have one, how the hell am I going to fit into it? I look like a whale. And the worst thing of all, my face. It's still a black and blue mess. I can't take wedding photos looking like this. This is going to be a freaking disaster.

"Stop," Amber says sternly. "Everything is being taken care of. Stop freaking out." There's no way they thought of everything in less than twenty-four hours.

"What about my face?"

"Chelsie can cover up anything with make-up. You won't see the bruises in the pictures.

"What about a—"

"We have a rack full of maternity wedding dresses downstairs waiting for you to try on."

"Fine. Then, when and—"

"I can only tell you it's around sunset. The rest is a surprise. I promise you, it's going to be perfect," she says while giving me a look that's daring me to come up with something else. I'm sure I could, but I think she might knock me into next week if I did. I give up. I'll leave it in their capable hands. They'll make sure the day is perfect. I know they will because it's what I would do for any one of them.

"Okay. I give up. What do I do first?" I ask her.

"Go take a shower. We'll all be in the kitchen making you a breakfast fit for a bride," Amber says, and bounces out of the room.

I take my time in the shower. The hot water soothes my battered body and calms my nerves. I'm not nervous about marrying Paul at all. My nerves are from not being in control or even not knowing what's going on. I know it's not rational, especially in this case, but I just can't help it. Ray was always so unpredictable that there was always this fear in me. I never knew what would happen next. Now, the unknown tends to frazzle my nerves. Again, an irrational thought in this case, but it seems to be hardwired into me now.

As if on cue, the baby kicks and all the negative thoughts leave me. I'm filled with pure love and joy. I've found a good man. A man who loves me. A man who would rather die before he did anything that would hurt me. He makes me feel safe even when I know there's danger lurking about. And this little girl. She renews my faith that maybe I can have a happy ending. I've beat my demons and I can move on and be happy. With my family. I'll finally have a real family. Something I've always dreamed of, but never thought was possible.

A knock on the bathroom door startles me from my thoughts. "Hurry up in there. We have a lot to do today," Becky yells from the other side of the bathroom door. Turning off the water, I grab a towel and quickly dry off. Wrapping the towel around me, I go into the bedroom to find some clothes. What do I wear? I have no idea what we'll be doing, but if I'm trying on dresses, I need something comfortable and easy to get off.

On the bed is a white t-shirt with "bride" all blinged out across the front and next to it is a pair of very comfy looking black yoga pants. God, I love these girls. I slip into my new clothes and of course, they fit perfectly. Sometimes I think Amber knows me better than I know myself. After throwing my hair up into a high ponytail, I begin to make my way downstairs.

As soon as I hit the stairs, I can smell the food and my mouth begins to water. Everyone is chatting away when I enter into the kitchen. The amount and variety of foods they have spread out is unbelievable. A large platter of fresh fruits is in the center of the table, but it's the food surrounding it that really get my taste buds excited. Pancakes, eggs, grits, toast, and, my absolute favorite, bacon. There's lots of bacon. "Wow, ladies. This looks delicious. What are you all eating?" I say, grabbing the plate filled with bacon. They all look at me and laugh as if I'm kidding.

After overstuffing myself on breakfast, Amber announces it's time to try on dresses. Just what I want to do now. I already feel fat and swollen as it is. Add the five pounds of bacon and other assorted food I just ate and nothing is going to fit. I reluctantly follow her into the living room. The rest of the girls stay in the kitchen to clean up. As we walk into the living room, I'm in complete shock. There's a rack that takes up the whole length of the room filled with beautiful white dresses. Happy tears sting my eyes. How did they pull all of this off so quickly? When the Greek god with a name that fits to a tee comes into the room, it's very clear. Zeus is the owner of the bridal boutique *Princess Weddings*. It's the same place we went to with Amber to find her wedding dress. This man is beautiful. Coal black hair, eyes as blue as the sky, and a body that looks like it was carved from marble. Every woman would kill for a man like this, but he only seems to have eyes for Paul. I'm guessing my baby flashed him that gorgeous smile of his and that's all it took for this favor.

"Hello, Miss Holly. If you ever get tired of that sensational looking man, you can just send him my way," Zeus laughs as he hugs me. Becky spits her mimosa all over the back of Chelsie's head. I forgot they weren't part of our previous interaction with Zeus. Both girls were probably fantasizing about this gorgeous Greek god and now their bubbles have been burst.

"Why are all the really hot guys either taken or gay?" Chelsie asks, wiping mimosa out of her hair. Her inquiry has us all laughing.

"Uh, some of us really hot guys aren't," Angel says as he struts into the room. I notice Chelsie blushing and Zeus drooling. Oh, this is going to be fun. In a flash, Zeus is leaving my side to go to Angel. Immediately, Angel starts to look a little uncomfortable. I don't think I've ever seen this side of Angel. He's always so damn cocky and confident. When Zeus extends his hand to him, I swear I see drops of sweat forming on his forehead. You'd think as sexy as Angel is he'd be used to getting hit on by both women and men. By his behavior, I think it's safe to say that's so not the case.

"Hello, stud. I'm Zeus and you are?" Zeus coos. Poor Angel looks like a deer caught in headlights. It's priceless. Grabbing my phone, I snap a picture. I just can't help myself. The guys are going to love this. Amber locks onto Angel's discomfort and quickly rescues him.

"Zeus, this is Angel. I hate to push, but we really need to get a dress picked out. The clock is ticking."

"Of course. It was so nice meeting you, Angel," Zeus says, ogling him. "If you ever decide to switch teams, call me. I'll take real good care of you," Zeus says while slipping his card into a speechless Angel's pocket. Again, everyone in the room is laughing. When Zeus winks at Angel, even he starts to laugh. Angel practically runs out of the living room toward the kitchen.

"Let's go, girl. We only have a couple hours left to get you ready and we still have a lot left to do," Amber says as she ushers me into a makeshift dressing room.

Ten dresses later, I finally find the perfect one. It's just like the one I imagined I would wear as a little girl. I never thought it would happen, but that didn't stop me from wishing. It has long, lace sleeves and puffy shoulders. The front is a low cut V-neck, all lace and pearl. The bottom is a poufy satin skirt with lace and pearl inlays. The back is a heart-shaped cut out with strings of pearls going across the open gap. It's beautiful and being in it makes me feel beautiful. Especially when I walk out of the dressing room and all the girls' mouths drop open in awe. Zeus squeals and claps his hands while jumping up and down. And then, Angel walks into the room and lets out a long whistle followed with his signature wink. But, the one reaction that surprises and touches me the most, is from Beasley. He just came through the front door and when he looks up, he stops dead in his tracks. A wide smile spreads across his face as his eyes fill with tears.

"Wow. Holly, you look beautiful," Beasley sputters. He walks over and gently kisses my cheek. "I came by to ask you something." He sounds nervous, which isn't like him. He looks around the room when he gets to Amber and she nods to him, encouraging him to continue. "I think of you like another daughter and I was hoping you'd allow me to escort you down the aisle." I'm speechless. I love Beasley and think of him like a father. He's the closest I've ever had to one. I can't believe he wants to do this for me. "If you'd rather me not, its okay. You—" I stop his nervous babbling.

"I would be honored to have you walk me down the aisle. You are the closest I've ever come to having a father and I'm so grateful to have you in my life. Thank you," I tell him as I wrap my arms around him and squeeze tight. Amber comes and wraps her arms around the both of us. When I pull away, all three of us have tears running down our faces. I'm so glad my make-up hasn't been done yet.

Paul

KYLE AND I are on our way to the lake to make sure Angel's wedding planner is as good as he says. If not, I'll knock his block off. I chose this place because it's where I first made love to her. That's one of my favorite memories of us. Here, at this lake, Holly laid out in the back of my truck, the rain pouring down on our hot, naked bodies…my pants are getting tighter from just picturing a sexy wet Holly.

"What's got you smiling like the Joker?" Kyle asks.

"Just thinking about the couple times I've brought Holly here."

"This is a magical place. I have several memories of Amber and I here, too. We had our first time together here," he says with a smile I can only assume matches the one I am sporting. He's right, there's something magical about this place. I could feel it that first night I brought Holly here. That night changed our lives forever. She opened up to me. Trusted me enough to tell me about a past she would love to just bury away and never think of again. Thanks to the strength and trust she found that night, her past no longer haunted her when she'd sleep.

Pulling onto the dirt road that leads back to the lake causes my heart to beat quicker. *Please, let it be perfect*, I plead in my head. She deserves the best of everything. She's been through so much bad lately. I want this to be a day she looks back on and can't help but smile. I want it to be one of the stories she tells our daughter. Most of all, I want this day to be the door to our past closing. Putting to bed all of the demons we struggle with and have fought so hard to overcome. We have both come so far. As the lake comes into view, I can see I'm not going to be disappointed and neither will my bride.

It's perfect. There are black chairs set up in rows with pink bows attached to the backs. A pink velvet runner lays as an aisle between the rows of chairs. A beautiful archway stands in front of the chairs. With the view of the lake behind it, it's perfect. Over to the side, in a clearing, a huge reception area is all set up. There are tables with black table clothes and pink accents. There's also a sizable bar, buffet table, and stage. She's even had wood put down to make a floor for dancing and the tables to sit on. I can see twinkle lights strung all over the place. I bet it'll be beautiful when the sun starts to set. She's going to love it. It's exactly how she'd set it up if she were throwing it. Angel came through. He owes Sasha one hell of a night for pulling this off with such little notice.

"Everything looks amazing, man. I think it's time to go home and get into our penguin suits. You won't want to keep your Bride waiting," Kyle says. He's right, I don't want to keep her waiting. She's been waiting for this day her whole life. The day she can finally feel completely loved, safe, and protected. I won't force her to wait even a second longer for that.

I let Kyle drive us back to his house, my mind too focused on Holly to concentrate on the road. I can't believe she'll be my wife in a couple hours. I wish my mom were here to share this day with us. She would have really liked Holly. They're a lot alike, both very strong women who feel anything but. All because an asshole of a man kept them from seeing their true selves. I wish my mom could've been a little more like Holly and gotten away from my dad. Maybe if she had met someone who would've loved her like I do Holly, she'd be celebrating with us today. She might have had a chance to get to know her granddaughter.

"What's got you so deep in thought over there?" Kyle questions. He's my best friend and I've talked to him countless times about my parents. He just doesn't fully get what I'm feeling. How could he? He grew up in a perfect family. At least, compared to mine it was perfect. He had two parents who loved each other and him. There was no yelling and screaming. There were no beatings. His father didn't kill his mother.

Every time we talk about my past, he always has this look of pity on his face. It's the same look everyone in town gave me after my parents died. I know Kyle is only concerned, but I just can't take the pity look.

"Everything," I laugh. "Today, I'll be a husband, and in a few short months, I'll be a father. If I'm being honest, I'm a little scared." He nods his head in understanding. He was in my shoes not too long ago.

"It's perfectly normal. I'd be worried if you weren't nervous and scared. You want to do what's best for Holly and the baby. That shows you love them. As long as you hold on to that love, you'll be just fine. I was terrified when Cody was born. Hell, I still am at times. I don't want to be a bad father and mess things up," Kyle says, his face lighting up from thinking about his son. "You and Holly will be awesome parents. I can see how much you both love that baby already and how great you are with Cody. Besides, you have all of us around to keep you in line." That makes me smile and calms my nerves. I'm so lucky to have all these amazing people in my life. We may not be related by blood, but this connection we all have with one another makes us family. A very strange family, but still a family, nonetheless. I couldn't ask for a better group of people to be by my side.

When we pull up to the house, Angel and Beasley are just getting out of their cars. I'm anxious to know how Beasley's talk with Holly went. Last night, he told me he wanted to walk her down the aisle. The moment he said it, I knew Holly would be all for it. Beasley is like a father to all us misfits. He's the only father figure some of us in this group have ever had. No matter what the situation, Beasley is always there with a way to help.

He turns toward me and his eyes are red. I immediately know he's been crying. Not that I'd ever say that out loud to him, though. He may be old enough to be my father, but I bet he could kick my ass without breaking a sweat. The dude scares me when he's angry. He's definitely the guy you want on your side.

Before I can say a word to Beasley, Angel walks up and slaps me upside my head. "What the fuck was that for?"

"Like you don't know. Sending me over to your house so I can be hit on by a man who's bigger and hotter than me," Angel barks. I have no idea what he's talking about, but I have a feeling I know who does. Kyle bursts out laughing so hard, he doubles over.

"Kyle, would you like to fill us in? I have no clue as to what's going on." He continues laughing, unable to stop. When he finally catches his breath, tears are rolling down his face.

"I arranged to have Zeus bring dresses to Holly so she could choose the wedding dress of her dreams." Well, that was a wonderful thing to do. I hope she feels like a princess today with all the pampering and attention she's getting. "I thought it would be funny to send Angel over to meet him. I knew how much he liked you, so I figured he'd really like Angel," he confesses, breaking out in a fit of laughter again.

"Oh, he liked me alright, you asshole. He made me look like an idiot in front of—" he abruptly stops himself before finishing that sentence. We all know he was going to say Chelsie. The chemistry between those two is so obvious and they both fight it with all they have. I was really bad when it came to steering clear of any kind of relationship or emotional connection, but Angel puts my ass to shame. He won't talk about his past at all, no matter how hard we try to get him to. Judging by the nightmares he has almost every night, I think it's safe to say he may have had it worse than any of us. "I do have a reputation to uphold," Angel huffs and storms into the house. His little fit causes Beasley and I to join Kyle in laughter.

Once we contain our laughter, we go inside to get dressed. It won't be too long before I'll be watching my doll face walking down the aisle to me. My pace quickens so I can get ready faster. I can't wait to see her. The beautiful Holly in my head is nothing compared to what the real one will look like.

CHAPTER
Fifteen

Paul

As I stand here waiting for the music to announce the entrance of my bride, butterflies invade my stomach. I don't think it's so much nerves as it is excitement. I'm so ready to make Holly my wife. I have no doubts that this is the right thing. That she's the perfect woman for me. No doubt that we were made for each other.

I turn to my left and look at my bandmates, my best friends, who are beside me. Without them, I wouldn't be here. I never would've been able to get my life together enough to allow myself to give in to my feelings for Holly.

When the music starts to play, my chest tightens in anticipation. I feel like this is the moment I've been waiting for my whole life. When she walks into view, all the pieces of my shattered heart suddenly begin falling back into their proper place. My heart finally feels whole again. The sight of her gliding down the aisle, arm in arm, with a very proud Beasley, steals my breath away. She's absolutely the most beautiful woman I've ever seen. What did I do in my life to deserve this angelic woman?

She looks a little nervous, but when her eyes meet mine, a bright, beautiful smile graces her face. A smile that causes my knees to go weak. Kyle notices and grabs my shoulder. He leans over and whispers in my ear, "How did two bums like us get so damn lucky?"

"I was just thinking the very same thing," I whisper back, still unable to take my eyes off the beauty walking toward me. Everyone is completely silent and in total awe of Holly. Then, Angel lets out a whistle, breaking through the silence and causing everyone to laugh, including Holly. When I look over at him, he just shrugs his shoulders and gives me his signature wink. What an ass.

When Beasley and Holly reach me, he places her hand in mine and kisses her cheek. "I love you like a son, but I also love her like a daughter. So, if you hurt her in any way, you'll have me to deal with," Beasley threatens, loud enough for the handful of people attending to hear. He then smiles at me and takes his seat.

"Hi, handsome," Holly says as she leans in so close, our noses are touching.

I rub my nose against hers. "You are the most beautiful bride I've ever seen," I tell her. She crushes her lips to mine, making everything around us fade away.

The pastor clears his throat. "I'll chalk that up to those pregnancy hormones I hear so much about," he jokes, causing yet another round of laughter from our friends. Holly gives him a sheepish look and backs away a little bit, still keeping her hands in mine. The pastor starts the ceremony but I can't take my eyes off Holly. It's still hard for me to believe how much this redheaded spitfire has changed my life. The last time I remember being this happy was when I was a little boy. Back before my dad changed and became so angry all the time. I'm going to be a husband and soon a father. I'm going to do everything in my power to make sure I'm doing my best at both.

"Dude, you're up," Kyle whispers and nudges me. I can feel my face heat from embarrassment. I glance over at Kyle with a quizzical expression on my face.

"Your vows, dumbass," Angel whispers loudly. Again, bringing about laughter from everyone. At this rate, people will think this is a standup comedy act, not a wedding ceremony. With every eye on me, the nervousness begins to set in. I pull the folded piece of paper out of my jacket pocket and fumble, trying to get it open. Quickly scanning over what I've written, I decide it's not as good as I had thought. Crumbling it up into a ball, I throw it over my shoulder.

"Holly, you crashed into my life."

"Literally. You knocked him right on his ass," Angel throws in. When I glare at him, trying to tell him to shut the fuck up, he shrugs his shoulders. "Well, that's what happened," he grumbles.

"You were like a hurricane blowing in and turning me upside down. I never wanted to fall in love. To be a husband or even a father. That was, until I met you. All of a sudden, you made me want all of these things and more. I didn't think I could love someone as much as I do you. Nor did I think I'd ever truly be happy again. So, thank you. Thank you for loving me, trusting in me, and most of all, for making me the happiest man alive," I say, getting a little choked up with the immense emotions I feel at this moment. Amber passes a tissue to a tearful Holly. She softly dabs at her eyes, careful not to smudge her make-up. It takes her a minute to get herself together. Taking a deep, shaky breath, she starts to speak.

"How am I supposed to top that?" she says with a giggle. "People say everything happens for a reason, but I could never understand what kind of reason would require me going through so much pain and misery. Until now. The day I crashed into you, it all became so clear. We were destined to meet so we could put each other back together. You have healed my broken soul. You've given me things I'd never thought possible. True love, trust, and most of all, the constant feeling of being safe. You've given me the chance to have a family. To be a wife and a mother. My whole life, I hoped and prayed for the life you're giving me. I'll never be able to thank you enough for that, but I promise to spend the rest of our lives showing you how much I love you and how much you mean to me," she says as tears stream down her cheeks.

And she was worried she couldn't top what I said? She just blew me out of the water. The fact that I'm standing here in front of all these people crying like a little bitch proves it. I don't care. Let the guys make fun of me. No more hiding my feelings. I love this woman. I love that I can make her feel the same way I do, thanks to her.

The pastor is talking, but I'm no longer paying attention. I'm lost in Holly's eyes. Both of us saying so much to each other without uttering a single word. It's all in her eyes. Kyle nudges me and hands me a ring.

"I do," I blurt out, causing a huge eruption of laughter. I'm puzzled as to what was so funny.

"We're not quite there yet, son. Almost," the pastor says with a smile. I look over at Kyle, who rolls his eyes at me and smiles. He's been in my shoes, so he gets it. When I look at Angel, he just mouths, "dumbass". Typical Angel. He'll see. One day, he's going to meet a woman who turns his brain to mush. The only thing he'll be able to think about will be her. I can't wait for that day to arrive, because I'm going to razz his ass about it constantly.

The rest of the ceremony goes smoothly. When the pastor announces it's time to kiss my bride, I don't waste any time. I take her in my arms and crash my lips to hers. This is our first kiss as husband and wife. I know it sounds crazy, but this kiss feels different. It's more intense. Just a preview of what I have to look forward to for the rest of my life.

Holly

FINALLY, PAUL and I are able to sit. My poor feet ache from holding up my rather large belly. I didn't think that photographer would ever finish taking pictures. Even my cheeks hurt from smiling so much. Not that it has been an effort to smile. I can't imagine being happier than I am right now. So far, this day has been amazing. More incredible than I could've ever imagined.

"What has you smiling so big?" Paul questions, leaning in close to my ear. He brushes his lips against the sensitive spot behind my ear, causing me to break out in goose bumps. Closing my eyes, I take a deep breath, trying to calm my racing heart. I wonder if anyone would even notice if the two of us left. I sure wouldn't mind getting the honeymoon started. That kiss at the end of the ceremony was amazing. It felt different than all the other kisses we've shared. It was more passionate. More demanding. More intense. I want to find out if everything between us has gotten better.

"I was just wondering if we could sneak out of here without anyone noticing," I tell him honestly, causing him to laugh. "What's so funny? I'm serious. I can't wait to get home to bed."

"Me, too. I'm exhausted. Sleep sounds really good," Paul says, feigning sleepiness, making me want to slap the fake yawn right off his face.

"Don't even think about leaving yet," Amber scolds, pointing her finger at us both. "You still need to have your first dance, cut the cake, and throw the bouquet. When all that is done, you can leave."

Her no nonsense tone makes me laugh. When she shoots me a "don't fuck with me" look, I cover my mouth with my hand to try to control my giggles. I'm usually the bossy party planning bitch. It's really funny seeing Amber in that roll. I have to admit, she's pretty good at it. Maybe I've rubbed off on her a bit. As if on cue, here comes Angel to throw out his smartass remarks.

"Holly, what have you done to the normally sweet and quiet little Amber? She sounds more like you," Angel teases. He slaps Paul on the back and bends down to kiss my cheek. He then does the sweetest thing I've ever seen. Slowly, his hand lands on my swollen belly. As it gently glides along, a look of awe comes over his face. Suddenly, the baby kicks right against his hand, causing Angel to jump. He doesn't take his hand away as he stares at my belly, waiting to see if it happens again. I glance over to Paul and when our eyes meet, a huge smile crosses his face. The baby kicks once more and Angel grins wide. Slowly, he looks up at me with an amazed expression on his face.

"Sorry. I just wanted to say hi, but feeling her kick was unbelievable. I never realized how incredible that would be," he says, looking from me to Paul and back again.

"You can say hi to her anytime you want to. After all, she is your niece," I encourage.

"Uncle Angel, huh? Doesn't sound too bad. I suppose we all are like a bunch of misfit puzzle pieces that by some miracle seem to fit perfectly together," he says with a far off look in his eyes. Almost as if he's lost somewhere else in this moment. Deep in thought maybe? His past haunts him, but he's tightlipped about it. Maybe someday we'll be able to get him to open up, but today is not that day.

Amber places her hands on her hips as she begins to tap her foot. No doubt she's waiting impatiently for our reassurance that we'll stay and perform the duties she feels are necessary. It's not that I don't want to do all of the usual wedding reception tradition, but I've done all this once before. Had the so-called perfect fairy tale wedding. That marriage didn't work out so well. I don't need all of the pomp and circumstance, I just need Paul.

Amber starts to tap her foot harder, causing it to make a loud clicking sound against the wooden flooring. This tells me her patience is wearing thin. I can't help giggling at her. She really has turned into a mini me.

"This is a day you'll remember forever. It needs to be perfect. If I have to wear your usual shoes for a night and be the party planning drill sergeant, then so be it. You'll be thanking me later," Amber pleads. As if I'm going to tell her no and get up and leave. No matter how much I'd rather skip the normal traditions, I couldn't do that to her. She means so much to me and if going through all the typical wedding reception hoops is what will make her happy, then I'm all for it.

"Okay. Okay. Geesh," I concede. I'm not sure if I should be insulted by her referring to me as the party planning drill sergeant or flattered that she's trying so hard to make this the perfect day for me. For now, I'll go with flattered, but you can be sure I won't let the drill sergeant comment go. "You're in charge, boss. Just tell us what to do." A huge smile graces her face as she claps her hands and jumps up and down like an excited child.

We've just finished dancing and all I want to do is sit. My poor feet are protesting. They were just not meant to support my fat pregnant ass. The chair looks like an oasis in the desert to me right now. Right as I'm about to plop down into the chair, Amber grabs my arm, announcing it's time to cut the cake. I groan as I'm dragged farther away from the comfort that chair can provide.

"Can I do it sitting down?" I ask, even though I know her answer will be no. She looks over at me like I have two heads.

"Um...NO!" she snaps. I look at Paul, pleading for him to do something. He just grins and shrugs. Well, that was a big help. Not! Married only two hours and he's already leaving me to fend for myself. Or...maybe not. He looks at me sympathetically then scoops me into his arms. When we catch up to Amber, she shakes her head with a smile.

"We'll cut the cake, but only if I can hold my bride," he tells a laughing Amber. And this is one of the reasons why I love him so much — his need to make sure everyone around him is happy. He's making both Amber and I happy at the same time without worrying about how badly my fat ass is probably killing his back.

"I expected some amount of crazy from you two, so if this is the worst, I'm good," she states, still laughing. Paul follows behind her toward a table set up with a large three-tiered cake. It's absolutely gorgeous. It's decorated with pink bows just like the ones on the backs of all the chairs. Sitting on top is a bride and groom decoration. I smile when I notice the bride on the cake has red hair.

Paul lowers his lips to my ear, and whispers, "I had to paint the hair on her. A blonde or brunette just wouldn't do." With his words, my heart melts. The lengths he's gone to in order to make this night perfect has me in awe.

"It's perfect and so are you," I whisper softly, afraid if I say it too loud, I'll break out in happy tears. He smiles wide at me and I can see the love he has for me in his eyes. Normally, this would have me weak in the knees, but since he's carrying me, I'm safe.

As we reach the cake table, all of our guests are gathering around to witness this tradition. Amber places a beautiful crystal-handled cake knife in my hand. I recognize it as the same one I bought for her and Kyle. This one has, "To our best friends, we wish you all the happiness in the world. Love, Kyle and Amber," engraved on the blade. I can feel the tears building up in my eyes. These two people are amazing. When I first moved here, I intended on living a life alone. Never did I imagine I'd find such wonderful friends and meet the man of my dreams. The whole thing feels too good to be true. I give Amber a smile and mouth, "Thank you" to her. Smiling back, she nods then wipes tears from her eyes.

Paul sits down in the chair Kyle places in front of the cake table. I reach over, slice a large piece, and set it on the plate Clark holds out to me. Taking the cake knife from me, he hands me the plate and a fork. I laugh to myself as I try to decide whether I should be nice or smash the delicious looking cake in his face. When I look over to Paul, his eyebrow is arched and a slight smile is on his lips. He knows exactly what I'm debating. Behind him, all the guys are making hand gestures, telling me to smash the cake into his face. Well, I can't let everyone down, now can I?

I pick up a chunk of the slice of cake and slowly move it toward his lips as I give him a sweet and innocent smile. I don't want him to see it coming. A relieved look crosses his handsome face and I know I have him fooled. I just hope he doesn't drop me accidentally. Just as the cake touches his lips, I shove it into his mouth. Using my palm, I smoosh it all over his face. I can feel his chest vibrating against me from his laughter. The crowd behind us explodes into fits of laughter. I bite my lip, trying to contain my own amusement over the situation. He has cake everywhere, even in his nostrils. The sight is hilarious.

Paul picks up the other chunk of cake with a wicked smile. Suddenly, I'm nervous. My heart is racing, but I have nowhere to run.

He has me held tightly in one arm, ensuring I cannot leave his lap. He turns and looks behind him at the cheering crowd, encouraging him to copy my actions. I should have made him feed me first. He slowly starts to move the cake to my lips. I brace myself and wait for the impact, but it never comes. He runs the cake along my lips and when I open my mouth, he gently feeds me the cake. I take a nice big bite. It smells so good and I am eating for two, after all. After I've taken my bite, Paul drops the rest of the cake back onto the plate. Some of the guys are booing. They wanted a show and to my surprise, they get it. As soon as the plate is on the table, Paul grabs my face and smashes his lips to mine. He sprinkles kisses all over my face, spreading the smeared cake from his face to mine. At this point, I don't mind. As long as his lips are kissing all over my face, I'm a happy girl.

Both of us are laughing hysterically by the time Amber hands us napkins. While we clean ourselves off, the gang heads back to the dance floor. A yawn escapes my lips and I realize I'm exhausted. Keeping my eyes open at this point is a fight. Paul notices and leans in close to my ear.

"Lay your head on my shoulder and get some rest. I promise to wake you when we get home," he says in his sexy, husky voice. The thought has my lady bits all tingly. I decide it's probably not a bad idea to get myself rested before we get home. I plan on taking my sweet ass time with him.

"I think I will. I'll need to be rested for the things I have in store for you later," I tell him as I snuggle into his hard, warm chest. A groan escapes his lips and I can feel him harden beneath me. It makes me smile.

Amber trying to slip my bouquet into my hand wakes me. I have no idea how long I've been sleeping, but I know this is not how I expected to be woken up.

"Please, Holly, just toss it over Paul's shoulder before you go," Amber pleads with me. If I didn't love this girl as much as I do, I'd be telling her where she could shove this bouquet. Because I do love her like a sister, I decide to appease her.

"Okay, Amber, but then I get to go home to bed," I state, and she nods her head in agreement. Paul steps in front of all the awaiting single girls. I toss the bouquet over his shoulder and watch the girls reaching for it. No one stands a chance against Chelsie. She's taller than all of them and catches it with ease. I'm glad. I'd really like to see her find what Amber and I have. She's such a sweet girl.

"We thank you all for being here with us. We love you all. But it's time I get my exhausted pregnant bride home to bed," Paul announces with a wicked little smile. Oh, I can't wait for him to take me to bed. I have a feeling my exhaustion will be nonexistent by then. Paul carries me over to the truck with all our friends saying their congratulations and goodbyes in tow. Best. Wedding. Ever.

CHAPTER
Sixteen

Holly

I ROLL OVER and see my handsome husband. The view causes a warmth to fill my insides. So, this is what happiness feels like? I know now that even the few times in my life when I believed I was happy, I wasn't. Life couldn't get any better than it is right now. I never knew it was possible to be this happy. The last few weeks being Mrs. Paul Walters have been beyond my wildest dreams. I still have no idea how I got so lucky.

A week ago, I called Tanya, the only friend I had when I was with Ray. I figured now that Ray already knows where I am, it's safe for me to reach out to her. I asked her to come for a visit. I've missed her so much. She seemed so excited to hear from me and even more excited when I asked her to come see me. She was my only light during a very dark time in my life. The two of us instantly connected when we met. It felt like we had known each other for years.

"Good morning, doll face," Paul says in his husky voice. With his eyes still closed, he rolls over and pulls me securely into his arms. His hands instantly gravitate to my swollen thirty-week belly. He can't seem to keep his hands off my belly. Not that I mind. I love that he wants to be close to our daughter. "What are you thinking about?"

"Tanya. I'm so excited she's coming for a visit. I can't believe I'll get to see her tomorrow," I tell him excitedly. He looks at me with a grin that makes me think he has a secret. And, of course, he does.

"I have a surprise for you," he says with a sly smile. He knows I hate surprises, and he's enjoying that he knows something I don't.

"You know how much I hate surprises," I whine, running my hand up and down his muscled chest. Maybe I can seduce him into telling me what's up. "Maybe you should just tell me now." He closes his eyes when I begin running my hand along the waistband of his boxers.

"Not going to happen, doll face. But nice try," he laughs as he jumps up out of the bed and out of my reach. Damn him and his willpower. "I promise. It's a good surprise. You'll love it." Rolling over, I bury my head into the pillow and groan. "Let's go, woman. Amber and Kyle are waiting," Paul yells from the bathroom. I should have known those two would have a hand in any type of surprise. I roll out of bed so I can get ready, wondering what the three of them have planned this time.

After getting ready, we drive to the bar. Paul gets out and walks around to my side. Opening my door, he helps me out of the truck. When my feet hit the gravel, my vision spins a little and I lose my balance. Before I can fall to the ground, Paul's arms are around my waist, holding me up. This has happened a couple times over the last few days.

"Are you okay, doll face?" Paul questions, fear lacing his voice, concern evident on his face.

"I think I'm just going too long without eating and it's causing me to get lightheaded," I explain to him, but it doesn't seem to ease his worry. "We have a doctor appointment tomorrow, I will mention it then. I'm fine. Let's go inside so I can see what you've planned," I say, hoping to get him focused on something else. He looks at me for a moment longer and then takes my hand and leads me into the bar.

As we walk in the bar, I notice it's covered in pink baby shower decorations. Streamers, balloons, table centerpieces, and a huge *"It's a Girl"* banner fills the room. I laugh because it seriously looks like a couple gallons of Pepto Bismol exploded all over everything in the bar. Now I know what they're all talking about when they say I go overboard. Tears fill my eyes, because this is exactly how I would have decorated it. I've taught them all well. A large cake decorated like building blocks sits front and center on a table.

I glance around at all our friends scattered throughout the bar, but one redhead in particular catches my eye. It can't be. She wasn't supposed to be here until tomorrow. Paul leans downs and whispers, "Surprise, doll face." I love this man so much. Giving him a beaming smile, I waddle off to get ahold of Tanya.

She looks up just before I get to her. As soon as she sees me, a smile crosses her face and tears fill her eyes. I never noticed this before, but we could pass for sisters. How did I not see that? All thoughts leave my head when she crashes into me. As she hugs the life out of me, I try to catch my breath enough to speak. The only thing I can manage, however, is laughter. I really missed this woman something fierce.

Paul steps next to us, and says, "Maybe you should let her go, Tanya. She's either gonna pass out from lack of oxygen or pee her pants from laughing so hard. Neither scenario is very desirable." Paul chuckles and moves out of the way so as not to get smacked by either one of us.

I pull back from Tanya so I can get a good look at her. "I can't believe you're actually here. I missed you so much," I squeal with excitement.

"I'm so glad you called. I'm sorry to hear about what Ray did, but happy that we can now stay in touch," Tanya says with a wide smile.

I talk with Tanya for a few more minutes before making my rounds to say hi to the rest of our friends. Before long, Amber is ushering me to a chair that sits next to a large table filled with beautifully wrapped gifts. At first, I feel a little self-conscious up here in front of everyone. If you counted every gift I've ever gotten over my lifetime, it wouldn't come close to the stack on this table.

"Here, open this one first," Amber demands, shoving a box wrapped in sparkly pink paper in my lap. *Please tell me I'm not this pushy when I throw parties.* Sadly, I most likely am and it's rubbed off on Amber.

"You've created a little mini you. Another party planning demon," Angel yells from the crowd. Everyone, including me, howls out in laughter. My face heats, probably turning beet red from embarrassment. I think I may need to tone myself down a bit in the future when it comes to planning parties.

For the next hour, I open gift after gift. This is going to be one spoiled little girl. I hold up a hilarious onsie I just opened up from Angel. I'm not sure whether my daughter will ever wear it, though. It's white with a large barcode in the center. The writing on top says, "Made in," and below the barcode, "vachina". As I look over at a proud Angel to tell him thanks, suddenly everything in front of me is a blur. A sharp stabbing pain spreads across my abdomen, causing me to whimper. Immediately, Paul and everyone else is out of their seats and by my side. Panic sets in when I feel like I'm sitting in a puddle of water. Did my water just break? If so, it's too early. I still have ten weeks to go. Something is wrong, I can feel it. My terrified eyes meet Paul's, which look just as scared.

"Something's wrong, Paul. I think we better go to the hospital," I say as calmly as I can. If my shaky voice doesn't give away just how frightened I am, then my quaking body and racing heart will. He reaches his hand out to help me off the chair. As I stand up, I see all the blood drain from Paul's face. He's as white as a ghost. Amber is beside me and gasps loudly, causing me to look in the direction she is. Slowly, I glance at the chair below me. When I see that it's covered in blood, my hand instantly goes to cradle my belly. Silently, I begin to pray, *God, please. Please, don't take my baby. Keep her safe.*

I glance around the room at all of the horrified faces, none of them knowing what to do. Another stabbing pain releases, causing me to bend forward, and I feel a gush of blood coming from between my legs. The last thing I see is my husband's pained expression and then everything goes black.

Paul

THE ONLY sound I can hear is my racing heart and Holly's frightened voice saying, "Something's wrong, Paul. I think we better go to the hospital." Watching her collapse into a heap in my arms is too much to bear. There's commotion around me, but my only focus is my wife. Everything else is just background noise. I'm so scared of what will happen to her and our baby. I'm afraid if I wish too hard for one to be okay, the other will have to suffer. I want them both to be just fine.

She is pale, lifeless, and covered in blood by the time the ambulance arrives. It feels like an eternity in this ambulance. I never thought we'd make it here. I've heard bits and pieces of the discussion between the paramedics on the ride over. Enough to terrify me even more. Hemorrhaging, deprivation of oxygen to the baby, emergency C-section. I'm too scared to ask questions I may not want the answers to.

Running alongside the gurney as we enter the emergency room, everything is a blur. I'm holding Holly's hand and begging for her to be okay. We get to a set of double doors and the paramedic turns to me with a sympathetic look. "I'm sorry, sir, but you can't come in. Go to the waiting area and someone will come speak with you soon," she says and lightly touches my shoulder, trying to give me some comfort. I know she means well, but it doesn't do any good. At this point, the only thing that will bring me comfort is hearing my wife and daughter will be just fine, that this all looks so much worse than it is, but I don't think that's going to happen. I have a really bad feeling in my gut. Something is wrong. Terribly wrong.

A hand touches my shoulder and I turn to see a crying Becky and Amber behind me. "I'll go find out what's going on. Why don't you follow Amber to the waiting room? I'll come in as soon as I know what it is," she says between her tears. The worry and concern I see in her face scares me even more. She's a nurse. She knows this isn't good. I nod to them. That's is all I can do. I fear if I open my mouth to talk, I'll completely break down.

Amber leads me to the waiting room where everyone is already seated. All eyes are on me the second I walk into the room. All of them looking at me with worry. A million questions, I'm sure, swirling around in their heads. Thankfully, no one makes a move to talk to me right now. I'm hanging onto my sanity by such a thin thread as it is. I take a seat between Amber and Kyle, my eyes never leaving the door as I wait to find out what is going on with my girls.

I have no idea how much time has passed. My eyes are dry and hurting from staring at the door, trying to will the doctors to come out with some good news. As if on cue, the doors begin to open and in walks Becky with Dr. Monty in tow. I try to scan their faces for any hint of whether or not Holly and the baby are okay, but they give away nothing. When they get in front of me, I stand, as does everyone in the waiting room.

Dr. Monty gives me a sad smile and shakes my hand. I just know whatever he's about to say isn't good. "Just give it to me straight, Doc," I say, even though I'm not sure whether I can take it. He takes a deep breath and scans the room.

"Holly has a Placental Abruption. It's when the placenta peels away from the inner wall of the uterus, causing a very serious complication," he states loud enough for everyone to hear. "It's depriving the baby of oxygen and nutrients, as well as causing Holly to hemorrhage. The only way to stop it is to perform an emergency C-section." Immediately, I fall back into the chair. My head is spinning from the fact that both my girls are in danger. After a minute, my mouth is finally able to form the words I need.

"She's only thirty weeks along. Can our baby survive if she's delivered this early?" I question, terrified of the answer.

"She should be fine. She'll need some help breathing for a while. Barring any other complications, there's a ninety percent survival rate for babies born at this stage. They are both in more danger if we don't get the baby out." He looks at me, waiting for a response. I nod my head, because there is obviously no choice.

"Can I be with her when you do it?" I ask. She needs me. I can't allow her to go through this alone.

"Of course you can. Come with me," he answers, putting an arm around my shoulders and leading me through the same doors he just came into. We walk down a long hallway and enter another set of doors. "The nurse will get you set up and bring you into the OR when you're ready," he tells me before walking into the adjoining room where I'm guessing he'll be scrubbing in for the surgery.

The nurse hands me a pair of scrubs along with a mask, booties, and a hair cap. "You can put them on in the bathroom right there. I'll get you some gloves when you come out, because you'll need to scrub up," she says, pointing to the door marked restroom. I nod as I take the blue scrubs from her and go into the bathroom. I can feel the tears threatening to fall, but I will them away. My girls need me to be strong for them right now. I have no time to break down.

After I get all my gear on, I meet the nurse back in the hallway. When she turns around, I'm surprised to see its Becky all suited up. She gives me a small smile. "One of the perks of working here. I thought you could use a friend in there with you," she says.

"Thank you," is all I can say. Anything more and I'll lose it. We go into the room with the sinks and Becky guides me through scrubbing my hands and arms. Another nurse places the gloves on my hands. Becky then guides me to the operating room. The second I see Holly laying on a table in the center of the room, my chest begins to ache. She's motionless and pale. Machines are beeping all around me. Taking a deep breath, I will my feet to move toward my wife. Becky never takes her hand off me, as if she knows my legs feel like they're going to give out at any moment.

Becky motions to the stool situated next to the table by Holly's head. "Sit here. You can hold her hand and talk to her. She's awake but groggy. She's lost so much blood." She points to the sheet hiding her belly from view. "That will keep you from seeing anything that's going on," she explains. I'm so glad she's here with me. When this is all over, I'll have to make sure I tell her. Right now, Holly needs my full attention.

I take Holly's hand in mine and kiss her cheek softly. "I'm right here with you, doll face. Everything's going to be okay, I promise," I whisper in her ear. Her eyes flutter open and she turns her head to look at me.

"Paul? Is our baby okay?" she asks with a groggy voice.

"She'll be fine. I'll be right here to make sure of it," I assure her and she closes her eyes again, but I see her lips tip up into a small smile. I'm so glad I've been able to put her at ease a little. I continue to hold her hand and soothe her, telling her everything will be fine. "Becky is here with us. Should we tell her what name we've chosen?" I ask her, trying to keep her mind on happy thoughts. Another smile crosses her lips as she gently nods her head.

"Hope," Holly croaks.

"That's beautiful and very fitting," Becky beams.

Looking over at Holly, I see a tear slip from her eye, causing my heart to shatter. I know she's scared and I have no idea how to make it all go away for her. So, I do the only thing I can, I reach over and kiss her tear away. I'm startled when I hear a faint whimper. I look up at Becky, questioning with my eyes if that noise was what I think it was. Her face confirms it was. She has tears streaming down her smiling face. Seconds later, a loud cry rings out. That's my girl.

A nurse walks over with the most beautiful baby girl I've ever laid my eyes on. The floodgates open and I have no control, nor do I care at this point. She's so tiny and pink. The nurse leans down and rests the baby on Holly's chest. Her eyes pop open and she begins to sob. Gently, with her hand, she strokes Hope's cheek.

"Beautiful," Holly whispers. Then, all hell breaks loose. Machines begin beeping loudly as doctors whisper and scramble around frantically. When I look back at Hope, I notice she's turning a light shade of blue. When the nurse notices, she swiftly wisps Hope away from us.

Just then, I hear the doctor say, "We're losing her. There's too much bleeding."

I'm torn between following my daughter and watching over my wife. Holly squeezes my hand. Her tear-filled eyes and a look of pure fear on her face scares the shit out of me. "Go. Please, go with Hope. She's so little and probably scared. She needs her daddy," Holly pleads. I glance up at Becky, hoping she'll tell me what to do.

"Go. They won't let you stay in here anyway. I'll be here with her the whole time. I promise," Becky says as she moves over to take my seat. I stand and kiss Holly lightly on the lips.

"I love you, doll face. I'll stay with her and make sure she's okay. I need you to promise me you'll hang on. You can't leave us. Promise me," I beg, cradling her face in my hands.

"I promise I'll do my best. Now, go," she says before passing out completely. Pulling myself away from her, I follow behind the nurse racing out the doors with Hope in her arms.

I watch through a glass window as the nurses and doctors in the NICU hook Hope up to the machine to help her breath. They also insert an IV into her tiny little arm. Watching this threatens to break me. My poor little angel is so fragile and only a few minutes old. She shouldn't have to go through this. I feel so fucking helpless. I can't do anything but sit here and watch.

"She's a fighter like her mom," Angel says from behind me.

"Yes, she is. They say she'll be fine in a day or two. Has there been any news yet on Holly? I'm going crazy here."

"Nothing yet, man. I'm sorry," Angel says sadly. "She'll be okay. I know it. She loves you and that sweet little girl too much to go anywhere." God, I pray he's right. The thought of losing Holly causes an unbearable pain in my chest. I'm so worried about her, but I promised to stay with Hope.

"Paul." I turn around to see Dr. Monty standing behind me. He looks worn out. My legs threaten to give out on me and I wobble when I go to take a step forward. Angel catches me and keeps a tight grip on my arm to keep me upright. "She's okay. They are moving her to a room now," he says with only a half-smile. Something else is wrong, I can see it in his eyes. "She lost a lot of blood and we were able to give her a transfusion with what we had on hand. Holly's blood type is AB negative, which is very rare. We only had a small amount. She'll need more. Her friend Tanya is a match and is up donating as we speak," he explains. He takes a deep breath and I can see this is where he's going to tell me whatever bad news he has. "In order to stop the bleeding, we had to perform a total hysterectomy. I'm sorry, but she won't be able to have any more children."

I can't seem to catch my breath. This is going to destroy Holly. I find a chair and sit in it before I fall down. I close my eyes and try to get my breathing under control. "Can I see her?" I ask.

"Yes. It may take a little longer for her to wake up, but you can wait in her room so you're there when she does. Follow me," Dr. Monty says. I'm not sure I should leave Hope, but I need to see Holly.

"I'll stay. I won't leave her," Angel says, moving back to the window. Relief washes over me. I'll have to remember to thank him later, too. Right now, I need to get to Holly. I follow Dr. Monty to the elevator and up to the fourth floor. The elevator doors open to absolute chaos. An alarm is sounding as doctors, nurses, and security guards scramble in all directions. The feeling that something is terribly wrong returns in my gut. I step out of the elevator and brace myself along the wall. I see Beasley walking toward me. He's dressed in his uniform, meaning whatever is going on is bad enough that they called in the sheriff.

"Paul, its Holly. The nurses who were bringing her to her room were found knocked out in the elevator. There's footage of her being wheeled out of the hospital on a gurney. She was put into a medical transport van. We're trying to find it, but as of now, it's seemed to disappear," he says regretfully. Just like that, my entire world goes black. I can no longer hold it all together. My legs give out and I drop to the floor. A howling scream escapes me. I begin sobbing uncontrollably. I can't stop it and I don't care who's watching. I'm at my breaking point. I've failed to protect her yet again and that's not something I can handle. Beasley kneels beside me and wraps me up into his arms.

"I know what you're feeling, son. Let it out and then pull yourself together so we can find her," Beasley firmly states.

I don't know how long I'm crying on the floor, but just as quickly as it came on, it stops. I need to help find her. I not only owe it to Holly, but also Hope. She needs her mommy. There's only one person who would do this. I know I should have killed him when I had the chance. Ray Marconi is going to pay for this, that's a promise.

CHAPTER
Seventeen

Holly

MY EYES flutter open and I try to take in my surroundings. The room is dimly lit and I hear beeping from a machine next to me. As I try to sit up, a stabbing pain radiates in my abdomen and I immediately lay back down. Looking around, I can see I'm not in a hospital. An eerie feeling comes over me. This can't be right. Why am I here and not in a normal hospital? Nothing in here is familiar to me. The last thing I can remember is telling Paul to go with Hope and watch over her. Oh my God! Hope. Where's my baby girl? Did something happen to her? Where's Paul? He wouldn't just leave me.

I attempt to sit up again, but the pain is more than I can bear, causing me to scream out. I'm too weak, too sore, to move. After taking a few deep breaths to ease the pain and calm my nerves, I try to remember how I got here. The last place I remember being was in the operating room. How did I get here? Tears begin to fall from my eyes. Something is wrong. I just don't know what.

When I hear voices outside the door, I freeze. They seem to be arguing. The female voice sounds familiar, but I just can't place it. When the arguing grows louder, a chill runs down my spine the second I recognize the man's voice. This can't be happening. My heart begins beating so fast, it causes the machine to beep frantically. The door flies open and Ray runs in. The sight of him makes me want to vomit.

"Holly, baby, are you okay?" he inquires. If I didn't know better, he might actually have me believing he's concerned. I'm just a possession to him, nothing more. "Shut that fucking beeping off!" he screams at the woman dressed in scrubs, reading what looks like a hospital chart. I've seen her before. She was one of the nurses in the operating room. She tried to soothe me. I can't remember her name. I'm so lightheaded, I can't think straight.

She turns off the machine, ending the annoying beeping. "She needs a blood transfusion. Her blood type is very rare and I was only able to grab a little bit. She needs to be in a hospital. This place is not set up to take care of her needs," she snaps at Ray. I like the fact that she's standing up to him. It's obvious she doesn't seem to like him, I can tell that much by the disdain on her face every time she looks at him. I don't miss the fat lip and black eye she's sporting either. I have a feeling she's not here under her own free will. I'd know Ray's handy work anywhere.

Ray smacks her hard across the face, sending her falling to the floor. "Just remember you are here to take care of her. If you can't do that, you're no longer needed and I'll have to get rid of you," he snarls as he stands over her shivering body. She lets out a small whimper. My heart breaks for this woman. I've been in her shoes. Naive and scared. Not believing anything like this can actually happen to you. Wondering what he'll do next. I know exactly how she feels. I need to get him to focus on me.

"Ray, leave her alone. She can't do anything if she's scared to death," I reason. His expression softens as he turns and looks at me and it makes my stomach turn. How did I not see through him from day one? I can't believe I ever loved this man enough to marry him. He's a monster.

"I have some supplies to get, but someone is watching the house. If you try to leave, I'll know. I promise you won't get very far before I put a bullet in your head," he says, his voice filled with so much venom, you don't doubt he's capable of carrying out his threat. I feel like vomiting when he bends down and kisses my forehead. His lips on my skin feel like acid. He glances down at the frightened nurse. "Don't try anything stupid," he barks out before walking through the door.

"I'm K-Kelly. He forced me to help him take you from the hospital.

I'm so sorry," she sobs. That revelation isn't a surprise to me. I've needed to know something since I woke up, but was too afraid to bring it up around an already agitated Ray.

"My baby. Do you know if she's okay?" I ask Kelly, who's now by my side, holding my hand. I'm so afraid of what her answer may be. I don't even realize I'm crying until she reaches over and gently wipes away a tear sliding down my cheek. Her face breaks out into a huge smile.

"She's perfect and beautiful. She'll be on a ventilator for a day or so, but she'll be fine," Kelly assures me. I close my eyes and thank God for keeping her safe. At least now I don't have to worry about her. Paul will do anything to protect that little girl. Then, there's always the gang who will love and protect her, as if she were their own. I know she'll be well taken care of if something happens to me. I'm not foolish enough to think I'm making it out of here alive. I refuse to let Ray cause me to live in fear another day. Now that I know Hope is okay, I'm no longer concerned about myself.

"How bad off am I?" I ask while watching her beautiful smile turn into a sad frown. "Please, be straight with me." She takes a deep breath and squeezes my hand.

"You've been out for three days. I was afraid you weren't going to wake up. There were complications during the C-section. You were bleeding out. In order to stop it, the doctors had to perform a complete hysterectomy. I'm so sorry, Holly." She watches me carefully, waiting to see if she's giving me more information than I can handle. Devastated is the only word I can use to describe what I'm feeling. Paul and I talked about having at least three children. We both wanted a big family, something neither of us had growing up. I can't help but wonder if all the efforts they made to save me on that table weren't all a total waste of time.

I give Kelly a nod, reassuring her it's okay to continue. "You lost a lot of blood and needed a transfusion, but you have a very rare blood type and there wasn't much on hand at the hospital. By some miracle, your friend Tanya is a match and she donated as much as she could, but it just wasn't enough. You've developed a small fever, which usually is a sign of infection, so we'll have to keep an eye on that. I promise, I'll do everything I can for you."

"Thank you." Tears puddle in my eyes, threatening to fall. I have to be strong. This sweet woman shouldn't be here. She shouldn't have been brought into this mess, and if it weren't for me, she wouldn't have been. I have to do whatever it takes to get her out of this unharmed. Or, at least, not harmed any more than she already has been. "I'm sorry you've been forced into this mess and exposed to the monster that is my ex-husband. I'll figure out some way to get us out of this," I tell her. She gives me a kind smile.

"We'll get through this together. Obviously, I'm not going anywhere," Kelly says with a laugh. At least she still has a sense of humor.

"Just be careful. It doesn't take much to set Ray off. It might also be a good idea to make him think my condition is worse than it is." She gives me a questioning look. After all these years, I have at least learned how to deal with Ray. "If he thinks I'm weak and fragile, he'll let his guard down. Plus, it will force him to keep you around," I explain and I see the moment she understands what I'm saying.

"He has a gun and some goon helping him. That's how he forced me to help him take you from the hospital. And this..." she says, motioning to her black eye and fat lip, "was what I got when I tried to refuse." I can see the pain in her eyes as she relives the memory. I know that look all too well. I've seen it in the mirror hundreds of times before. I'm going to do anything I can to make sure she doesn't have to go through that again. Now, I just need to figure out a plan.

"Do you have any idea where we are?" I ask, praying we're still in Oakville.

"No. There's nothing but woods around us. They blindfolded me in the van, but I looked at my watch before and we only drove for about twenty-five minutes. We aren't far from home," she states. Being so close to home should make it a lot easier for Paul to find us. I'm sure by now he's going crazy, trying to figure out where Ray took me. Knowing my Paul, he's also kicking himself in the ass thinking this is all his fault. He'll be blaming himself for not protecting me. As if he could have seen something like this coming. I hate that my past has come back a second time to cause him pain.

Paul

I sit here in this rocking chair, feeding my beautiful baby girl for the

Protect Me

first time. How is it possible to be the happiest I've ever been and breaking into a million pieces at the same time? The only thing keeping me from completely falling apart is this little girl in my arms. I can already see so much of Holly in her. She has a full head of dark red hair and sparkling green eyes. I can't look at her without smiling, especially when she makes that sweet little cooing sound. Only three days old and she already has me wrapped around her teeny, tiny, little finger.

I made a promise to Holly...a promise to stay with Hope and watch over her. It's killing me not to be out looking for her, but Beasley swears he's doing everything possible. He even asked Liam to come to help. He helped out a great deal before, so I'm hoping that's the case this time. I need Holly. Hope needs Holly. Living without her just isn't an option. We have to find her.

"It's Uncle Angel's turn," Angel says quietly from over my shoulder. I turn to meet his eyes, finding them fixed on Hope with a huge smile on his face. Of all the guys, I never imagined Angel would be the one who would be all sappy and dopey around babies. When he's around Kyle's son, and now Hope, he turns into a totally different person. I think these kids could get him to do just about anything. "Beasley and Liam are in the hall with an update. I'll stay with the little munchkin," he says with his arms out, ready to hold my baby girl.

I hand my precious girl over to Angel. I start to tell him she'll need to be burped, but he's already a step ahead of me. Like a pro, he has the burp cloth on his shoulder and he's gently patting Hope's back. "Looks like you're all set here," I tell him with a chuckle.

"Uncle Angel has it all under control, doesn't he, Hope?" Angel coos. Who the hell is this guy and what has he done with the real Angel? When did he become so fucking maternal? I shake my head and smile as I walk out of the NICU. When I step out into the hallway, Beasley and Liam look to be deep in a discussion.

"Please tell me you guys have been able to find something to get us closer," I blurt out, interrupting their conversation. They both look over at me with sorrow-filled eyes and I know instantly they haven't. My heart hurts and I want to get back to Hope. She's the only one who can make me feel better right now. One look at that beautiful angelic face of hers, and my heart is whole and full. It no longer feels as if it's breaking into a million tiny pieces.

"He's gonna need medical supplies. I have notified all drug stores and medical supply stores within a hundred mile radius. The second

169

Ray or anyone suspicious turns up, we'll know about it," Liam explains as he shakes my hand. There's something about this guys that makes me think he always gets the bad guy. He's also intimidating as hell. I'd hate to be the guys he's hunting. "The son of a bitch won't get away with this. That, I can guarantee," he says, determination showing in his eyes. He makes me believe…believe we'll actually get her back.

"I just want my wife back safely. Who knows what kind of shape she's in. I can't lose her, neither can our daughter."

"I want to bring her home to you both. I promise, I won't stop until I do," Liam states with conviction in his voice. "We'll keep you in the loop every step of the way. The hospital allowed me to set up in a vacant office downstairs, so if I hear anything, I'll come up and let you know." He shakes my hand.

Beasley gives my shoulder a squeeze. "That is one beautiful little girl you have," he says, glancing through the window at Angel holding Hope. I can't help but smile.

"She most definitely is," I tell him. He nods before following Liam into the elevator. Sneaky bastard. He brought her up knowing it would take my mind off Holly for a brief moment. I appreciate it. I'm driving myself insane with worry. The only thing keeping me going is that precious little girl in Angel's arms.

"Hey, man. Any news?" Kyle asks as he walks up to me. He looks almost as bad as I do. Everyone is worried about Holly. I shake my head at him and notice his fists clench at his sides. "If I ever get my hands on that son of a bitch."

"Stand in line. He's mine first," I tell him. I'll be the one who gets the satisfaction of pounding the shit out of that asshole. The rest of the guys can do what they want to him after I'm done. One thing is for sure, he's not walking away again. We let him go once and that's proving to be a grave mistake. I never should have left him breathing.

"I know this is tough. I've been there, remember? I'm here. Anything you need, just like you were for me." I walk over to the window of the nursery and look at my little girl. Instantly, I the anger washes away. Kyle comes up beside me. "How did we end up with such beautiful kids?" Kyle jokes. The answer to that is simple.

"Look at their mothers."

"That explains it," he laughs. "You know, if our wives have their way, we'll be in-laws."

"I guess it could be worse," I tell him. We stand there talking for a while. Kyle keeps the conversation light and away from the topic of Holly. Not that it really makes a difference; she's always on my mind. If that's not enough, the ache in my heart is a constant reminder.

The dinging of the elevator doors opening gets my attention. When I see Beasley and Liam rush out of the elevator and in my direction, I freeze. My heart is beating against my chest with such force, I'm afraid it'll come right out. I can't decide whether I'm excited or scared by the fact that they obviously have some news. My legs threaten to give out when I attempt to take a step toward the two men. Luckily, Kyle grabs a hold of me, steadying me. He guides me over to the row of chairs lining the wall behind us. I sit and pray that whatever I'm about to hear is good news.

Liam reaches me and a smile appears. "We just got a call from a pharmacy about forty minutes from here. Ray came in with a prescription for antibiotics. The pharmacist recognized Ray from a picture I faxed. He was smart enough to tell Ray it would take about two hours to get the medication and asked him to come back," Liam says in one breath. I'm on my feet within seconds. This is it. We've got him.

"We're going to follow him from the pharmacy so we know where he's keeping Holly and the nurse. Once we know where he has them, we can move in and take him," Beasley says, a hint of excitement in his voice.

"Let's go," Kyle and I say at the same time. Beasley eyes Kyle warily. I know he's afraid to have Kyle involved. I don't blame him. He's thinking about his daughter and grandson. He knows this could get dangerous. Ray isn't going without a fight. Kyle sees the apprehension on Beasley's face.

"I'll hang back. I won't put myself in unnecessary danger. I just want to be there in case I'm needed," he assures Beasley. After a moment of thinking it over, Beasley nods and agrees. I fill Angel in on what's going on. He offers to stay with Hope until I get back and I'm thankful because I promised Holly Hope wouldn't be left alone.

Taking my daughter in my arms, I kiss her forehead and whisper, "I'm going to get your momma, baby girl. I'll be back soon. Love you." After placing one more kiss on her chubby little face, I hand her back to Angel.

"Go get our girl. We'll be waiting," Angel says, smiling down at Hope. Before I open the door, he calls out, "Be careful, Paul. Remember you have this little girl here waiting. Remember her face when you get a hold of Ray." I know exactly what he's trying to say. He wants to make sure I don't do anything that will take me away from my family. I nod, letting him know I understand. Then, I'm out the door. I sure hope seeing my daughters face in my head will control my temper when I get my hands on that fucker.

CHAPTER
Eighteen

Holly

As I wake, I can hear the pounding of rain on the roof. I keep my eyes closed, hoping when I open them, I'll be home in my own bed. Even the hospital would be better than where I was when I fell asleep. I take a deep breath and slowly open my eyes. My heart plummets into my stomach when I see I'm still here. Normally, the sound of rain is soothing to me, but not today. Today, it just makes me feel worse.

As I glance around the room, I spot Kelly sleeping soundly in the armchair in the corner of the room. A wave of guilt washes over me. She's in this mess because of me. Maybe not directly, but still because of me.

I wish I knew what Ray actually thinks he'll accomplish with this. Does he really think there's anything he can say or do that will send me running into his open arms? For God's sake, he has kidnapped me along with an innocent woman. And, to top it off, he's physically assaulted her. There's nothing he could possibly say or do that would change my opinion of him. Nothing that would ever make me feel anything but pure loathing and hatred for him.

As if on cue, the door leisurely opens with a loud creak. Turing my head in that direction, I see Ray casually walk in. He looks as if nothing's wrong. Like this is all so normal, just like any other average day. He's a psychopath. I always thought I was so smart. So good at spotting the evil ones. Foster home after foster home, I survived by being able to see through the facades people tried so hard to keep up. How could I be so blindingly stupid with Ray? Because I wanted so badly to be loved, to fit in.

His face is hard as he looks over at a sleeping Kelly, but when his attention turns to me, it instantly softens. Bile rises in my throat. In his own sick, twisted way, he loves me. However, it's not the kind of love I want or need. Not really love at all, outside of his fucked up mind.

He walks up to the side of the bed, a grin plastered on his evil face. I'd like to punch that grin right off his damn face. He reaches down, placing his hand on mine and squeezing it. Immediately, I yank my hand from his grip. Hurt flashes in his eyes, but it's quickly replaced with anger. His hand balls up into a tight fist at his side while the other swiftly grips a hold of my neck. He squeezes his fingers tightly, biting into my skin. I'm struggling to catch my breath and try to wiggle from his grip, but the sharp pain from my abdomen stops me in my tracks. He watches my face intently, waiting for a reaction. He wants me to beg him to stop. I know this sick game. I won't do it. I'll die before I ever beg him for anything ever again. This is it. He's finally going to kill me. I've always thought he would, I just pushed it to the back of my mind. Hoping if I didn't dwell on it, I could keep it from happening.

My head begins to spin. Closing my eyes, I think of Paul and how much this must be hurting him. And Hope. Oh, God, Hope. I don't want her to grow up without a mom. I can't control the tears falling from my eyes. Ray loosens his grip.

"That's more like it. There's the Holly I love. You're still afraid of me, just like it should be," Ray says in almost a whisper. Only in this man's sick and twisted mind could this be mistaken for love.

"I'm not afraid of you, Ray. You don't scare me anymore. Do whatever you want to me, but I refuse to allow you the satisfaction of seeing me scared," I snap at him. I glance quickly at Kelly, who's staring at me with wide, panicked eyes. Shit! I hope he doesn't get any ideas about getting to me through Kelly. That type of cowardly shit is right up his alley. So help me, if he lays another hand on that poor girl. Oh, who am I kidding, I won't be able to do a damn thing in this condition.

"Don't start with that smartass mouth of yours. Learn to start controlling yourself, or..." he pauses and turns to Kelly. Slowly, he stalks toward her. I can see all of the blood drain from her face. Poor girl. She is so frightened. "I know you, Holly, you may not act properly when your life and wellbeing is at risk, but you will if someone else's is," he says with a wickedly evil grin. Damn it! Now what do I do? Physically, I can't do anything. I'm still too sore and weak. So, he gets what he wants. As always.

"What do you want from me, Ray?" I ask trying my damnedest to sound sincere. When Ray grins, I can see I've succeeded.

"First, you have to get better. Once that happens, we can get rid of the little nurse here," he says maliciously. I don't like the sound of that. "Then, you and I are going on a little trip. Consider it a second honeymoon, if you will. And don't you worry, I'll make sure no one can find us." He runs his hand across my cheek. I want to scream. Tell him he's fucking delirious if he thinks I'm going anywhere willingly with him. But for Kelly's sake, I can't open my mouth.

Ray leans down and kisses my forehead. I stiffen instantly. It takes everything I have to keep from punching him in the face. When his lips touch my skin, it feels like acid is being dripped on me. I can't stand him being so close to me. My stomach begins churning. I try to hold it back, but I can't. All of a sudden, I lean over the bed and vomit all over him. I really don't mean to do it. He looks horrified. I'm finding it difficult not to laugh. I lay back in bed and cover my face with my hands.

"I'm so sorry, Ray," I say as I try to hide the laughter behind my hands. I can feel the anger and disgust radiating off him in waves as he stands there with his arms out. Kelly comes over and hands him a towel. He yanks it from her hands.

"Get this mess cleaned up," he snaps pointing to Kelly. "And, you, this is strike one. Trust me, you don't want to get to three. Now, I have to take a shower so I can go back to get the medical supplies we need." He storms out of the room, slamming the door behind him.

"I'm sorry, Kelly. It happened before I knew it was coming," I apologize. I feel so bad that she's stuck cleaning up after me.

"I'm a nurse, this is not new territory. Besides, I'd gladly clean up if it meant seeing that ass getting puked on," she giggles. I join in. It is funny. That look of pure disgust on his face. Kelly and I can't seem to stop laughing.

We finally get ourselves under control and Kelly finishes cleaning up the mess on the floor. I lay back, realizing laughing right now is still quite painful, but it seems to release some of the tension and anguish that's been building inside me. I still have no idea how to get out of this mess, but for a brief moment, I don't think about that.

A knock on the door halts my easy feeling. A chill runs down my spine at the thought of being faced with Ray again so soon. I'm surprised when I see a very tall and muscular man peek around the door as he slowly opens it.

"Ah...Mr. Marconi wanted me to bring in your lunch while he's out. Are you hungry, Mrs. Marconi?" he asks nervously. Mrs. Marconi? He thinks I'm Ray's wife? Does he even realize he's holding us here against our will? Maybe if I tell him the truth, he'll let us go. He looks young, probably somewhere in his early twenties.

"Please, call me Holly," I tell him. He blushes and gives me a shy smile as he nods his head. "What's your name?" I feel bad for this guy. He doesn't belong here mixed up with Ray, especially if he has no idea what's going on.

"I'm Peter."

"Did Ray tell you we're married?" He looks confused.

"Yes, ma'am, he did."

"What explanation did he give you for why he's keeping us locked up?"

"Locked up? He said you're sick and someone is after you. I'm here to protect you." Now, I'm the one looking at him with a confused expression. Ray sure can pull the wool over people's eyes. He has this guy believing he's protecting me.

"I haven't been Ray's wife for a long time. Kelly and I are here against our will." I can see he's thinking it all over and what I've said has him confused. He has no idea who the real Ray is. "Peter, I have a husband and a baby girl. Ray isn't a good man. I don't think you are anything like him. Please, help us get out of here." He keeps looking between the two of us and the door. Is he afraid of Ray? Well, I can definitely understand that feeling.

"I'm sorry. I truly didn't know. I had no reason not to believe him. He hired me a month ago. He said someone was after him and he needed security," he explains, remorse and shock evident on his face.

"Where did he say I was?"

"He told me he sent you to stay with family in order to protect you." I can't believe what I'm hearing. I just don't understand why Ray would want someone who clearly hates him.

"Please, help us get out of here before he gets back," I beg him once more. I glance over to Kelly. She's hanging on every word, most likely praying Peter will help get us the hell out of here. Ray's already been gone a while. We don't have much time and I still don't know if I can walk.

"Okay. Can you get her up? I'm going to make sure he's not back yet," Peter says and leaves the bedroom. Excitement blooms inside of me. The thought of seeing Paul and Hope brings a smile to my face.

I wince as I sit up. This is going to be harder than I thought. Kelly is by my side, ready to help. Very slowly, I move my legs so that they're dangling over the side of the bed. Pain radiates through me as I straighten out my legs and try to plant them on the floor. A cold sweat is building on my forehead from all the energy this simple task is taking. Setting my feet on the floor, I stand halfway up before screaming out in pain. My legs begin to give out beneath me and Kelly quickly holds me up. It's just no use. Between the severe pain and being so weak, I won't make it across the room, let alone out the front door. My earlier wave of excitement quickly turns to disappointment.

Peter runs back into the room. "The coast is clear for now. We need to get going." I want to tell the two of them to go get help. I'll only slow them down. He must sense what I'm thinking. Sweet, kind eyes look into mine. In a flash, he scoops me effortlessly into his arms. My abdomen screams in pain so I bite my lip, attempting to will it away. I try to keep telling myself it will all be over soon. Just hold on a little longer.

Peter carries me through the tiny cabin with Kelly close behind. I notice candles burning throughout the living area. Ray was a stickler for having the house smell good. I always thought it was a strange obsession. Right as we get to the door, it opens. My heart plunges into my stomach when I see Ray coming through the door. Everything seems to happen in slow motion. Ray is scowling. The veins on his temples are protruding, looking like they might explode at any moment. He's beyond pissed. I've only seen him like this one other time and it was the worst beating I ever took. The night he killed my baby. My mouth goes dry and I'm finding it hard to breathe. The fear and panic are overwhelming me.

Ray reaches behind him, pulls out a gun, and slams it into the side of Peter's head. There's a loud crack and he tumbles to the floor, taking me with him. The air is knocked out of my lungs as soon as I hit the cold, hard floor. A stinging pain from my abdomen brings tears to my eyes. It takes a minute to catch my breath. When I look over at Peter, he's lying in a heap with a nasty gash on his head. Kelly is standing there shocked, her face as white as a ghost. I look back to Ray and the anger I see in his eyes causes me to shiver. He sets the gun and bag on a nearby table. My vision begins to blur and the last thing I remember is the sting of his fist as it crashes into my temple.

Paul

BEASLEY, LIAM, and I drive over to the pharmacy. We wait in the car for Ray to return for his supplies. The plan is to follow him back to where he's keeping Holly and the nurse. Beasley has back up on standby if needed. So far, it's been the longest forty-five minutes of my life.

"There's the son of a bitch now," Liam says, pulling me from my thoughts. Ray casually strolls into the pharmacy, as if it's just another day. If we didn't need him to lead us to Holly, I'd go beat the shit out of him now. My entire body is shaking, my fists clenching and unclenching. I want to wrap my hands around his scrawny little neck while witnessing him take his last breath.

Liam grabs a small black box off the seat and gets out of the car. What is he doing? I watch as he goes over next to Ray's car. Bending down on one knee, he places the little black box underneath the car.

"You okay back there?" Beasley questions.

"I will be once I get my wife back." He nods in understanding. I know Beasley's been in my shoes before with Amber. And knowing him the way I do, he won't stop me from a little payback before they slap the cuffs on Ray's ass.

Liam comes back to our car and slips in with a satisfied grin on his face. He opens an app on his phone and holds it up for us to see. It's a map with a blinking red dot on it. Oh — he put a GPS tracker on Ray's car. I never would have thought about that. I'm thankful to have people like Beasley and Liam. In situations like this, I wouldn't have a clue.

"Here we go," Liam says, starting the car. Ray comes out of the store and is walking to his car. Again, he looks as if he hasn't a care in the world. To see him, you'd think he was a normal average guy, not the kind who beats women and holds them against their will.

My stomach is twisting in knots as we follow a few cars behind Ray. I'm terrified he's going to get away and we'll be back at square one. I keep my eyes trained on Ray's car, silently praying this will all go smoothly.

We follow him through town. When we turn onto an old country road, I know where he's going. There's an old plantation out here that was turned into a B & B a few years back. They also have about five cabins spread out over the fifty or so acres of land. It's a popular honeymoon or romantic getaway spot. The cabins are very secluded, so it makes it the perfect place to hide out. I explain all this to Liam and Beasley. This way they know what we're getting into.

"This is actually a good thing," Liam states. He sees my confused expression when he glances at me in the rearview mirror. "From a tactical standpoint, it's good. The woods and the fact it's secluded will make it much easier to sneak up on him. He'll never see us coming," he clarifies. I relax only a little. He's right, this is a good thing.

Ray turns right onto a dirt road. When Liam keeps driving, I begin to panic. What the fuck is he doing? I scoot to the edge of the seat so I can see them both. "What are you doing? Shouldn't we be following him?" I ask, my voice laced with a mixture of confusion and panic.

"Relax, Paul. We have the tracker on his car. If we follow him down that little dirt drive, he'll get suspicious," he says just as he pulls over in a small clearing. "We'll go by foot from here."

He's right. Again. Taking a calming breath, I exit the car. My legs feel like Jell-O, thanks to being so anxious and nervous. *Please, let her be okay*, I keep repeating over and over in my head as we begin our trek through the woods. We're careful about how much noise our footsteps are making as we walk. I'm more afraid he'll hear the rapid thumping of my heart.

The woods are nice and thick, making it easy to hide ourselves. It doesn't take long before I can see the small cabin. My body begins to shake. This is it. Liam turns to us and holds his hand up, forcing us to stop. He puts his finger to his lips to ensure we don't make a sound. He stalks ahead just a bit to get a closer view while Beasley and I remain frozen in place. It seems like hours, but it's only minutes before he comes back to where we are.

"It looked like there was a man trying to help the girls escape. I saw

Ray hit him with a gun." Liam looks at me with worried eyes. "Paul, this is your wife. Do you want to be the one going up against Ray? If so, Beasley and I will get the man and the nurse out. It's your choice."

I look to Beasley and he gives me a nod, telling me he's on board with whatever I choose. I just want Holly safe. But, I also want to make that son of a bitch suffer. Last time, he didn't get the message. I need to be more persuasive this time around. "I want Ray. Get the other two out and if I'm not out in ten minutes, come help me." They both agree. My main concern is Holly. I need to keep that in mind and not put her in any unnecessary danger just to get Ray. My daughter is counting on me to bring her mama back to her.

We slowly make our way to the cabin. The front door is now closed so we have no idea what's going on inside. Liam's plan is for us all to barge in and take him by surprise so that he's off guard. He'll go first followed by Beasley and then me. Makes sense, the two of them have guns and can probably assess the situation a lot faster than I could.

"Ready?" Liam asks. He waits for both of us to acknowledge we are and the three of us sprint toward the cabin. My stomach is filled with butterflies. I'm afraid of what we'll find once we get inside. Just before Liam turns the knob on the door, I whisper to myself, "Daddy loves you, Hope."

Liam bursts through the door. I get in and see Liam grabbing a gun from the table. I scan the room and see a very frightened woman curled into a ball in the corner. There's a young guy laying on the floor, bleeding from a nasty looking head wound. But it's what I see a couple feet away from him that knocks the air from my lungs. A sharp pain radiates through my chest when I see Holly laying lifeless on the floor. There's blood seeping through her hospital gown. For a second, I'm frozen in place, afraid of what I'll discover when I get to her. Beasley is by her side in an instant with his fingers on her neck checking for a pulse. I hold my breath. When he smiles at me, I can finally breathe. Thank God! Liam and Beasley begin getting everyone out of the house.

Knowing she's okay, my feet start moving again. I lunge at Ray, knocking us both to the floor. I pin him down and slam my fist into his face. Seeing the blood trickle from his split lip fuels the angry fire raging in my belly. I hit him, over and over again. There are moments when I see my father's face in place of Ray's.

At first, he's so stunned, he can't fight back. It only takes a moment for him to snap out of it. He lands a good punch to my ribs, causing me to roll off him. I stand up as I catch my breath. Ray comes at me and tackles me, sending us falling into an end table and its contents flying across the room. Neither one of us relents. We both keep beating on the other with everything we've got. Everything around me is a blur. The only thing I see is this fucker in front of me.

Each blow I deliver has a purpose. I'm punishing him for all the times he laid his hands on Holly. For taking her unborn baby from her. For taking her from me and our daughter. I'm also punishing him for all of the things my father did to my mom and I. After all, he is just like my father and my father isn't here for me to take my anger out on. Every beating I took, every beating I saw my mom take, and all the beatings Holly had to endure play over and over in my head. I'm making Ray pay for them all. He may not be responsible for some of it, but he is the same type of man.

Out of nowhere, Ray head-butts me hard. The force knocks us both to the ground. My head is spinning and my vision is blurry. I close my eyes, unsure whether I have any fight left in me. I'm bloody and in pain, but I bet I'm in much better shape than my opponent, who has knocked himself out cold. Something catches my attention out of the corner of my eye. I turn my head slowly to see what it is. Panic immediately sets in when I notice a fire has broken out. *Holly!*

Dragging myself on floor, I try to make it over to Holly. My head is still throbbing and spinning. Every bone in my body hurts and my strength it totally depleted. I have to get her out of here, though. I have no choice. The flames are spreading. The room is filling with smoke, making it more difficult for me to concentrate. When I get halfway to her, I feel myself being lifted to my feet. I look back to see that Beasley's helping me. Thank God. When I turn back to Holly, I see her being lifted into Liam's arms. Relief washes over me. My baby is getting out of here.

Liam lays Holly down on a waiting gurney and the paramedics begin checking her over. Beasley helps me over to another empty gurney. Suddenly, I remember Ray is still inside. As much as I hate the man, I can't leave him inside a burning house. He should be in jail left to suffer. I wiggle from Beasley's grasp and start back to the cabin. I know they'll all think I'm fucking looney, but I don't think I can live with myself knowing I allowed a man to die. Not even a man as evil as Ray.

I get about twenty feet from the cabin and stumble, falling to my knees. Before I can get up, I hear a loud boom. Instinctively, I cover my head. When I open my eyes, I realize the cabin has exploded. It's engulfed in flames and debris has fallen all around us. I don't have time to think about what's happened because I hear Holly's panicked scream, "Paul!"

I get up with a little help from Liam and make it over to Holly. "I'm here, doll face. I'm here," I tell her as I gently kiss her lips. A heart-stopping smile spreads across her beautiful face.

"I love you," she whispers. "Kelly and Peter? Are they okay?" she asks as she tries to look around.

"They're fine. How about you?"

"I'm great now. I'll be even better when I get to see Hope."

"She's been waiting on you. She's so beautiful. Just like her mama," I tell her and kiss her again.

CHAPTER
Nineteen

Holly

I'M SITTING in a hospital room filled with dozens of flower arrangements from all of our friends. Everyone around us has been amazing. In the ambulance the other day, Paul filled me in on our daughter's progress and how everyone has helped him care for her. He said Angel barely leaves her side, even when it's not his turn to be there. He has the biggest heart out of them all. I wonder why he tries so hard to keep that hidden.

He also told me about Ray. To my surprise, I'm not jumping for joy that he's gone. I hate him for all of the times he's hurt me, but I had also loved him once. It's like a double-edged sword. I am happy that I no longer have to wonder what he'll do to hurt me next, or that he'll bring harm to my family and friends.

When we arrived at the hospital, I was in worse shape than I thought. It's been two days now since I arrived back here. Everyone has been in to see me, but I haven't been able to go visit our daughter yet. Today, I'm feeling much better and the doctor cleared me for travel to the NICU. I'm a bundle of nerves as I sit and wait for Paul to bring me to see our baby girl. What if she doesn't like me? What if I'm really bad at this whole mom thing?

"Stop that, doll face," Paul says as he comes in, pushing a wheelchair. How does he know I'm worrying? "I can see worry all over your face." Damn, he's good. Maybe he should go into fortune telling on the side. "You are going to be the best mama ever and our daughter loves you. There's nothing to worry about. Are you ready to go meet our daughter?" I can only nod. It feels like I've been waiting my whole life for this single moment.

Tears begin to fill my eyes and slowly slip down my cheeks. Paul is right by my side, wiping them away. "Those better be happy tears, doll face," he says with a grin that melts my heart.

"They most definitely are. And they're all thanks to you. You're amazing and I am the luckiest girl in the world."

"No, doll face, I'm the one who's lucky," he says, and kisses my cheek sweetly. "You and our baby girl are my world. I never knew how happy I could be, but you've shown me." I'm lost in his eyes and my heart swells from his words. We've saved each other. We've shown one another what true, unconditional love really is, and that we are both worthy of it.

"Your chariot awaits, Mrs. Walters," Paul says as he carefully helps me into the wheelchair. He's very cautious with me, worried he might hurt me if he makes a wrong move. Never would he intentionally hurt me. Protecting me. Keeping me safe. Loving me. Making me happy. These are his priorities and what makes me love him the most.

After a brief elevator ride, he's wheeling me into the NICU. My hands are shaking and my heart is about to beat out of my chest. I'm both afraid and elated as we pass through the double doors. My heart swells when I see Angel in a rocking chair holding my beautiful baby girl. He's softly singing to her. It's one of the most touching things I've ever seen. He's looking into her eyes as he sings, a sweet loving smile on his face. It's obvious our little girl already has him wrapped around her little finger.

Tears flow freely from my eyes as I take in the sight of how much our friend loves and cares for our daughter and from the sight of the most beautiful little girl in the world. She's even more beautiful than I remember from the brief moment I saw her in the delivery room. She makes a small whimpering noise and I can no longer hold it together. I start to whimper as tears flow heavily from my eyes.

Angel's head whips around and his singing ceases. He turns back to Hope. "You have a very special visitor, baby girl. I told you your daddy would bring her back to you." Hope lets out a little squeak of a cry. "Don't worry, Uncle Angel isn't going anywhere. I promise you. I'll be here for you always. Anything you need," Angel whispers. The connection between the two of them is so beautiful, it causes me to cry even harder.

Angel stands up and carries Hope to me. With the utmost care, he places my beautiful girl in my arms and kisses me on the cheek. "Welcome home, mama." I look up and smile my thanks. My attention is quickly directed to my daughter.

It's almost as if she was made especially to fit in my arms. I place soft sweet kisses on her forehead, nose, cheeks, and lips. I then count all ten perfect little fingers and toes. I'm in awe of her angelic face. She has Paul's exquisite green eyes and my red hair.

"She'll be able to go home with you tomorrow," Angel says from behind me. "Her doctor says she's a very strong little girl. I can't possibly imagine where she gets that from." I give Angel a smile as he claps Paul on the shoulder and walks out the doors. I have a feeling he hasn't left this room or our daughter too many times. For that, I'm so grateful.

After a while, they allow us to bring Hope to my room. She is perfect in every way and I am so in love with her. I haven't put her down since Angel placed her in my arms. I just can't bring myself to let go of her. The nurses keep saying I'll spoil her. To be honest, I really don't care. She's our miracle. And the fact that she'll be an only child pretty much ensures she'll be spoiled.

A light knock on the door drags me from my thoughts. Tanya's head peeks around the corner. She has an enormous smile on her face, but her eyes look sad. "Hey there, are you up for some company?" she asks as she quietly walks over to look at Hope in my arms.

"Of course. Would you like to hold her?" I ask. She looks so mesmerized by Hope, but so sad at the same time.

"I'd love, too. It's been a very long time since I've held a baby so tiny." I hand Hope to her and see a tear slip down Tanya's cheek.

"Why do you look so sad? You can talk to me about anything," I encourage her. This woman helped me through the worst time in my life. We became great friends and I would do anything to help her if she needed it. I don't know a whole lot about her, just that she came from a very strict and abusive home. When she was eighteen, she married, thinking it would take her away from the abuse. Unfortunately, her husband was worse than her father. She never talked about kids so I imagine she never had them, which is too bad. I know she would've made a great mother.

"Just remembering a time long ago," she says with a faraway look in her eyes. "I had a baby girl when I was a teenager. I was forced to give her away. It was the only way I could keep her safe. I've thought about her every single day since."

"Have you ever thought about looking for her?"

"I have, but I'm afraid she'd hate me. I was a coward. Instead of taking her and running away from my family, I left her to be raised by strangers. At the time, I really thought I was doing what was best for her. Who's to say she wouldn't feel the same way you do about your birth mom." She has a point. I never went into detail about my situation with Tanya, but I did tell her I was abandoned by my birth mom. I never had any kind words for that woman either, so I can see where she'd be reluctant to seek out her own daughter.

"To be honest, Tanya, I've started to rethink my feelings toward my birth mom. I have no idea what was happening in her life, so I can't judge. Who knows, my life could have been a whole lot worse if she kept me." My confession has made her eyes brighten a little. "If you ever decide to look for her, I'll help you every step of the way."

"I'll think about it. Thank you."

The adoption subject is finished and the rest of Tanya's visit is filled with fun topics of conversations. She asks a lot of questions about Beasley and every time she does, she blushes. I'm starting to think she has a bit of a crush on him. Personally, I think they'd be great together. They both need someone who will treat the other well. She's also informed me that she wants to stay in Oakville. This news makes me very happy. I've missed her so much since I came here. She was my first real friend ever. I'm going to love having her here all the time. Plus, with Amber's help, maybe we can get Tanya and Beasley together. We spend an hour or so just talking, laughing, and enjoying Hope.

Paul comes in and smiles when he sees how happy I am. "I hate to break up all the fun, but I think it's time for my girls to get some sleep. After all, tomorrow will be a big day." Tanya agrees and hugs Paul and I goodbye. Paul takes Hope from me and lays her in her bed.

"Where are you sleeping?" I ask him.

"With my wife, of course. As long as it's okay with you. I don't want to hurt you."

"It would hurt me more to have you out of my reach. I need you holding me tonight. It's the last piece needed to put us back together." He smiles, takes off his shoes, and pushes Hope's bed close to my side. Then, Paul climbs in bed with me, pulling me into the safety of his arms. Like Hope fits perfectly in my arms, I fit perfectly into Paul's. This is happy. This is where I was destined to be. Wrapped in the arms of a man I love with every fiber of my being and watching the most beautiful baby girl in the world sleeping soundly next to us. This is the family I've always dreamed of having and now, I have it.

Paul

THE SUN is shining bright and the sky is blue as I drive my lovely girls home from the hospital. I can honestly say this is the happiest I have ever been in my entire life. Glancing in the rearview mirror, I'm met with a glowing smile from Holly. I think it's safe to say she's feeling the same as I am.

We have both been through a ton of shit in our lives, but now we are finally getting the happiness we deserve. I have to laugh at myself for that thought. Before I met Holly, I didn't think I deserved anything good in my life. I always felt like I would destroy anyone who tried to love me. Just like I did my parents. They were happy once, too. In love and blissfully happy. At least, that's what my mom used to tell me. That all changed after meeting Holly, though. She made me feel worthy of love. She also showed me that by loving her, I made her life better. I wasn't destroying her, I was helping to put her back together again.

"So, who all will be at the surprise welcome home party?" Holly asks with amusement in her voice. I laugh. I tried to tell Amber she'd never be able to surprise Holly with a party, but she was bound and determined to try it anyway. I don't think the two of them realize how much alike they are.

"You know, just the usual. But you didn't hear it from me. Amber threatened to cut my balls off if I spilled the beans," I tell her with a chuckle. I'm pretty sure she was only half joking when she said it.

"Don't worry, baby, my lips are sealed. I'll act surprised. Besides, who do you think taught her?" she says with a hearty laugh. God, I love that laugh. It's the kind of laugh that warms you from the inside out. When I hear that laugh, it reminds me of how happy she is and that I'm part of the reason why.

I glance into the rearview mirror again as we pull into our driveway. She has a smile from ear to ear as she watches all of our friends come to greet us. My smile mirrors hers. We never imagined we'd have a family at all, now we have an enormous one filled with the most amazing people. I couldn't have picked a better family if I tried.

Not surprisingly, Angel is the first one to the car the second we come to a stop. I'm amazed to see how much he has taken to Hope and how protective he is over her. He has a massive bottle of hand sanitizer in his front pocket. He forces anyone who wants to hold Hope to sanitize their hands. It's pretty fucking funny.

"Dude, what are you doing?" I ask him.

"You can't be too careful. What if someone gets her sick? You have no idea the amount of germs that are floating around here." I'm laughing so hard, my eyes are watering. He's so serious. A small part of me wonders if I'm a shitty dad for not thinking of that myself.

"Don't sweat it, baby. I didn't think of that either. I never imagined we'd be getting schooled on baby care from Angel," Holly says with a chuckle. At least now I don't feel so bad.

We're sitting in the back porch watching everyone talk and laugh. Marcus' boys and Clark's boys are playing football in the back yard. Holly is next to me on the porch swing. She grabs my hand and squeezes it. "Are you upset that I can't give you any more children?" she asks with sadness in her voice.

"Doll face, I feel blessed to have Hope. I'm perfectly happy with just having her. Besides, there's nothing stopping us from adopting later on. I think it would be nice to give a child a loving home when their natural parents couldn't." Before I know it, she's in my lap and grabbing my face in her hands. Her lips crash to mine and she begins passionately kissing me.

When Holly pulls away, her eyes are filled with tears. "You'd be willing to adopt a baby someday?" she asks with surprise in her voice. "I've always wanted to give a child the opportunity for a family I never had growing up."

"Of course I would. I think we should have a very big family." I kiss her smiling lips and hold her tight. I have to be the happiest man alive in this moment. I have a beautiful, loving wife. A sweet, beautiful baby girl. The possibilities for our future are endless. I'm going to enjoy every day I have with my girls and I look forward to where the future will take us.

THE END

Acknowledgments

John and Cody, thank you for standing by me and helping me do something I truly love and enjoy. You two mean the world to me. I couldn't ask for a better husband and son. I love you both so much. Mom, thank you isn't enough. I love you and I'm so thankful for all of your support and encouragement.

Kelly Williams and **Tanya Turner**, what can I say? You girls rock! You both encourage me, make me laugh, keep me sane, and act as my sounding board. Without you I wouldn't be able to do this. There just are not enough words to tell you how much I appreciate everything you do. I love you both.

Monica James, I am so happy to call you my friend. I can't wait to end up at a signing with you and actually have a chance to hang out.

Monica Black, I thank my lucky stars everyday that our paths crossed. I couldn't ask for a better Editor and friend. Thank you so much for helping me grow.

Becky Schmidt and **Chelsie Leverette**, you both have been by my side since day one. I am so lucky to have your support and friendship.

To all my beautiful Betas, thank you for all your time and supprt. You girls are amazing!! **Kelly, Tanya, Chelsie, Brandy, Becky, Angel, Amanda, Courtney, Mary, Tobi, Candi, and Jamie**.

To the wonderful ladies who are part of my Street Team, I can't thank you enough for all the pimping and promoting you do. **Kelly, Tanya, Chelsie, Becky, Angel, Mary, Tobi, Candi, Jamie, Courtney, and Mary** I love you ladies!!

To all the **blogs** and **readers** none of this would be possible without you. Thank you for all of your support, great reviews, and simply for enjoying my stories.

Stephen Thomas, thank you so much for being my very first cover model. **Heather Hill**, thank you for letting all the readers out there ogle him.(haha) You both have been a pleasure to work with and I hope we can work together again on future projects.

Protect Me Playlist

Scars - Papa Roach

Never Again - Nickelback

Dear Agony - Breaking Benjamin

Learning To Love - Cinder Road

Don't Be Scared - Cinder Road

Halo- Beyonce

Carry On Wayward Son - Kansas

Perfect Storm - Brad Paisley

Goodbye - Absence of Concern

Breaking Me - Cinder Road

Contact Author

Kathy-Jo would love to hear from you:

Facebook www.facebook.com/authorkathyjoreinhart
Twitter twitter.com/KathyJoReinhart
Website kathyjoreinhart.com
Goodreads www.goodreads.com/author/show/7890595.Kathy_Jo_Reinhart

Other Books By Kathy-Jo Reinhart

The Oakville Series

First Love - Kyle and Amber's Story (Book #1 Part 1)
Remember Me- Kyle and Amber's Story (Book #2 Part 2)
Protect Me- Paul and Holly's Story (Book #3)

Coming Soon (in no particular order)

Redeem Me - Angel and Chelsie's Story
Save Me - Liam and Kelly's Story
Forgive Me - Beasley and Tanya's Story
Marcus and Taryn's Story
Clark and Becky's Story